INFERNO IN CHAOS

A GUILDS OF CHAOS NOVEL

by
Malfera Sinclair

GUILDS OF CHAOS MAP

CONTENTS

NIX

BRIDGES BURNING

F lames burst forth in my room, transforming the once-familiar space into a nightmarish inferno. The hungry blaze devoured the walls and floor, reducing them to a swirling abyss of ash and ember. I stood frozen in horror as the relentless flames ignited the hallway outside, creating a lattice of blazing wood that crackled and popped with malevolent glee. I thought I spied a way to dash through—

The fire's fury blasted me, a wall of heat forcing me back like an invisible hand. The monstrous flames roared with deafening intensity as overhead beams plummeted nearby, each deafening crash a death knell that signaled the disintegration of the only home I'd ever known.

Shit! This is not good.

With any luck, Dad would hear me over the voice of the ravenous fire.

"Fire! Dad, get out of the house! Get Mom out! Fir-reee!" My desperate scream tore at my throat as acrid smoke billowed around me, the pungent scents of burning wood and melting plastic stinging my eyes and filling my nostrils.

I desperately wanted to rush to my parents, to ensure their safety, but the wall of fire stood between us like a malevolent sentinel. Transfixed, I couldn't tear my gaze away from the scene unfolding before me. The flames' searing heat enveloped my body in an oppressive embrace. It didn't hurt, but the intensity of it—its insatiable hunger—terrified me to my core.

Covering my mouth with my hand, I struggled to keep the noxious smoke from invading my lungs. Panic coursed through my veins, intertwining with the guilty thoughts that raced through my mind.

What the hell was I thinking? I should have tried to practice with the flames outside, somewhere that wasn't a tinderbox waiting to ignite. But late in the evening, I couldn't risk someone seeing me.

Magic was forbidden in our town—in the whole Mortal Realm, actually. Getting caught meant facing punishments that still gave me nightmares. Dad mentioned outlaws from other Realms hiding out here before, but I barely knew anything about those places. Mom and Dad never talked about them, like staying silent about them would somehow protect me from the unknown.

Unfortunately, when I was a child, I discovered an unpredictable magical ability within myself. It manifested at various times without me even trying. I thought practicing would help me learn to control it, but Mom and Dad had forbidden it, citing the grave consequences of defying the law.

So, I practiced in secret, driven by the fear that my power might reveal itself in the middle of town, forcing my family to pay the price for my transgression. Now, they were paying the price regardless, our home consumed by the same flames I had sought to master.

I surveyed my surroundings, a sense of eerie calm enveloping me as I observed the spot where I stood. For some reason, I remained untouched by the ravenous flames. From what I could see through the haze of smoke and ember, the rest of the house was a blazing inferno, a nightmarish landscape of destruction.

Knowing my parents were in grave danger, their lives and our home being consumed by the fire, my heart clenched with worry. The impending fallout from the town loomed over me like a suffocating shadow.

Smoke invaded my lungs, its tendrils choking me and wracking my body with violent coughing fits. My mind raced to find a way out of this hellish nightmare.

My eyes darted to the window, where flames roared through the open space. The extra air fueled the fire's voracious appetite as if it were a living, breathing entity hell-bent on devouring everything in its path.

Desperate to ease my breathing, I grabbed a t-shirt from the floor. I wiped my face and arms, hoping the moisture would create a barrier against the suffocating smoke. Tying the shirt around my face with trembling hands, I created a makeshift filter against the noxious fumes.

From downstairs, the anxious shouts and heavy footsteps of my parents rose through the air, their voices laced with desperation. Shit. They thought they could reach me. They'd risk their lives in the process.

"Nix!" Dad's rough voice reached my ears, a lifeline in the chaos.

"No, no, no!" I coughed out, my chest heaving with the effort. I couldn't bear the thought of him risking his life or Mom's. I crawled toward the hallway, desperate to get as close as possible despite the heat.

"Dad!" I called out, my voice strained and barely audible above the roar of the flames. "I'm—" A violent fit of coughing seized me, my lungs burning with each labored breath. "I'm okay! Get outside. I'm fine!"

My heart leaped in my chest when I heard another voice outside, one that sent a chill down my spine despite the oppressive heat. "Dad, come back!" It was Melian, my older brother, his presence a double-edged sword.

Had Melian witnessed me practicing? I wasn't sure. Thinking back, I realized my door had been partly open, a detail I hadn't paid attention to in my concentration. He might have seen the eerie change in my eyes as they turned a blazing red or the sparks that danced along my skin like fireflies. If he learned about my power now, then he had to turn me in—expose the secret my parents had tried so desperately to keep from him.

If I survived this hellish ordeal, what awaited me in Drade was a life of ostracism and imprisonment. The town would throw away the key. They'd never accept me as one of their own again. Never.

Sweat coated my body, every second in this house pushing me closer to the brink of death. Even if I made it past the wall of flames, I didn't want to face what waited for me outside. A sea of horrified faces, their eyes filled with judgment and fear.

I knelt on the floor, the cloth pressed against my face, and I was emotionally torn. If I didn't leave this room, I would die. If I did leave the room, I would probably die, and my family would suffer as well.

Anger welled up inside me, my maelstrom of emotions fueling the flames with renewed vigor. The fire roared, a deafening symphony of destruction. I realized I was an undeniable threat to my family. The town wouldn't want me after this—but I had one way out—an escape hatch Dad had prepared for me in case I needed it.

On my knees among the flames, a childhood memory surfaced, its edges blurred by time and smoke. My parents arguing, their raised voices filling the house while Melian was out with friends. I remembered the discomfort of hearing their heated words, coupled with my feelings of resentment toward Melian—for his freedom to enjoy the company of others while I stayed home alone.

I had pulled the blankets over my head and cried, my emotions so overwhelming that I didn't realize I was burning until I heard my dad's panicked yell. The scene replayed in my mind, a haunting reminder of the power I possessed and the consequences it could bring.

My dad discovering the flames, using a fire extinguisher, and buckets of water to put them out. He'd yelled to my mom, his eyes staring at me with a mixture of terror and wonder. My mom, racing up the stairs with more water, urgency in her eyes.

My Dad's eyes, filling with fear—fear for me—once he realized the fire hadn't even burned me. He'd grabbed a paper and pen from my desk, cautioning me as he wrote, "Nix, you can never let anyone know what happened today, understand? This can't happen again. If it does—if we don't catch it in time—The Law will come. They'll take you away. This is important.

"Drade is in an Outskirts Realm. The Arcane Alliance—the guardians of all magic at the Guilds of Chaos in Arnexis—they call our Realm the Mortal Realm. They despise Mortals, but if you need a place to go, if you are threatened with anyone finding out what you can do, travel there." He'd scrawled words on the paper, folded the note, and pressed it firmly in my hand. "Don't hesitate to go if you're in trouble. Say the words on this paper to get you there. Don't ever say them out loud until you're ready to go. Remember!"

He never mentioned it again. Neither did I. The silence hung between us like a heavy curtain, the weight of those unspoken words a constant reminder of the secret we shared.

I'd etched each syllable of that note into my mind like a sacred incantation, the words a mantra I mentally repeated in the quiet moments when the world closed

in around me. And now, as the flames consumed everything I had ever known, there was no escaping the repercussions of my fire. The note, along with most of my posses-
sions, was nothing more than ashes, a reminder of the power I
wielded but could not control.

"Shit, shit, shit." I didn't have much time. I'd have to use the
damn escape hatch, even though I didn't know what the spell
would do, or exactly where it would take me. It was supposed to
lead me to the Guilds of Chaos—to the Skia Guild, whatever that was, a place shrouded in mystery and intrigue.

The tears that streamed down my face evaporated as quickly as they hit my cheeks, the heat of the flames licking at my skin
like a cruel caress. I wanted to tell my parents goodbye, to hold
them close and never let go, but I knew it was impossible.

Dad would know where I'd gone, but that didn't make
me feel any better. Guilt and shame clung to me tighter than the
sweat on my skin, a suffocating blanket of emotions that threatened to drag me under. A deep well of sadness poured into me,
choking me harder than the smoke invading my lungs.

I didn't want my parents to risk their lives for a lost
cause. "I'm okay!" I yelled through the thick smoke, my voice
strained. "Get out of here now!"

This is all my fault. If I hadn't . . .

I heard shouting voices that faded away from me, growing distant like a half-remembered dream. Dad, Mom,
and Melian had to be out of the house now, safe from
the flames that threatened to consume us all. I hoped
they were okay, that they would find a way to move on without
me.

Time to go.

As I stood up for a moment, surrounded by a hellish landscape of my own making, I closed my eyes and pictured the
words on the note Dad had given me. The Guilds of Chaos.
The Skia Guild. He'd written words below the names, alien

words that were supposed to get me there, a lifeline in a sea of uncertainty. I was good at memorizing and good at languages. I clung to that knowledge like a drowning man to a piece of driftwood.

Squeezing my eyelids tight, I recited the words, nearly certain I was saying them right, each syllable a prayer, a plea for salvation. When the last syllable left my lips, I opened my eyes—and there was . . . nothing.

I pictured the paper again, my mind's eye tracing over each line, each curve of the letters, and I realized there'd been an accent mark over one of the words. I tried once more, using a different pronunciation, my tongue curling around the unfamiliar sounds.

I opened my eyes.

Relief poured through my heart as a dark mist swirled in front of me, a portal to the unknown, a gateway to a new life. A broad golden band arched over the mist like a doorway, and the billowing swirls within it glittered like stars in the night sky, beckoning me forward. This had to be the way into the Guilds of Chaos, the path to a future I couldn't even begin to imagine.

I inhaled as deeply as I dared, unsure if there'd be air in there—I knew nothing about this thing, this portal that promised to take me away from everything I had ever known. I got back down on my hands and knees where there was less smoke and crawled, the t-shirt slipping from my face as I entered the mist, passing under the archway, my body trembling with a mixture of fear and anticipation.

It had been close to a minute, and I still wasn't through. The seconds stretched out like an eternity as I held my breath, counting each one as it passed.

Sixty-one, sixty-two . . .

Then, the searing heat disappeared, replaced by a coolness that seeped into my bones, a balm to my battered soul. An adrenaline surge forced me to go faster, and I was crawling for one second, then my hands found lush, cool grass, the blades tickling my palms like a gentle caress. It was dark here, the sun having already set. The world was bathed in shadows and secrets.

I stood up, too rapidly I guess, because I promptly stumbled, fell, and smashed my head on a rock. Pain exploded behind my eyes like a supernova.

Or did someone push me? No, that's ridiculous. I brushed the thought away, my mind reeling from the impact of the events of the day. So much for my quick reflexes and martial arts training.

If Chicken could see me now. Ah, he'd start lecturing me about being aware of my surroundings at all times.

Chicken was my martial arts sensei and part-time sitter. As a kid, I stayed with him whenever my parents and brother went away on business or school trips. When we weren't training, we watched martial arts films.

My parents were extremely cautious, but I learned most of my distrust of others from my sensei. He wasn't bitter toward people, but taught me that, in general, even though most people had good natures, they were also unreliable. Chicken showed me examples of that over and over again during our lessons. I saw it, too, with my own eyes.

And tonight? Yeah, Chicken would have shaken his head at me and, with a wry smile on his face, said, "Fail. Get up. Go do it again."

The hot, sticky sensation of blood trickling down the side of my face tried to grab my attention, but I ignored it. I'd made it here. And I was alive!

The crisp, clear air felt blessedly cool—a stark contrast to the smoke that had filled my lungs only moments before. My lungs still rebelled from being assaulted with smoke. Another coughing fit took hold of me, my body shaking with the force of it.

I stared up, my eyes widening in wonder at the sight that greeted me. I couldn't remember ever seeing so many stars, the night sky, a canvas of twinkling lights, each one a promise of hope, of possibility. Drade was over an hour away from San Francisco, but the light pollution still affected the sky, dimming the beauty of the cosmos above.

But here, the constellations spun overhead like a kaleidoscope, a celestial display that left me breathless. I marveled at their beauty and at the sheer magnitude of the universe that stretched out before me.

My vision faded in and out, and the world around me turned into a hazy blur as a wave of dizziness washed over me. Lowering my gaze, I spied tall buildings in the distance, their silhouettes piercing the darkened sky like ancient sentinels. Some had lighted windows, glowing like beacons in the night, beckoning me forward. An alabaster dome rose high above them all, its surface gleaming like a celestial orb, casting an ethereal glow over the landscape.

The Guilds of Chaos—it had to be.

And somewhere nearby, the Skia Guild waited, promising salvation and answers to the questions that burned within me. I got up and tried to take some steps, but my body failed. My knees collapsed, and I crumpled to the ground, the cool grass soft against my battered form.

So close. I'm so close.

It felt like swimming in cool, thick water, the sensation both soothing and disorienting. A cacophony of voices surrounded me, their muffled and distant words intruding on my sleep like a morning alarm.

"Oh, dear Celestials, Daris, is she dead?" said a high-pitched voice laced with concern.

Another voice, deep, steady, and comforting, cut through the haze: "She's alive. Head injury. I don't know what else." Then, quickly, a note of authority ringing clear. "You! Call someone at Immaru. Everyone else, back to your classes!"

An uncontrollable groan escaped me as strong, warm arms lifted my body, cradling me against a solid chest. The muscles of my neck felt too weak to support my head, and I rested it against a firm chest, relaxing as the scent of cinnamon and cedar enveloped me. A flicker of hope sparked in my heart, and a faint smile found my lips.

I plummeted into darkness, the voices fading away like echoes in a vast cavern. I dreamed of firebombs decimating cities in front of me, the landscape a hellish wasteland. Dead eyes stared up at me from charred and smoking bodies covered by urban rubble, their lifeless gaze a silent reminder of my failure.

Frantic, I rushed towards a group of children, shouting in a desperate attempt to warn them, but each step became a Herculean effort. My feet dragged as if mired in quicksand, and I struggled to lift them—tried to make them run, to escape the nightmare engulfing me. Another firebomb landed on the group of children and exploded. the blast a searing flash of light that tore through the darkness of sleep.

I jolted awake, my eyes flying open as my breath raced and my heart pounded. I glanced around, disoriented and confused, wondering where the hell I was then I remembered. The Guilds of Chaos.

Tremors coursed through me from the nightmare's aftershocks. Maybe I was imagining it, but my mouth still tasted like ashes, and the scent of smoke clung to me like a second skin. It hurt to breathe, like someone had stuffed broken glass into my lungs.

I tried to focus, my eyes adjusting to the soft light that filled the room. Beautiful stone walls surrounded me, their smooth polished surfaces reflecting the warm, clinging light. I didn't see any lamps—it was like the walls themselves were alive, pulsing with a gentle radiance. I wasn't dreaming. I was really here, in this place of wonder and mystery. Soft fabric covered me in a bed, the white sheets smelling soothingly of lavender.

A man sat across from me, short locks of curly black hair framing his face. His presence was both comforting and unsettling.

A small gasp escaped me as I met the man's gaze, a flicker of recognition sparking in my mind. Did I know him? No. We'd never met, but his face seemed so familiar. I wondered if I'd seen it in a dream, though I never remembered dreams.

My eyes drifted to his plush, parted lips and the neatly trimmed beard adorning his jaw, his dark hair contrast starkly against his pale skin. He rubbed his chin, thoughtful, but paused when he realized I was fully awake, his maroon eyes locking with mine.

"Who are you?" I recognized his voice, gravelly with concern and suspicion, as the one that had been giving orders when I first arrived. It was a voice that commanded attention and respect.

Is this Daris?

Yes. This was the man who had carried me—the one who had brought me to safety. Even from a distance I caught his unmistakable scent of cinnamon and cedar.

My gaze shifted to his strange, maroon-colored eyes, their depths holding secrets I longed to unravel. I'd never seen eyes such a dark red before. I couldn't help myself as I focused on all of him, noting how his long-sleeved gray shirt hugged his broad chest and thick biceps, the fabric stretching taut over his muscular frame.

My pulse quickened, a heat rising within me that had nothing to do with fire. My mouth was dry, my tongue like sandpaper. I tried to swallow, instead erupting into a fit of coughing as my lungs rebelled.

The smoke. The fire!

The man rose from his chair and knelt by my side in an instant, his fluid and graceful movements belying the strength that rippled beneath his skin. He reached for a glass of water from the white stone dresser next to the bed, the crystal catching the light and throwing tiny rainbows across the room.

"Here. Drink. Take small sips for now." He offered me the glass, his voice gentle, almost tender.

The speed in which he moved shocked me. He placed his hand against the back of my head, his touch both electric and soothing. With a gentle touch, he helped me lean forward, supporting my weight as I brought the glass to my lips. The cool liquid soothed my parched throat, though I found it a challenge to swallow the first few times.

I was hyper-aware of the warmth emanating from his touch, the heat of his skin seeping into mine. I felt alive in a way I hadn't felt for a long time.

The pain receded from my chest, and the ache in my lungs eased with each sip of water. Something about the man's proximity calmed me. My muscles relaxed as the tension drained from my body. I fought the urge to surrender to the comfort he offered. Then, I remembered his question, and my lips pressed together, a flicker of uncertainty crossing my mind.

What if I'm not wanted here? What if my father didn't know this place well? I pushed the concern away, burying it deep within my mind.

My father wouldn't send me into harm's way. He'd be sure to send me to a place where I'd find help. My first action should be to find out what I'm dealing with, to assess the situation and gather information.

I asked, "Am I safe here?" My voice shook, charred and unrecognizable to my ears. I couldn't help it, the vulnerability in my tone betraying my heart.

Instead of answering me, he returned a question. "What happened to you?" He pulled back, his startling eyes searching mine for answers. Answers I wasn't ready to give.

When I hesitated, he settled into his seat and leaned forward with interest, his elbows against his knees. The strength and gentleness in his gaze pulled at me, even as I wished he'd provided me with some information first.

I'd be crazy to trust a stranger, someone I'd just met, even if he did help save me. How could I trust anyone right away? Certainly not before I understood my situation and what this place really was.

I huffed, annoyed. "Is this a custom here? Are we supposed to answer every question with a question?"

Laugh lines scored his cheeks and he pressed his lips together, a hint of amusement dancing in his eyes. He tried once more. "I only want—"

A new voice interrupted: "Oh, dove, I'm so glad you're awake! It's late evening. We wanted you to rest, but we must get going!"

A plump girl, close to my age, with quick steps and dark auburn hair popped into view.

Late evening? Confusion washed over me.

"How long have I been asleep?" I still found it difficult to talk, but I'd at least managed the question.

The girl paused as if perplexed and then touched the tips of her fingers as if counting the hours. "I believe twenty or so in all. But part of that was in Beauty Sleep—a little pun we stole from the Mortal Realm, "she chuckled. "Our Immaru placed you in a suspended sleep state, if you will, while he checked you and made sure you were okay. Speaking of okay, is there anything you need before your trial? Food, perhaps, or a change of clothes? Oh—I'm the silly one. You will definitely need clothes!"

As the girl gestured toward me, I realized I no longer wore my shirt and pants, but someone had placed me in a modest black slip. My boots were near my bedside. I caught her disconcerted stare at what I was wearing but ignored the clothing issue for the moment. I had bigger concerns.

"My—trial?" More questions. I looked from the girl to the man; neither of them could look away, but they wouldn't meet my eyes.

"My brother didn't tell you yet? I see. You don't know anything about this world, do you?" She tapped her toe thoughtfully. "You came here through a portal, with your own spell, apparently. That's amazing. Only Magisars, Guildmasters, and Archgnos—the graduate Apprentices—can do that. You have some magic, but you've never Apprenticed. You haven't been properly ignited and trained. This is not allowed in the Realms, you see, so the Arcane Alliance must hear your case and decide what to do with you."

I tried very hard not to look surprised and frustrated but slowly shook my head. Dad had never mentioned this. Melian's words echoed in my mind—'*Reveal only what is necessary to strangers—no more.*' This was true with anything. Being seen—being known—that was dangerous, I'd learned.

In Drade, people didn't ask questions because they were curious about you. No, they had other motives. People in town were paranoid about anything that resembled magic.

"You are safe here." The maroon-eyed man finally answered one of my questions.

Well, yay. Thanks for that.

The man raised his tattooed wrist, glancing at a gleaming silver watch adorned with moonstones. I wanted to see his tattoo, but he stood, his eyes fixed on mine.

"Speaking of the trial, I must make arrangements. My sister will explain the procedures." As the man's gaze averted, a strange desperation surged within me, and I wanted to follow him, but his sister's radiant expression interrupted my view as she stuck her face right in front of mine. Her bright green eyes sparkled, and she grinned.

"Oh yes! Don't you worry! I'm Elena, by the way." Words tumbled out of her mouth. "That was Daris, my older brother. He's a Guildmaster and a mentor for Apprentices at the Skia Guild—that's where we are. How are you feeling? An Immaru cleared you. We needed someone more advanced to check you over since you aren't from here. The Immaru Guildmaster came to us to learn more about what happened, and well—now you're all better!"

I slowly nodded along, trying to learn what I could while reeling as if her speech had taken me on a rollercoaster ride. I looked at her, finding her pattern of freckles engaging.

"I'm Phoenix. I prefer the name Nix," I told her, making an effort to sound friendly, though my voice sounded flat and dull. I so felt drained. Still, I figured since I was here now, at the Guilds of Chaos, it was best to get down to making friends. Better that than enemies. "What's an Immaru?"

"Oh, they are our healers, among other things," she answered with a chuckle. "This is Leander. He's a very high-level Immaru—the head of his Guild here. Their group is called Vivomance. Not that you needed a high-level Immaru, mind you. Your wounds were superficial, and you would have been just fine. You were dehydrated, too. As Guildmaster, Leander is familiar with many different species, we only wanted to be sure you were okay before taking you to your room."

I suspected there was more to it than that. I was a stranger. They'd kept me sleeping for twenty hours. Surely, someone assessed that I wasn't a threat, but I didn't want to challenge her.

My gaze shifted to Leander. He was a tall and ageless man, his willowy figure, clad in white, reminding me of wispy clouds in an azure sky. He glided toward me like a gentle breeze, and he smelled like the freshest open air.

I inhaled deeply as he approached and somehow felt better. His pale blue eyes were large and calm. If he had any hair, it was tucked under his white cap.

Using a palm-sized clear crystal, he conducted a final check on me before allowing us to leave. I observed with curiosity as he pulled something from his robes that looked a lot like a cell phone, only it shimmered, pretty, and almost translucent.

Elena saw me staring and quickly explained. "Oh! That's our Celcom. Named after our dear Celestials—we love them so! Celcoms help us communicate across any distance, to any Realm. They're life savers, really.

Our Oscuro Guild gave us this gift of magic creation. We have Tessar Pads, too, but we use them mostly during our classes and in residence. They're portable, but they're difficult magic to maintain on the go. Celcoms are better."

My brain buzzed as I pushed my feet into my boots, the sensation of feeling grounded once more flooding me with relief. Elena handed me a full-length cardigan to wrap around the slip I wore. A chill caused me to shiver, and I crossed my arms close to my chest and followed Elena through the dark hallways of the Skia Guild.

Orbs of soft light clung to the walls, and Leander's fresh scent was replaced by something that smelled earthy, ancient, and full of minerals. Not unpleasant. I sensed that the stones—welcomed me if such a thing were possible.

After a few more moments, Elena guided me through a large archway and common room, then up the spiraling stairs of a wide tower and past a row of impossibly tall windows that shimmered with their own soft light, their stained-glass designs rearranging themselves every few seconds.

And that wasn't all. Gargoyle statues nestled into intermittent niches along the inside tower wall. At least, I thought they were statues—but then one of them moved its hand to scratch a pointed ear. I gasped, nearly falling down the steps in surprise.

Elena burst out laughing. "Ah yes! Don't be afraid. The goyles are regulars. They don't bother anyone—usually." She paused, her gaze lingering on one of them. "You'll get used to them. Just don't feed them. You'll never get rid of them. *Never.*"

She said her last word, *never,* with such a serious face that I nearly laughed out loud. I had a vision of someone feeding tons of "goyles" and having a flock of them following that person everywhere. Then, I couldn't hold it in. I did burst out with laughter. Elena turned toward me, curious.

Still laughing, I just shook my head, my eyes streaming with tears. I chalked my reaction up to delirium, exhaustion, and perhaps more dehydration. It didn't stop me from continuing to smile, picturing hordes of gargoyles following someone around.

The tower's stone stairs were wide enough for groups of people to ascend at a time. The passage was nearly empty now except for two young individuals wearing dark robes. They huddled together, peering over some kind of scroll. One seemed to be taking pictures of it or scanning it with their Celcom.

"Apprentices," Elena explained. "And up very late." She shook her head.

Elena chattered the rest of the way up the steps. "I'm sure you have nothing to worry about regarding your trial. You'll stay here until you're officially assigned to a Guild. Oh, I do hope you stay! Believe it or not, despite our reputation, Bloodwraith welcomes new Apprentices. And there are plenty of programs to help you catch up with lessons—you have excellent timing; we started this term only last month. It's entering our spring session—right after the New Year, and the new Apprentices just had their Blaze Ceremony . . ." She carried on like she thought I'd planned to come here.

"Do you get to choose your Guild?" As the words left my lips, I thought my question was stupid. Did I really have a choice where I went? I had no clue. I wanted to be in a place where someone would teach me how to control my crazy powers. Somewhere I couldn't hurt anyone.

"Not exactly. But there are other wonderful Guilds here, in case you don't stay with us. Did I already mention the Teravites of the Terra Guild? They have strong Earth magic. We're Bloodwraith, of course, and then there's the Casterfire of the Magus Guild. They're arrogant because all the Apprentices there have widespread abilities, and many are legacies from rich families. And the Neptanos, you probably guessed they're water-based —the Mernai Guild—and well, they are very welcoming and wouldn't even call for a trial if you'd shown up there. Watch out for them, though. They can get a little too friendly. Let's see," Elena finally paused and took a breath. "If you're good at being stealthy and like discovering secrets, the Phorates might take you in the Oscuro Guild. Next to us, they make some of the best spies . . . "

I let her ramble on, feeling as if I wouldn't remember a thing, she told me even though I wanted to. I still wondered how someone was assigned to a Guild. Elena hadn't said.

The cold night air made me shiver as we headed outside. Elena's black slip was not designed for warmth. The sweater was some comfort at least.

We emerged onto a path that wound around the upper levels of the tower. Though the view was spectacular, I kept my eyes closely trained on the path in front of us. I noticed with a glance that, even in the sunlight, the tower had a translucent skull shining brightly above it. Skia Guild's tower.

Why did we have to go to the top of the building? Why couldn't a portal take us where we needed to go?

I thought of the spell I'd learned from my father, and I wondered how it worked. He'd titled it the *Anywhere Spell*. After cracking my head on a rock from using it last time, the thought of trying it again was daunting, but if I practiced, maybe it would be worth it. I shivered again.

Elena glided ahead, unfazed by my internal turmoil. She turned to look at me, and with an encouraging smile, she gestured to the walkway in front of us. "Trust your feet to carry you, as they always have, and you won't fall. There are sets of stairs that descend from each top wall so Apprentices can find their proper corridor. Don't worry. I got you!"

In general, I hated two things. Heights and water. My fear of heights was irrational, maybe, but I didn't like the thought of falling and my body being smashed into bits everywhere. And water—well—I never learned how to swim. We lived inland, away from San Francisco, and I'd never known anyone with a pool. The closest I came to water immersion was a bathtub and a stream or small river up to my waist. I couldn't imagine what it would be like to be in water where you couldn't touch the bottom.

I peered down and swallowed my fear. Elena held out her hand for me, and I took it, happy to feel more anchored to the building as the wind gusted around us.

With tentative steps, I followed her until we reached the second side of the building, my hair whipping around my face making it difficult to see. She guided me through the entrance and down the staircase. It was dark at first, but then soft lights flickered to life as we passed over the threshold to the second level, cheerful voices echoing ahead of us.

"We don't have much time, so I'll introduce you to the other girls in our wing later." Elena led me through a common room, acknowledging others with nods and brief greetings. In the center of the room, girls lounged on plush red couches or nestled in comfy chairs while another sat on a bench and played soft and haunting music on a grand piano.

Elena ushered me into another hallway. We rounded a few corners until she stopped in front of a plain black door decorated with a silver pentagram enclosed in a circle. The design was larger than the size of my palm and was about head height. Elena stopped and waved her hand, and a flash of glittery silver light appeared as her door opened.

As we entered, she pointed to a large closet. "Take anything you'd like. You can try things on, and I'll wait out here. I do hate to rush you after all you've been through, but you need to be quick. There's a little relief room to the right if you need it."

As she stepped back outside, I reached out to lay my hand on her arm.

"Thank you, Elena. Truly. You've been so kind to me." Her eyes gleamed, but she shrugged off my words with a smile and a wink as she closed the door. Acts of kindness like hers were unfamiliar to me, and her assistance helping me by holding my hand on top of the building, well that was a gesture beyond the ordinary.

Elena's room featured one untouched bed and another piled high with blankets and pillows. Neatly tucked wardrobes flanked a desk, creating an atmosphere of both comfort and extravagance.

I stepped into the closet and surveyed the clothing. There were only dresses here—no pants or boots in sight. I sighed but selected a lush green dress, which fell a little below my knees, and a set of matching shoes. I put them on, worried about the fit, but the both the shoes and dress surprised me by automatically adjusting to my size.

I did a quick clean-up with a fresh washcloth, combed through my hair with my fingers, and then dressed. I examined myself in the full-length mirror, determining I looked presentable. Elena nodded her approval when I emerged.

On our way, Elena waved her hand over me, and when we passed by a mirror. I noted she'd done my hair in a matching green bow. I cringed. I didn't do bows, but it did look nice.

Following Elena up the stairs I hurried ahead, only stumbling twice as I tried walking in the heels. She led me around the top of the building, down the tower, and out of the Skia building. The alabaster building with the enormous, round dome I'd seen when I first arrived loomed before me. Its gold-trimmed windows, gleaming in the sunlight, seemed ominous now.

We entered an expansive room with pentagonal stone walls inside. The main level Elena and I entered was lined with rows of chairs on the main floor which nearly empty with exception to the first two rows up front where a few people sat, then more seating ascended going up the walls, and that seating was also empty.

On a raised dais were eight imposing chairs set before a rounded white area that looked as large as a stage and as intimidating as a boxing ring. To the right of those chairs and set just back of larger seats were smaller chairs. I assumed they were for assistants or the second person in charge.

Elena placed a gentle hand on mine. "Only address them once they've spoken to you, understand? Don't tell them anything more than what they ask, but don't be evasive, or they'll ask more. As long as you tell the truth, you'll be fine. Good luck, dove."

I squeezed Elena's hand. She bowed her head to the figures before hurrying on. Silence enveloped the room as the eight cloaked figures loomed on a dais a few steps higher than me. Undaunted, I raised my head as high as possible, straightening my back, and resisting the urge to fidget.

As long as I tell the truth. Right. Well, they'll find out soon enough.

Call it a mutation, a curse—call it what you will—but whenever I lie, my skin turns scarlet. And I don't mean like I'm blushing. Oh no. It turns the full-on siren color. It's beyond blood red—we're talking ruby-throat hummingbird "Look, I'm lying" scarlet.

My parents loved it–I'd had to unlearn lying because the Town Council of Drade would have charged me with magic use. They'd have taken me away, maybe sentenced me to death if they found out about my fire. My curse was the bane of my brother's existence. I could never lie for him, and I had to get damn creative when it came to telling the truth. So, I learned to push the boundaries of truths and lies.

Seconds ticked by—

Twenty, twenty-one, twenty-two . . .

The two central figures stood, pushing back their hoods. To my relief, the one to my left was Daris. His was a reassuring presence my heart warmed to see. I refrained from smiling at him, not knowing the protocol here. I redirected my attention to the stern woman on the right who had also risen.

Her penetrating gaze bored into me, sending spidery chills up my spine. I didn't sense a spark of warmth or the slightest dryer lint of fuzzy feelings coming from her. For some reason, my mind went back to an image of Leander—the Immaru. I inhaled, pretending I had that fresh air scent he gave off right in front of me and his calm, large eyes. That felt better.

Now. What the hell was next?

DARIS

SCARLET

The girl Nix masked her nerves adeptly, but I saw anxiety in the subtle dance of her body language, her weight shifting anxiously as she stood. I barely recognized the girl after Elena had clothed her in a new green dress with matching heels. She tucked her plump bottom lip behind her teeth as she mentally prepared for questions.

Elena's influence was apparent. She'd counseled the girl on the proper way to provide her self-introduction.

The court's administrator, Uli Umber, a man of small stature who was of mixed human and halfling blood, entered the Court Arena—the flat round platform in front of the Arcane Alliance members and the Gallery—and announced Nix's case. He brought out his Tessar Pad, calling up the information he needed.

"Good morning, Alliance members. I present to you the case of Ms. Phoenix Emberwind, of an Unknown Realm. Ms. Emberwind came to us wounded last night. She is staying at the

Skia Guild and is seeking admittance to the Guilds of Chaos. She is charged with possessing magic before it was properly ignited and not attending the Guilds of Chaos as an Apprentice at the appointed time. This is all we know." He turned his head to Nix, gesturing that she should come now to state her case.

Nix took a deep breath and stepped forward. Though she'd fidgeted before, she seemed in full command of herself now. I judged her to be no more than eighteen or nineteen, and I wondered why she hadn't been brought to us beforehand so she could be properly introduced.

Her father obviously knew about us because he gave her the spell. He had to know Realm laws. Nix should have attended the Blaze Ceremony and had her power ignited so she could have Apprenticed. He'd placed her at great risk.

Nix's voice was, for the most part, strong, containing only the slightest quaver. I tried not to find her flaming hair distracting, the way it framed her face—or note how her pulse thrummed at her neck, inviting me to sip there so easily.

And her scent—so unique—I had a hard time describing the essence of it! It wasn't anything typically feminine, not herbal, floral, or fruity, and it wasn't exotic like an incense or animal musk.

Hers was like that pleasant scent of a burning fire you huddle over when you feel too cold like the crackly air after lightning has just zapped the sky. Oh—hers was the odor of the newest pine needles on the wind mixed with the breath of a baby Agon just hatched from an egg. Bind all of that, mix it with sea spray and a sunset by the Observatree in Autumn, and . . . I was so lost in watching and smelling her that I nearly fell out of my chair when she spoke.

"Good morning, Arcane Alliance members," she began, using the full Alliance name. "I go by the name of Nix. I am from a town in one of the Outskirts Realms, one which harshly penalizes anyone who displays magic. I come here seeking refuge and ask your permission to train at the Guilds of Chaos. Recent tragedy struck my home. Yesterday, it burned to the ground. My father assured me I could find safety—and find answers to my type of magic."

Nix's gaze swept around the room, and she took time to look at every member. "My parents are not well off. They have basic living and meager supplies—unlike this fine building and the rich foods I saw this morning. Our town does have enemies, though, and so my dad taught me how to get here in case I needed your help. Yesterday, I needed your help very much."

I kept myself silent and unmoving as the High Inquisitor, Guildmaster Devereux, stood from his gold-trimmed chair and strode toward the stand. The rest of the Alliance remained seated, their attention focused on the unfolding scene.

Short, polished horns protruded from Devereux's head, gleaming under the courtroom's bright lights. His immaculate blond hair and trimmed goatee gave him the look of a serious man intent on his prize. The black suit he wore was tailored to perfection, and I could not detect a trace of dust or lint on it.

My colleague was obsessed with his appearance. He'd once called his impeccable style his armor.

However, Devereux's clothing was not in keeping with his Guild for this occasion. He was the Magus Guildmaster. His Guild collected the most versatile of all Apprentices, and its main symbol was the element of fire.

The Magus Guild's colors were gold and red, and its house name at the Guilds of Chaos in Arnexis was Castafire. I suspected he felt theatrical tonight and desired to separate his look from the Grand Guildmaster's.

Technically, Seraphina was the Magus Guildmaster, but since she'd been elected to the position of Grand Guildmaster, she appointed Devereux to oversee the Magus Guild in her stead. Many new conflicts plagued the Realms, and many magic violations occurred—often related to Demomancers. Too many for Seraphina to pay attention to her Guild and also serve as Magus Guildmaster.

Ignoring Nix's name preference, Devereux launched into his questions about her origins.

"One Who Calls Herself Phoenix," he started, addressing her in a ridiculous manner, "please answer for the Alliance. Where exactly do you come from? Be specific."

I watched Nix's internal struggle as she remained silent. Her fear was evident in the quickening of her pulse. Few people understand how well Sangors hear, how even covert spells designed to keep conversations secret are nothing to us, our powers stretching through and beyond them.

Unfortunately, the girl either knew nothing about Compulsion magic or was goading Devereux to use the spell. I winced internally, knowing that if he compelled her, she'd suffer some significant pain. Devereux was highly accomplished in that art. Given what Nix had already been through, she might tolerate it, or she might not.

"I will ask you again," Deveraux said, placing his fingers together below his chin, his glare boring into her. "Where do you come from?"

The girl remained silent, lifting her chin ever so slightly in defiance. I sighed, recognizing the futility of her resistance.

Devereux's face was stoic, but I saw the glint in his eye. He parted his fingers and made an intricate motion with his hand. The girl looked genuinely surprised as her eyes widened. She dropped to her knees, gripping her abdomen, the blast of pain overwhelming her. Slowly, she stood, regaining her footing as she straightened her dress.

"Well, that hurt. Thank you for your kind introduction to your capabilities." Nix threw an incinerating glare toward Devereux. I thought it was fortunate that she didn't know how to use her powers yet, whatever they were. "I come from . . . an Outskirt Realm," Nix finished, her voice strained but resolute.

It was clear the girl was not going to give up answers easily.

Devereux pressed, "Tell us the name of your Realm, girl," his tone demanding and unyielding.

Nix hesitated, and this time, Devereux gave no quarter. With another motion of his hand, Nix dropped to the ground once more. Gauging from the emotions crossing her face, I suspected she understood this session would be long and painful unless she cooperated. She seemed to be deciding if the information she had was worth keeping a secret. Sparks glinted in her eyes.

Nix pressed her lips together, pushed her shoulders back, and her glorious red hair swung slightly. A defiant answer burst from her lips: "I am from . . . home."

My jaw nearly dropped. I thought for sure the girl would give in. She was suffering. I knew it. And yet, I was powerless to step in until it was my turn. Apprentice attendees in the gallery shifted in their seats uncomfortably.

Compulsion spells brought forth immediate answers that required the truth, but everyone knew the spells could not compel what truth the person chose to reveal. Our protocol within the Alliance was for Devereux to extract what information he could, first, out of respect for his position as High Inquisitor. He was not a cruel man, usually, but one who valued authority and rules. In his eyes, he was simply doing his job.

The verbal exchange escalated as a determined Nix glowered at Devereux, prompting my internal struggle to suppress laughter at the gravity of the situation while experiencing serious concern for Nix. I knew she was no threat. How I knew, I couldn't explain.

But that was something I might have to ask the Faen Astral Temporal Element Sisters, known by most as The FATES. I'd have to work myself up to see them if I had to, though. Encounters with them required preparation, and they demanded special services as payment.

Devereux pressed Nix for more information about her Realm, escalating the tension in the room. Nix remained resolute, describing her Realm without naming it.

"It has great trees—oaks. Do you have oaks? I used to climb them all the time."

The seriousness of the matter heightened, and the Alliance's disapproval grew like thunderclouds on a summer afternoon. Nix's steadfast refusal to provide direct answers was akin to placing an iron rod upright in the middle of a field and holding it tight as a lightning storm blew in on Ur. Not a good idea.

Devereux, strong in his stance, argued the importance of recognizing Realms that refused Guild acknowledgment and ferreting out infiltrators. He cited the work of Demomancers as part of his argument. This line of questioning was becoming pejorative, and if the girl was going to stay here—for however long—she deserved to feel safe.

"Am I safe?" When she'd asked me that earlier, I'd thought it was a silly question, but now I wasn't sure. Was it possible that she didn't know much about where she really was? Was it possible that, where she came from, she didn't feel safe?

Part of me admired her, though, and I wondered if she'd ever been coached. This was what we taught our spies and warriors if they were ever captured: answer without answering. It was one way to get through an interrogation.

I raised a brow at the Grand Guildmaster, catching her eye, and received her bored nod. She was flipping through messages on her Celcom. It seemed she felt she had better things to do, which told me she didn't think Nix had anything to do with Demomancers. At last, I could intervene.

I rose and strode to stand beside Devereux, who reluctantly relinquished his position to sit in the Inquisitor chair.

"Alliance members," I addressed them, "one of the purposes of our allied Guilds is to serve as a safe haven for magic folk misunderstood in their Realms. We have never turned away those sincerely seeking sanctuary." I noted several heads nodding as they surveyed the young Nix.

My thoughts revisited the haunting image of Nix's frail form, clad in burned and tattered clothes, gasping for air—though oddly, not a space on her skin suffered burns anywhere. Memories of her whimpering as I carried her to receive care from the Immaru echoed in my mind.

The delicate balance of power and the clash of perspectives among Guilds weighed heavy on me. I was the Guildmaster of Bloodwraith, the name of our Skia Guild. The Alliance's impending decision would not only shape Nix's fate but also ripple through the intricate web of the Alliance's dynamics.

I decided on a different approach with the girl. "Nix." Chaos and Celestials, how I enjoyed the sound of her name. "Please describe to the Alliance, *in detail*, the situation that brought you to us." I emphasized the words 'in detail' using a dab of my Sangor seduction to influence her. Not a bone in my body felt guilty about it either.

Nix's hazel eyes met mine. Their green tone more prominent now, flecked with blue and red.

Caught between her desire not to say anything about her Realm and my seduction influence, her bemused reply was almost comical.

"My home caught fire." Nix addressed the entire gallery now, and her eyes caught on each Alliance member as she described her situation. "It was destroyed. I was trapped in the middle of the blaze. My father taught me a spell a long time ago that would transport me here if I were ever in trouble. I never needed it before now. For years, our family has been under the threat of magic that could easily destroy us. My parents tried to get me to come here before this, but I refused to leave them. Until now." Nix lowered her gaze, her face a transparent picture of confusion. Tears threatened to spill down her cheeks. She blinked quickly to stop them.

I hated myself, not wanting to press too hard. But extracting answers from her was for the girl's own good. If she didn't give the Alliance something, she'd end up in a place she would never come back from—and the Alliance would learn everything anyway. "Can you tell me more about your Realm?" The seduction in my voice wrapped around her like a warm blanket.

"Yes," she whispered, her voice barely audible. Then, she raised her head. "I live, or lived, in a small town. Nowhere important. It is filled with simple people. Farmers and artisans, mostly. We have very little interaction with the Guilds, though our people support their fight against keeping magic from the Mortal Realm and ensuring evil does not overtake the Outskirt Realms."

"And why do you feel it would threaten your town if you were to name it? There are only a handful of those who possess pure Orphic blood in the Mortal Realm, such as yourself."

With a sharp inhale, Devereux shot to his feet. "Objection! Orphic blood? Why wasn't I informed she had Orphic blood?" His face reddened, part in embarrassment, I surmised, and part in anger. Devereux did not like to be surprised. He prided himself in knowing everything. Me—I prided myself in keeping secrets.

Nix's incendiary glare washed over Devereux, and then she shifted her attention to me—her eyes filled with questions. "How do you know that? You're joking, right? My parents don't do magic, or whatever . . ."

I ignored Nix's outburst and answered Devereux.

"I had contact with the girl's blood shortly after she arrived. She was injured." I faced the Alliance members, intent on reassuring them. "As you all know, my abilities allow me to understand the nature of the blood I taste. She arrived injured, and I wiped the blood away from her face. I attempted to determine who she was so we could provide the correct medical treatment, and I can confirm that it is indeed pure Orphic blood."

No way could I tell them how delicious that taste was—how it made me want more. It took concentrated effort to divert my gaze from a pulsing vein in Nix's neck. And there was more—much more to tell—but they could not know any of it.

Devereux raised his voice, "This only goes to show that the girl's lack of transparency, combined with her strong magic nature, places us all at risk. She could be a spy or sent to infiltrate us by the Demomancers!"

Hisses and gasps rose from the gallery.

I nodded, conceding his point. It was a valid concern. Still, I countered. "Or she could simply need our help."

Devereux redirected his scrutiny toward Nix, who continued to stare back at him as if she were ready to call on Agon breath to reduce him to cinders. "There's an air of suspicion about you, One Who Calls Herself Nix. If you persist in keeping your origin veiled, I fear there might not be a place for you among us."

My jaw tightened. He 'feared.' I wanted to laugh. There was not an ounce of fear in Guildmaster Devereux. Regrettably, though, he wasn't wrong. The glances from the Alliance members reflected my doubts about trusting in Nix.

But the more I considered her, the more certain I felt I was right to support her. I recalled how I'd found her and how her Orphic blood tasted. The sound of truth in her words accompanied by a steady heartbeat—these things were undeniable.

At Nix's wide-eyed, uncertain gaze, I squared my shoulders and addressed the Alliance and their attendants one by one.

"Hemere," I uttered, turning to the head of Spell Theory and a fellow Sangor from the Skia Guild. "When you sought refuge in the Skia Guild, you were teetering on the brink of death. Your brother's misguided spell laid a powerful curse on you, and you had nowhere to go. Despite the risks to all who touched you, did you readily divulge your situation the moment you knew you'd survive with our help?"

Hemere tilted his head thoughtfully. His dark skin and black eyes shimmered with a deep blue tint. He slowly shook his head once.

"And you, Gauge," a Slay Orc and Guildmaster of Bellator who loved competing with me, stared back, "you were unfamiliar with the Guilds when your father brought you here after the wars of Madigan. Can you recall the terror that caused?" He grunted, leaned over, and whispered to Wyvana, his Second, and inwardly, I smiled.

Grand Guildmaster Seraphina growled. "What's your point, Guildmaster?"

I clasped my hands behind my back, directing my words to Devereux while keeping Nix in view. "We help those who need our help. Our ranks have grown stronger because of it. I say we grant Ms. Nix Emberwind two days to address our inquiries. Let her acclimate to Bloodwraith. Let her learn more about us. If she refuses to answer afterward, then we bar her from the Guilds. I'll personally assume responsibility to ensure she poses no threat." The last statement slipped from my lips as a strategic move to sway the decision, though it happened before I realized what I was saying.

Nix's head tilted, uncertain, but surprise filled her eyes when she heard my words.

She leveled her gaze at me. "Will it help if I demonstrate to the Alliance a weakness I have? What may be considered a curse or vulnerability that pushed me toward leaving my town?"

"It might," I answered and glanced around. The Alliance members had expressions of astonishment and mild approval on their faces. Many seemed curious about what this girl could possibly show them that could help gain their trust.

"Then, I will demonstrate to you that I am incapable of lying."

I was taken aback. The statement prompted gasps and whispers all around. How could we tell? Now, this would be interesting, and if it were true, I felt very sorry for the girl. There were very few species in all the Realms capable of complete honesty. It was the nature of all things to be dishonest about something sometime in their lives.

"Ask me something obvious right now that everyone can see," she said, encouraging me.

"Okay," immediately going for what some men always wonder. "What is the natural color of your hair?"

"Green," she announced loudly so everyone could hear. Those with sight, who saw color in the rainbow spectrum, clearly saw her hair as auburn or red.

The entire room held its breath—waiting to see what would happen. Before the entire room, Nix's skin turned the brightest shade of red I'd ever seen on a species. It was practically neon. The gallery sucked in its breath, and there were "ohs" and "ahhs" from the crowd.

I flicked a glance to Devereux, who had to feel a bit silly now, seeing the girl was incapable of lying.

The color red disappeared quickly from Nix's skin. I tried a couple more questions until her curse, mutation, or "tell"—whatever it was—became quite evident.

I turned to the Alliance. "Once more. All in favor of my proposal to allow Nix, Ms. Emberwind, two days to reconsider answering our questions appropriately, with me as her responsible interim mentor?"

"Concur!" The word echoed from each member of the Minor Alliance. Devereux hesitated, unable to maintain dissent against the masses, and nodded his agreement. His eyes held no warmth as they met mine. I could tell he felt the delay wasted time.

"Let us both hope you don't regret this."

I jutted my chin, defiant. "I'll never regret trying to save a life."

"It will never make up for the ones you've taken, Daris," Devereux snapped.

I sucked in a breath sharply, repressing my instant reflex to throw him down and rip his gleaming horns out of his head. He had no right to bring *that* up. That was long ago. He referred to a time of war. When the deaths were necessary.

But were they? Necessary? I should away the thought.

While Devereux and I shared disagreements, I believed we ultimately sought the Guild's best interests. I wanted to trust him as a challenging voice with a diverse perspective and, at the end of the day, a respected colleague. But sometimes, he stepped over the line.

Draped in Magus colors of gold and red, with a hood framing her dark curls, she surveyed the courtroom from her chair, maintaining her composure. Her hawkish eyes studied Nix and me. I'd convinced myself that the Grand Guildmaster wasn't concerned about this trial, but the fact that she'd bothered to be here meant something.

Seraphina clapped her hands, amplifying the sound so that all the voices stilled. Her gaze swept around the room, then landed on Nix. "We will reconvene in two days," she announced, "after which the Alliance will decide on the girl's fate."

The Grand Guildmaster had the power to cast Nix out of Arnexis without a second glance—and since Nix's power was already awakened, that meant a one-way trip to Lethenthril if she didn't stay here. Seraphina held out her hands in a gesture for silence.

"Please be aware, everyone—I've called for the Arcane Alliance to convene at the Cor in one week. Serious matters at hand may require immediate action on our part, so be ready. Each Guildmaster may bring two representatives with them, a Second and an Apprentice. You can ask your questions then. You are dismissed." Seraphina drew a circle with her right pointer finger and made as if placing her right palm and four upright fingers through the circle and out toward the members—her thumb curled across her palm. Members returned the gesture, including me.

The announcement of the continuation loomed heavy in the air. I stepped down from the Court Arena and moved toward Nix. The emotions crossing her face reminded me of when I confronted my prey. It was clear that she understood there was no escape.

"You'll be fine, Nix. Elena will help you settle in." I tried on a gentle smile and hoped my Sangor seduction power would fill her with confidence and warmth. Deceptive—but effective. "I have a final class to teach." Thankfully, Elena whisked her away.

A melodic hum interrupted us, preempting Seraphina's departure. The Grand Guildmaster's scrutiny, directed at both Nix as she left with Elena and toward me, gave me a sense of foreboding. I pondered Nix's safety and the enigmatic circumstances that had drawn Seraphina's attention to her. Seraphina took a moment to descend the stairs and come toward me.

"Grand Guildmaster," I acknowledged her with a slight bow of my head, "how may I assist you?"

As the other Alliance members dispersed, I noted Devereux cast a jealous glance our way as he exited, leaving me alone with the Maestra. I suspected he'd hoped for time alone with her as well—though for different reasons.

Too late, my friend.

I faced Seraphina, raising an eyebrow. Her scent reminded me of ancient pine forests, rich earth, and deep dark waters. And something else. Not quite unpleasant, just unsettling somehow.

"A few words, Guildmaster."

I nodded.

"Keep a close eye on your Apprentices. Everything we know is about to change, Daris. Everything." Seraphina closed her eyes, appearing oddly vulnerable.

Unsure of her meaning, I hesitated before reassuring her. "I always look out for my Apprentices. The building has sentries at night, and we have a good number of gargoyles this year."

gargoyles flew into their individual Guilds at night. They were loyal to their Guild and kept watch for anyone who trespassed—even other Guild members. They did tend to drop their excrement in different places inside and out, but since it was highly flammable and used in potions classes, there weren't many complaints about cleaning it up.

"Do you, Daris? Keep close eyes on your Apprentices?" She opened her eyes, her gaze now calculating—far from vulnerable. "I know you, *Sangor*. You are a prodigy—the youngest to ever become a Guildmaster. So skilled at siphoning blood from your prey that they aren't even aware of it. Your magic is legendary. Oh, now, don't look so surprised. I know everything about every Guildmaster. And the girl can do more than change colors when she lies—I know that much *now*, though I don't know what yet. I'll let the girl stay until we all make a decision, but I expect to be alerted if anything major happens. Do you understand?"

"What's drawn your attention to Ms. Emberwind, if I may, Maestra?"

A tight-lipped smile crossed Seraphina's face. "We'll discuss that another time. But the pure Orphic blood *that* surprised everyone. Don't do that again. I need to know what you know. Like how you suspect she might carry other traits similar to yours."

She narrowed her gaze at me, then glanced at an exquisite timepiece on her wrist, an almost-white metal I didn't recognize that formed a design of twisted snowflakes around the red face. Then she looked at her Celcom and swiped the face of it a couple of times. "Aren't you late to your class?"

Seraphina vanished. I hadn't even seen her cast the spell. The courtroom stood empty now, and I shivered. It wasn't the Grand Guildmaster's words that bothered me; it was how she knew details she shouldn't. I hadn't told anyone what I'd suspected about Nix. Adjusting my shirt collar, I headed to class.

My Apprentices eyed me curiously, their discussions obviously revolving around the new girl, Nix. I clenched my jaw and forced myself to relax, struggling to put the girl out of my head as I addressed the class.

"Apologies for my tardiness, everyone. Tonight's focus is on enhancement. Pair up with a person of different magic types or combinations and find ways in which you are similar. If you have Teragos, find Aquane. If Myrocans, find another Myrocans and compare which magic types you have and find those similarities. Then, look at those differences. After that, get out your battle-map. Plan how you would use these against each other and discuss the pros and cons. Tomorrow, we will try your strategies out at the Parabellum Arenas."

It never failed to give me a sense of pride and excitement when I watched Apprentices launch into this exercise, but today, my excitement was muted. My mind revisited Nix, her proud stature, the sound of her heartbeat, and the pulse of her neck.

I relived the momentary shock as I'd seen her skin turn scarlet when she'd lied about the color of her hair—and if I were a normal person, perhaps I'd feel embarrassed to know this secret of hers. Or feel pleased. But I wasn't.

Instead, my emotions were divided between awe and anger. Either Nix was very, very stupid to reveal her weakness, or she was brilliant. Time would tell.

I tried to recapture the experience of tasting her blood in my mind. That succulent, rich, full-bodied flavor. Did I have enough time to visit Nix tonight? I thanked the Celestials that I had the power to lie, and I savored the memory of dipping my fangs into her sweet neck while Leander was gone. There'd been no high like drinking her blood—not for a long time. It took all my strength to stop.

I'd healed my mark on her just in time. While my Sangor speed gave me an advantage, Leander's silence gave him his. But as I said, Sangors have excellent hearing, too.

NIX

SPARKS

Dawn broke the following day, and I couldn't help but be taken aback when I woke in this strange place. I'd dreamed of Daris, seeing him stand over me as I lay in bed. I had a strange sense of being watched right before I opened my eyes. I half-anticipated seeing fellow Bloodwraiths surrounding me, or something looming over me when my eyes fluttered open.

A pleasant vision greeted me instead. An empty room with serene daylight streaming in through a lovely framed window. I felt silly having such ridiculous thoughts.

My eyes swept the room. Nearby, a tall wooden chair cradled clothing on the arms and seat that seemed selected just for me. I rose from the bed and quickly held each item up.

Not a dress in sight. I sighed with relief. I'd learned clothing can be your armor, particularly in a new place—and the wrong clothes can be the opposite. A note on the table read:

'Dovey Nix,

I hope you slept well! Here are some clothes I think are your style and a new hairbrush. The relief room with towels and showers is to your right, and a new toothbrush and paste are also there. When you return, stand in front of my door, and say your name. Come downstairs before 1 p.m.!

I stared at her wall clock, a flat black circle with Roman numerals. It was just after noon; I'd slept very late. I inspected the clothes more carefully.

Black fitted pants, a white shirt with billowing sleeves, and a red belt. They were all well-made. There were also lacy black undergarments, which I raised an eyebrow at—I'd never owned such things—and a pair of red ankle boots.

I put everything down and took care of the essentials. Showered, then dressed, and after that, I had time to admire how the clothing fit me in Elena's full-length mirror. The clothes were very flattering, and I nodded with approval, though I missed the familiarity of my old boots, which sat in the corner of the room. There'd be time enough for them, I knew.

I styled my hair, leaving it loose and flowing, but brushing it well, mentally thanking Elena for taking care of these details. Because of her, I felt human again. Or was it proper to say Orphic now? Or Arnexin? I didn't know.

Daris's words yesterday rang in my head—"It is indeed pure Orphic blood."

I thought about that. First—eww. Why would he taste my blood? What kind of power did he have?

And then I thought of him overall. I hoped I'd see him today. Something about him made me feel like I'd been waiting for him for all my life. It was hard to explain. I didn't want to admit it, but I was attracted to him. He was intelligent. Capable.

And what he said about my blood—if my blood was pure Orphic, then didn't that mean my parents didn't come from the Mortal Realm? It wasn't their Realm of origin anyway. It had to mean that both of them had magic capabilities all of this time, and I'd never known it.

Was that why Dad made sure to tell me not to say what Realm I was from? Were they hiding from these people for some reason? Why?

Why had they never let me know about their past? They knew how hard I'd struggled with my secret. So many questions invaded my brain that I couldn't process them, and I sat down for a moment, cradling my head between my hands.

Leander's big blue eyes filled my mind, and his fresh air scent from yesterday overcame my senses. Geez—was it yesterday, or how long had it been now? Time was slipping away from me . . . but I inhaled, taking a deep breath, imagining Leander's scent and calm presence, then exhaled, and felt stress slip away from my body.

Why did my mind keep returning to Leander whenever I got anxious? As an advanced Immaru, did he do something to me to make this happen? I realized I wasn't getting answers asking myself questions. And I was going to be late.

I need to find Elena.

I stepped out of Elena's room and retraced my steps the way we'd come before. What seemed like an imposing place the past couple of days appeared less intimidating. I had sense enough now to pay attention to details.

This time, I took the stairs to the top of the building on my own and walked the high path around, gritting my teeth at the height. From above, I observed the layout of the Guilds of Chaos. I scanned the grounds as much as I dared.

A big round central building dominated the center of the area. Elena told me they call it the Omnipatos. Another blue-green building clung near the water. One building floated high in the sky, nearly covered by clouds. Another was covered by plants and flowers of every kind. Still, another seemed similar to Skia Guild but flaunted purple and blue colors over the turrets. I didn't look further, overwhelmed with the need to get down.

Pushing the door of the tower open, I descended the steps and admired the decor. The inner walls were decorated with beautiful paintings depicting magical beings casting furious spells during raging battles. Awe-inspiring paintings of mythical creatures I'd never heard of before hung on the walls, and the creatures moved, snorted, and made sounds as I passed by.

Sofas and soft, cushy chairs for lounging abounded on the main floor. Many were covered with opulent red or black velvet. Guild colors, I guessed. The scent of patchouli and cinnabar breezed through, making me wonder if Guilds had characteristic scents as well.

As I wandered through the main corridor, I realized that staying here would demand more from me than I was ready to admit. Revealing the truth about my house fire could unleash reactions from people that I didn't know how to address. They already knew I possessed a type of magic, or curse, with my inability to lie—but the fire. I bit my lip. I suspected that would be completely different.

Despite the Guild's supposed safety, I remembered the unease I felt radiating from the Alliance members when I mentioned the Outskirt Realms. I couldn't let them know I came from the Mortal Realm, not yet. My parents—the entire town—might be in danger.

My blood boiled while inner paranoia gripped my mind. People here wanted to kick me out of this place. Some, I felt sure, wanted to do much more than that.

I thought of Daris and his kindness and of Elena. There were also positive elements, being here.

Elena met me as I walked, offering me coffee in a cup that read "Hot FATES," along with a bottle of Aphrodite's Gold juice, and what I hoped was a normal bagel and egg sandwich.

"You missed breakfast," she tittered, "and I didn't have the heart to wake you. You were sleeping harder than an Agon after a herd-of-sheep meal."

"Thank you!" I imagine I eyed the food in her hands like a feral creature. I wolfed the thing down only moments after I accepted it.

The too-sweet coffee nearly caused me to choke as I drank it down. It tasted like pure caramel, but I was still grateful for its warmth and energy. I saved the juice for later. "But don't you mean 'dragon?'" I asked.

"You are very welcome," Elena grinned as she watched me inhale my food. "I wasn't sure what you'd like. I'll show you where to get your food in the common area later today. And, no, dear—misconception in the Mortal Realm. There are so many. Dragons are sort of like Agons, only they are very slow. Hence the name. If you ever meet an Agon—ah—well, then you'll be truly terrified."

I wanted to laugh, thinking she couldn't be serious, but apparently she was. I thought about the word Agon. I was very good at root words. In Latin, it meant 'conflict, contest or struggle.' Not terrifying, but that was something to consider. It was a word also used to create other words, such as 'agony,' and that gave me pause.

Elena guided me down more stone steps. "I'll walk with you today, and then you should find your way around quite easily. Our classes are mostly the same, except for my brother's. Family members are not permitted to teach each other."

I   remembered that Daris was Elena's   brother. Well, that sucked for her. I imagined she'd love to be in one of her brother's classes. They seemed to get on very well.

We strolled through some more corridors that turned and twisted and then we descended more stairs.

Out of curiosity and the need to know more about what amounted to my only friend here so far, I asked what her powers were. Her devilish grin stayed put as she morphed into a mirror image of myself, her shape-shifting abilities on full display.

I laughed at the sound of my own voice as she showed off her power. "Shapeshifting is one of my many talents," she admitted, reverting to her own form.

We reached a familiar-looking room, and she handed me a bag. "This should have everything you need for today," she said.

"Thank you," I mumbled, my voice shaky, as I entered the room. There were long tables with chairs along each one, rather than individual desks. At the front of the classroom, there stood Daris.

I found an empty chair in the back of the room, avoiding Daris's gaze. The room buzzed with Apprentices, but Daris's eyes were on me as I opened the bag Elena had given me. Daris clapped his hands together once, an amplified noise that I felt in my gut.

"Class—we have a new Apprentice joining us. This is Apprentice Nix Emberwind. Nix, will you please stand, introduce yourself, and tell us one thing about yourself that you like to do."

There was no help for it, but I'd already made this part of my life—pushing myself to face these situations head-on. I stood. "Hi everyone. I'm Nix. I enjoy gardening."

Some of the Apprentices giggled. A few—the ones studying herbology or potions, I guessed—smiled at me.

"Excellent, thank you, Nix. Now, everyone, back to the next lesson in 'Basics of the Inner Self.' Nix, there's a description, page 79 in the text you can go over later."

I had no time to prepare. The task at hand chilled me as Daris urged us to discuss and demonstrate our powers openly. A girl with a buzz cut who wore all black demonstrated her skill with weapons, pulling seven slim knives from her vest, naming her targets before she threw.

"Frog pic left eye back poster. Letter E on small print on front poster—" One knife arced around three Apprentices as she bent its trajectory with her fingers. When she finished, she took a bow. "They don't call me Points for nuthin'."

Other Apprentices completed their demonstrations. I could only watch. I couldn't perform anything like that in front of them. I couldn't even get my fire to ignite when I wanted it. And if I tried—and succeeded—I might kill them. My turn came.

My cheeks burned like molten lava. "Pass." It was obvious my one-word response wasn't appreciated as I glanced at Daris—who was now "Guildmaster Ravencroft" in my new GOC world.

He considered me, then motioned to me with his head. "Nix, step outside with me for a moment." When we stepped into the corridor, I heard Apprentices inside chuckling. Daris's enticing scent enveloped me as he leaned in close to me.

"You can do this, Nix. Just give it a try. The Apprentices in there, they all started where you are now. I'll cover you if things get out of hand. That's my role." His expression told me he expected me to take him up on his offer.

"Those Apprentices have never been where I am now," I snapped. I crossed my arms. "They never—" I stopped. I'd almost said too much. "And, I'm not doubting your skill, but—what are you going to cover? My ability to burn the retinas out of every student's eyes with my scarlet color after I lie?"

I had to keep my stories as close to true as possible—always. As far as he knew, I couldn't do anything else. If he suspected I had something to do with the fire, he couldn't prove it. Not yet. And if I flared, really flared—I wasn't sure he'd have the skill to stop me.

His expression softened. "Your second trial is tomorrow evening. Learning about your power before then could help you. Let me help you, Nix." He stretched out his hand like he was going to rest it on my shoulder.

Panic gripped me. I hated feeling like I was trapped, and I had no idea how to change that. But was certain of one thing. I was not going back into that classroom to expose my weakness in front of the others. I stepped back. "You can't help me! No one can!" I stormed away, not sure of the direction I was going and not caring.

I found solace on a bench by a statue of a satyr playing a flute. The seat and the statue were partially hidden by a multicolored tree that was willow-like, except its leaves were of various colors, cascading down like rainbows.

As I tried to steady my breath, the realization struck me. Telling the Alliance about Drade was my best chance at freedom. I should have asked Daris questions. I didn't think he'd reveal anything to anyone about my parents if I were careful. Why did I storm off when he was one of the few people who could help me stay here? My fist pounded the ground, and fiery sparks flew up, nearly singeing my hair.

Great. Look! I can wow the masses with my dismal display of fire sparks when I pound the dirt.

"Whoa, easy there," a voice interrupted my thoughts.

I lifted my gaze to find a golden-haired boy leaning casually against a blooming tree behind me. He radiated brilliance and shine. How had I missed him before?

"Excuse me?" I asked, irritated. A split second, beautiful yet perilous lights began to dance across my skin, and I shot up, gasping. My chest tightened, and memories of the flames engulfing my family home in Drade flooded my mind.

My untrained power was cruel and destructive. I needed to get a grip before I burned the trees down around us and turned them into cinders.

The golden boy sighed, threw an apple core into the dirt, and approached me. I started to get up, but his hands motioned me to stay.

I'd been so afraid this would happen, and now it was.

"What do I do?" The sparks from my fingertips grew larger and more frenetic.

"I'm no Magisar," he admitted, pausing like had all the time in the world. His slender eyes scanned me, and I thought I spied some humor in his eyes as well. He sat down in front of me. "But stay seated. Close your eyes."

The golden boy's voice was soothing, and I didn't question him or feel crazy or inept. I followed his directions. This was much like martial arts training. I needed to remember to use these principles when it came to fire exploding from my body.

"Travel into your body," he continued. "Start with your breathing—count to four as you inhale and then exhale for four counts—then let all of your breath out. Let it go."

I heard the sounds of birds and felt a slight breeze on my cheek. There were voices in the distance, but I let my mind pass over those, and I drifted over to hear the distant song of the river . . .

"Focus on something that relaxes you, like when you are swimming or walking in the forest—something related to your senses. A melody meant only for your ears. A masterpiece of art. A unique perfume. Anything."

Cinnamon and cedar.

I grasped at the memory of Daris's scent, and miraculously, my breathing became easier. My chest, which felt like a boa constrictor squeezing it into the size of a drinking straw, opened up.

The sparks on my skin retreated into the depths of my troubled soul. 'Golden Boy' continued to study me.

"Who are you?" I wondered if he was an Apprentice or a Guildmaster. His age was difficult for me to gauge.

"My name is Elias," he responded, lips curving into a smile as he extended a hand.

I shook it. "Please, don't tell anyone about this, Elias."

"Like I said, it's your business, although if I may . . . why the secrecy? Trust me, Sparks, you're not the worst person in this Guild."

I narrowed my eyes. "My name is Nix, not Sparks."

He smirked, a glint in his crystal-blue irises. "I think it suits you."

"Whatever, Goldie."

He chuckled and dropped onto a nearby bench. I settled beside him, fighting a smile. The silence between us felt surprisingly comfortable.

Glancing down at my hands, slightly embarrassed at my cracked, uneven nails, I pondered the lives of others and their pasts. Had Elias said those words to alleviate my concerns about my destructive nature or to encourage me to open up?

Why was it so challenging to believe I wasn't the worst person around? Then again, Points, the girl from class, aimed to become an assassin. I had never taken a life. If that kind of training was the norm here, perhaps I could find my place, even with the fiery aftermath I'd left behind.

"The Alliance wants me to reveal everything to them. This could put my family in danger," I confided.

Elias stopped tapping his foot, looking at me in wide-eyed surprise.

"On top of that, I had a confrontation with my brother. My flames spiraled out of control. I burned down my home, and I left before . . . before my town officials could arrest me. Magic isn't allowed in my Realm. They punish offenders and their families." I glanced at Elias. "How am I supposed to share all that with them?"

He shrugged. "The same way you just told me. Like I said, Sparks, it's not a big deal. I promise. We all go through the same thing, especially with the new Maestra. She expects a lot from each Guildmaster. And the alternative is worse."

I remembered the woman who led my trial, who'd scrutinized me like I was an annoyance and discarded me like trash. I clenched my jaw.

"What do you know about the Arcane Alliance? I heard her announce a meeting," I blurted.

That piqued Elias' interest. "What about?"

It was my turn to shrug. I leaned toward him. Whatever he was thinking, I wanted to know.

"Did she say when?"

I concentrated. At first, all I could remember was the immediate dislike I'd felt for the Maestra, but through that came the memory. "A week's time from last night, I think."

He grinned a foxlike grin. "What are you doing in six days, Sparks?"

I rolled my eyes at the nickname. "Why, Goldie?"

His eyes flashed with a mischievous glint. "How do you feel about getting into a little trouble?"

DARIS

PROTECTION

I wasn't expecting Nix to find me in my office that afternoon, but when she did, relief flooded through me. I'd been thinking about her since our fallout in my class. Was I too pushy?

She was right; I didn't know anything about her. What if she didn't want to stay and thought failing the trial was her way of escaping? She needed to be aware of the danger of that. There was no option. She didn't understand her Orphic blood awakening—or know about Lethenthril.

When she knocked on my door, my head snapped up from reorganizing my desk, and I cleared my throat in surprise. "Come in, Nix." I gestured to one of the seats at the wooden table opposite me, its surface worn smooth from years of use.

She shut the door behind her, the latch clicking softly. Something lively twinkled in her eyes, a spark of determination that hadn't been there before. "I'm sorry I've been so closed off to you and the Alliance. I just . . . in the Realm I came from, no one trusted anyone much, and for good reason."

I shook my head, my brow furrowing. "I shouldn't have pushed you. I want you to find a home here. That's what I want for all the Apprentices at Bloodwraith."

"I understand." She dropped down into one of the seats, the wooden chair creaking under her weight. Her eyes roved over various items remaining on my desk: binders, notebooks, a broken wand, some pens, and a collection of herbs I needed to drop off later. It was terribly messy, a reflection of my scattered thoughts. I swept my hand through the air, clearing the pens into the drawer and immediately tidying the desk with a flick of my wrist.

Awkward silence covered us like a heavy blanket, thick and oppressive. I needed to explain Lethenthril to her, but I wanted her to say what was on her mind first. "What can I help you with?"

Nix gazed at me as if sizing me up, her eyes narrowing slightly, then she pressed forward. "Tell me about the Arcane Alliance."

An idea came to mind, a way to build trust between us. I smiled at her and shifted forward till our knees barely touched under the table. "I'll make you a deal. Quid-pro-quo. You can ask me anything about the Arcane Alliance as long as I can ask you about your background. And no side-steps and half-truths."

She huffed and leaned back against her chair, the wooden frame creaking in protest. I worried I'd pushed too far again. She had the option to ask anyone else for information, but she'd come to me. I didn't want to lose that trust.

I was about to reconsider my offer when she nodded, a glint of challenge in her eyes. "Deal. What's the importance of the Arcane Alliance?" She was straight to the point, her voice firm.

"The Arcane Alliance is a collective of Guildmasters—there are eight. They are important for keeping balance among the Guilds, as well as interacting with the outside Realms and keeping the peace. They also head the Apprentice programs for all the Guilds across all of the Realms. While we have Apprentice programs here, other Realms have them, too. Skia Guild, for example, has Bloodwraiths here, like a team name, you see. In other Realms, like Zeleel, their name is Bodachcurse. At the Guilds of Chaos, we are fortunate, in some ways, because we are at the center of all activity. Guildmasters here are selected to serve on the Arcane Alliance and to teach Apprentices. It is a huge honor and an important duty."

I paused to think about the question I would ask her, my mind racing with possibilities. She leaned forward, arms crossed on my desk, her posture a silent challenge. This had become a game to her, a test of wills. "Why did you come to Bloodwraith?"

She hissed in a breath, the sound sharp in the quiet room. For a moment, the direction of her gaze scattered, her focus darting around the room, looking anywhere but at me. "I suppose I have to tell someone eventually , but promise me that I can trust you. Please. I . . . need to hear it."

"Yes. You can trust me." I tried very hard not to use my Sangor seduction, the temptation to manipulate her thoughts almost overwhelming. I wanted to be real with her as much as possible. "Nix, no matter what's happened, I'm on your side. My job as Guildmaster is to advocate for my Apprentices."

"What if that isn't enough?" she asked, her voice barely above a whisper. "What if what I tell you makes you choose between loyalty to the Guild and my safety?" I thought again of how vulnerable she'd been when I first helped her, the way she'd clung to me like a lifeline. I wanted nothing more than to protect her, to shield her from whatever demons haunted her past. That instinct burned inside of me, especially when she was close like this, her eyes searching mine for answers.

"It will be enough. And you don't understand this yet, but"—I didn't believe I was going to do this for a girl I had just met, but there was something about her, a pull I couldn't resist. She had already captured me, heart and soul. I removed a brilliant blue stone from a pouch around my neck and placed it in my palm. It pulsed and glowed, casting an eerie light across the room. "Your magic is not fully awakened, not yet. This is a Celestial stone. It binds a person to a promise."

I placed the stone in my palm and then brought her hand to mine so both our hands covered the stone, the heat of her skin searing into mine. "Clasp my hand," I told her, and she did, her eyes rising to mine with a question, uncertainty warring with hope. I stared into the whirlwind of her gaze, the colors shifting like a kaleidoscope, and said, "I swear to you, Nix Emberwind, before the Goddess Chaos and all the powers of the Celestials, that whatever you tell me here today is in confidence. I swear to place you and your safety above myself, my Guild—the Skia Guild, and above the Guilds of Chaos and the Arcane Alliance until death, or you, release me from this bond."

A gust of wind swept through the room, rustling the papers on my desk and sending a chill down my spine. Blue iridescent light arched over my head, crackling with energy. I wanted to explain to Nix what was happening—that this was going to be okay, but my body was paralyzed, frozen in place by the power of the stone. The pain of this binding was excruciating as it tore me—physically and psychically—and reformed me, molding me into something new. My soul was bound to her now, tethered by an unbreakable thread, and I felt the stone sink into my skin, branding me with its mark.

The energy dissipated as quickly as it had come. She pulled her hand away, and we both inspected our palms, identical tattoos etched into our skin. We bore the same Infinity

Cross, a never-ending knot that looked like four triangles on each corner with a square in the center. In the center of my square, there was the soft blue shimmer of the Celestial stone, a constant reminder of my bond. The stone would remind me of my bond if I ever came close to breaking it, and it would warn me if Nix were in danger. Nix's palm glittered in the center as if waiting for the stone to return, a promise of protection.

As her eyes lifted to mine, I almost expected a violent reaction from her, a furious outburst at my presumption. I hadn't told her about the extent of this bond I was making, the way it would tie us together forever. But Nix took a deep breath and exhaled, and I sensed—relief, a weight lifting from her shoulders. With a nod and deep breath, she launched right in, the words spilling out of her in a rush.

"I come from Drade, a town in the Mortal Realm. I have fire magic that I can't control. I escaped a fire I started by accident in my own home. I burned my whole house down. This was the only place I knew to go. I don't know what happened to my parents and my brother. I'm afraid to return home because the people in my town would put me in prison and might even kill me. They could even kill my parents."

Some part of me wanted to laugh. I'd heard far more severe cases from others: Sangors, like myself, who lost control of their appetites and drained cities of people. Metas who enjoyed hunting humans as prey—killing for fun. Monster hunters who messed up and killed innocent beasts, even sacred ones. The fact that Nix had been terrified to reveal something so trivial in the Guilds made me realize just how little she knew.

"Nix, I promise—you'll be just fine here." Before I could think, I reached my arm across the table toward her. What was more surprising was that she took my hand again, even after our crazy binding. Hers was small and warm under my fingers. Mine was calloused and hard.

"Nix . . . we must be careful," I advised. "We are bonded, yes. But I must tell you a couple of things that are important. First, because your magic has partially awakened before you ever had a Blaze Ceremony—an official ceremony to awaken your Orphic magic—you must stay at the Guilds of Chaos. If you do not, meaning if you are not accepted or refuse to stay, you will be sentenced to the Lethenthril Realm, which is a lifelong prison of forgetting. The Alliance . . ." I sighed. This was difficult to describe.

"They will remove your memories first. They place them in an archive underground. After that, they take you to Lethenthril, from which there is no escape. There is no portal, no way out of the Realm. You remember nothing there, and you would live out the rest of your days in mental oblivion until you die."

"The next thing," I pressed on, "is that if all goes well and you *are* accepted, you must choose a Guild. If you stay in the Skia Guild, then I will be your mentor—your Magisar." I paused to let that sink in. "That means I am 'Guildmaster Ravencroft' or 'Magisar Ravencroft' to you. I am not Daris. Our familiar relationship in front of others must end. Do you understand?"

Blood drained from her face. "How long would that last?"

I kept eye contact with her—I would not look away. "Six to eight, maybe even ten years, depending on the track you take."

This amazing woman—with fire-red hair and eyes that turned green and gold and could spark red and burn with the hottest blue—broke the steel bands of my heart as I watched the pain register in them. Tears pooled there, though she would not let them fall. My Sangor speed had me flying over the table and sweeping her up from her seat. My hand, which now bore the Celestial stone, caressed her cheek.

"Nix . . . I will be right here," My arm slipped around her waist, and my lips captured hers as I drank in her sweet breath. I reveled in the warmth of her skin against mine, the feel of her small, lean body against mine. The rising heat of her complimented what I knew about myself but dared not say yet. I melted into her and felt the heat of her flicker and flare as if she were fresh flames finding air, feeding off wind and dry kindling.

"Daris . . . " she murmured against my mouth.

My lips trailed down her neck, and oh, how I longed for another taste of her—a sweet drink, this time with her permission—and the stone tingled in my palm. My eyes widened and I scrutinized it behind her back, noting that it had turned pink just with my thought.

What had I done? I took a deep breath and hugged her close to me. I did what I had to do, and that was it.

I was the one to pull back first. Whatever I'd just started would be painful to finish, in one way or another, but the way she peered up at me told me she understood somehow. This feeling of being near her was so right, and I didn't think it would ever leave, no matter what the two of us faced.

We went back to our prior conversation like nothing had happened. She asked me about the meeting Grand Guildmaster Seraphina had called. I sighed, unable to hide my reluctance, which piqued Nix's curiosity. I told her there were four reasons an Arcane Alliance meeting was called: someone important died, a new threat came to light, including something like war, important information was received, or something needed to be settled between two or more Guilds.

In return, she told me about her family. Her mother and father secretly worked in InterRealm Relations, which dealt with Outer Realms, Inner Realms, and the Guilds combined. The people of the town thought they were Accountants.

She told me of her brother, Melian. He was in training, learning to hunt down those with magic powers in Drade and lock them up. She described how he'd seen her that night of the fire.

Some may have wanted to come to Arnexis, but if they were captured, then they never made it to the GOC. They never had a Blaze ceremony. Then, there were those who had their magic ignite without the Blaze ceremony but refused to be trained. Some committed crimes and suffered the consequences.

"That's twisted." I'd been alive for many, many years. I'd watched events take place that most couldn't imagine. The conditions in which potential Apprentices who refused to come to train among the Guilds were always the worst. Some were convinced they could learn their powers without training and got into so much trouble. Some were corrupted by evil forces.

In the end, the Alliance caught them if they could and banished them to Lethenthril. They could never trust them not to use their powers again. The Alliance would be turning their eyes on the Mortal Realm more often after this.

Nix shook her head when we talked about Lethenthril, and I got the sense she was like most of us in Arnexis. We disagreed with the procedure but understood that people couldn't be trusted once they were corrupted. And magic in corrupt hands was not a good thing. Ever.

We talked well into the afternoon in comfortable conversation. But my feelings were much more intense now that I'd held her hand in mine. She was all I could think about after she left.

I spent a lot of the early evening trying to decide how I'd explain my Celestial bond mark to Seraphina. She'd see it at the girl's trial later. And Nix would tell the truth about it if questioned. There'd be no sense in me lying about it. In the end, I figured I'd just deal with it as it came. What else could I do?

Later that evening, after some hard training at the Parabellum with Matarz, a Shadow-Elsh friend of mine from Oscuro Guild, I focused on quieting my mind. Prepared to grab a couple of hours of sleep. People often assume Sangors don't sleep, but we do. We just don't need as much of it.

But rest eluded me. Training should have helped tire me, but Nix's blood called to me. Unfortunately, my new bond made it impossible to drink from her now without her consent. And she was my new addiction. Blood itself was an addiction for me, but hers—it was worse than heroin in the Mortal Realm. I craved her.

I thought perhaps a run would help. I could strike out for the mountains. Pass by the Cave of Secrets. Maybe the Cave of Silence. Circle around the Oscuro Guild. That might do it.

As I stepped out onto the campus, taking in the soft glow of Hecade Guild's lights next door, I noted Apprentices still mingled about. Some practiced with light magic, and some with night flying. I couldn't help but search for Nix's bright, intelligent eyes and flaming hair, but I didn't find her anywhere.

I forced myself toward the Dream Waters fountain, across from the Omnipatos, which usually had few people meandering around at this hour. It was a great place for divination when the moon shone full, like tonight.

My ears perked as a scream filled the air, and I raced toward the sound. When I reached the bottom step of the main entrance, a terrible stench filled my nose, a mixture of rotten and burned flesh.

I raced up the steps as the scent grew stronger, and there, the corpse of a woman confronted me—splayed on the marble stairs in a contorted mass. She smelled of herbs, incense, rot, and char. Flames still burned vigorously in the center of her chest, and her vacant eyes stared blankly at the ceiling.

Who she was, I didn't know, but more important than that mystery was the fact that she was dead. Two Apprentices stood nearby, horrorstruck. They must have been the ones screaming—the victim being dead long before.

Shocked, I shouted for the Lupine Guardians. This incident had to have proper investigation procedures, and I needed to be sure Nix was safe. I wondered where she'd gone. For now, she was safe since the stone glowed calmly in my hand.

Whoever killed this woman didn't do it here. That much I knew. As High Inquisitor, Devereux maintained responsibility for all death investigations. I hated it, but he had to be notified.

Before I could lose my mind, I cautioned the Apprentices to remain at the scene until the Lupine Guardians arrived. Then I opened a Guildmaster Portal and stepped into Devereux's office at the Magus Guild. It was on the other side of campus. Only in extreme circumstances do we ever do this without prior notice.

"Devereux, forgive the intrusion," I said as I arrived. "There's a body on the steps of the Omnipatos . . ."

"I understand." Devereux had been sitting at his pristine desk, almost as if he'd been waiting for me. He stood calmly but promptly and opened his own portal. "Announce and enforce a curfew. Get word to the Magisars for a meeting."

"There's no need for a curfew. It was not a recent kill, Devereux," I stated. "The victim was an Apprentice, I believe. Horribly burned. But I smelled rot with the body. The stink was laced with herbs and incense. Someone tried to cover the body's decomposition with fire. Unsuccessfully. She died at least two days ago. I'm surprised she wasn't reported missing."

Devereux arched an eyebrow. "Are you sure?" For some reason, he almost seemed disappointed. I wasn't sure why. I watched as he nodded, stepped through his portal, and disappeared.

After noting a strange odor in Devereux's office and marking it in my memory, I focused on the stone in my palm. It still glowed softly, though it was its normal color.

What about Nix? Was she safe? Was she with Elena? I knew my sister could handle herself. She was a monster hunter, and she kept her weapons on her at all times. She'd never failed a mission or a bounty, though she did her best to appear unremarkable, so she had the element of surprise. But this death—this murder—seemed more sophisticated. More premeditated.

I wasn't sure how my bond worked or what the Celestial stone was telling me by glowing. I guessed that if there was something urgent needed of me, I'd be compelled to do something, but for now, all I had was a simple 'awareness.' If Nix was with Elena, she was probably safe. If not . . .

I decided it would look fine if I checked on my sister. I made my way toward Nix's wing, but someone grabbed my arm before I could get very far.

"What's going on?" The golden hair caught my eye first. It was Elias.

"Elias? Are you insane?" I yanked him roughly over to a more concealed part of the courtyard, checking that no one was around. "You should have been the first to go running to your room. Everyone's going to know sooner or later."

"What are you talking about? Know what?" His eyes darted from one of mine to the other. Where he still gripped me, his hand was shaking.

"I found a body, Elias. I should have examined the wound better, but it didn't look good. Did you try to cover it with the fire?"

"A body? Wounded, then covered with fire? Sounds like something a Homicidal-Pyromancer-Maniac would do." The tone of his voice indicated he didn't know what I meant. But I wasn't so sure.

I rolled my eyes. "Uh-huh. Go, Elias. I'll check on you later. If anyone questions you, ask for me, okay?"

"Thank you, sir." Elias tilted his head quizzically but took off toward his own wing. I watched him go, wondering what he was really doing here.

Many years ago, I'd been the one to advocate for Metas of monster origin to be welcomed into the Skia Guild. Before that, they were required to join Bellator if they had magic. If they had no magic, they were sometimes denied. But Skia Guild approved Meta monsters. Even so, because Elias had Orphic blood and magic gifts, not many knew that Elias was one of them. He'd entrusted me with that secret, and I'd never told a soul.

I didn't know if the rest of the Alliance was also aware of this or not, let alone Grand Guildmaster Seraphina, but from what I'd seen of her background checks on prospective Apprentices, I wouldn't have been surprised if she had guessed. One of Elias's monster powers included fire. He could have done this. But why? And why now?

As Elias disappeared, I turned toward Nix's wing. I needed to know that she was safe.

NIX

FOUR BELLS

I had just come back from an evening walk near the Omnipatos and was trying to familiarize myself with the Guilds of Chaos campus. I stopped in the common room for what they called Syceus cookies, which were awesome, and a cup of Campe Coco. The cookies were soft and chewy, with a hint of cinnamon and nutmeg, and the rich and creamy sweetness of the Campe Coco lingered pleasantly on my tongue.

When I entered my room, Elena gave me another clean outfit, along with some accessories. I hugged that girl so hard, feeling the warmth of her embrace and the softness of her hair against my cheek. I had never had a better friend in my whole life, and I'd only known her for a couple of days.

Elena and I were down the hall from our room looking at some of the Gorgon paintings when an alarm sounded. My heart leaped in my chest at the piercing noise as it echoed off the stone walls and made my ears ring.

"Let's get to our room quick." Elena quickened her pace, her footsteps echoing on the polished floor. One of her hands went to the hem of her shirt, resting against a small green hilt tucked into her waistband. The other pulled out her Celcom, the screen illuminating her face with a soft blue glow.

I felt a little left out by now. No cell phone like at home. No Celcom like the others.

"What happened?" I didn't like the worried look on her face, the way her brows furrowed, and her lips pressed together in a tight line. Elena almost always seemed happy even when not-happy things were happening, her smile as bright as the sun.

"I don't know, exactly, dove, but it isn't good. Let's talk when we're safe." We rounded a corner and nearly slammed into a boy dressed in all black, his clothes blending into the shadows. Darker bands wrapped around his collar, forearm, and hood's edge, like midnight ribbons against the inky fabric.

"Variant!" Elena hissed, her voice sharp and urgent. "What are you doing here?" She grabbed his wrist and continued dragging him with us, her grip firm and unyielding. "It isn't safe to go back to Oscuro. Come with us."

He ripped his wrist away from her grip, his eyes flashing with annoyance. "Four bells mean—"

"I know what they mean!" she snapped. My eyes went wide as I watched her shapeshift into a woman three times her size with huge biceps, her muscles rippling under her skin like coiled snakes. "I'm not asking. You are required to seek shelter, same as the rest of us. Now, come."

Too stunned to argue, he came with us, his footsteps reluctant and dragging. I caught his sharp eyes, the color of steel, and shrugged while Elena shifted back to normal size and herded us to our room. She slammed the door hard as though something was going to try its best to get in, the sound echoing through the room like a gunshot. I shivered at the thought and went to my bed, sinking onto the soft mattress with a sigh.

Even without this mess, it had been a long day. Classes were confusing, the lessons a jumble of unfamiliar terms and concepts. With each class I attended, the Magisar asked about my power, their eyes boring into me like lasers. Magisar Wylie wasn't subtle. He demanded to see what I could do, and he brought me to the front of the class, the eyes of my classmates heavy on my back.

It wasn't a pleasant experience, feeling all the student's eyes on me, their gazes a mix of curiosity and skepticism. My fingers had trembled as I'd managed a couple of sparks, the tiny flickers of flame dancing on my fingertips before sputtering out. But I was so afraid of letting my fire go—afraid of losing control—I'd shut down, my mind going blank and my body freezing up. Several of the Apprentices laughed out loud, the sound harsh and mocking in the quiet room.

But I raised my chin and gave Magisar Wylie my best smile, the expression feeling stiff and forced on my face. "I guess my powers don't want to come out and play. I haven't had the Blaze Ceremony, you know." When everyone heard that, some of them nodded sagely, their expressions shifting to understanding. Others were quiet, their faces unreadable. At any rate, the condescending comments stopped, with the exception of a whispered word I caught. "Lethenthril."

While Elena and Variant tried to pull up some news on their Celcoms via chats, their fingers flying over the screens, I decided it was time to get some education. I turned my head to Elena, my hair brushing against my cheek. "What does four bells mean?"

Poor thing. Elena always seemed like the one who held everyone together, but her face was paler than usual, especially in contrast with the dark auburn strands of hair hanging along her cheeks. The question did seem to pull her out of a funk, her green eyes slowly raising to mine, like emeralds catching the light. "Ah, well, it means someone on GOC grounds has been seriously hurt, or . . ."

"Someone died." It was Variant who spoke, his voice flat and emotionless. He kept staring at his screen, his eyes never leaving the glowing display. Across his long fingers danced a silver dagger, the blade flashing in the dim light. He rolled it back and forth over his knuckles and around to his palm, the movement smooth and practiced. It was mesmerizing the way he did it, the blade seeming to have a life of its own. He managed to do that with one hand while he scrolled on his Celcom with the other, his fingers moving in a blur.

"I see." My first thought was of Daris, and my heart quickened to a faster, more impossible pace than a moment ago, the blood pounding in my ears. Was he safe? I wanted to ask Elena, but I didn't want her to know how much I cared about her brother and the depth of my feelings for him. I wasn't sure how she'd feel about that. As far as I knew, she hadn't seen the tattoo on my palm yet, the mark of our bond. She'd see it eventually, though, and then the truth would be out.

"You mean, died like, they fell from a bridge, or like . . . murdered?"

"They wouldn't put us all on lockdown like this if someone had just fallen from a bridge." As soon as I caught Elena's tone, sharp and biting, she did, too, her eyes widening in apology. "I'm sorry, dove, I don't mean to be snappy. I'm worried about Daris."

My lips briefly quirked up, a small smile tugging at the corners of my mouth. She'd offered a way to ask about him without seeming suspicious, a lifeline in the sea of uncertainty. "He looks like he can take care of himself."

"He can. I don't know if he told you, but he's been a Sangor ever since he became an Apprentice. He's a very powerful one in terms of capabilities, so I'm not worried about him overall.

It's just that if whoever was hurt isn't dead—if they're bleeding—he'll hunger for their blood."

It wasn't what I'd been expecting to learn about Daris. I sat back down and rested my hands on my knees, my fingers gripping the fabric of my pants. I'd seen the creatures at Bloodwraith so far, the Metas, the monster hunters, and the assassins. I'd heard about them from some of the others in passing, whispered conversations in the hallways and the common room.

I didn't know why, but somehow, it was so much harder to believe in Sangors. They sounded like our Mortal Realm vampires, creatures of the night who fed on the blood of the living. But those were just myths. Weren't they?

"Oh, don't look so worried, dove. It's not like he doesn't have control. It's just that it makes it challenging for him, is all." She went back to her screen, catching her lip between her teeth as if she thought she'd said too much, revealing a secret she wasn't supposed to share.

I stared at the Celestial bond on my palm, the mark glowing softly in the dim light. I had so many questions about Sangors now, questions that burned in my mind like embers. Were they born? Were they made like Mortal Realm vampires?

Sangors seemed different than vampires. They were considered a species, not a monster. Daris had no problems with sunlight. His skin was warm. So, I guessed he wasn't 'dead.' I wondered about his age and if he hungered for my blood. Did he want to drink from me? When the time came, if he asked, would I let him? I wasn't sure how I felt about that.

Something flashed in the corner of my eye, a glimmer of light that caught my attention. I glanced at Variant as another glint sparked in the air by his shoulder, like a firefly dancing in the darkness. He seemed completely unconcerned and still focused on dancing his blade across his hand, the metal flashing as it caught the light. It seemed as if some of his messages could fly out of his Celcom like little fairies and whisper in his ear, their wings shimmering with iridescent colors. They sparkled, then disappeared, like stardust fading into the night. Cool feature.

"What were you doing on this side of campus, anyway?" Elena asked Variant, her voice tinged with suspicion. "Oscuro Guild is across Moriath Inlet. You looking for some Incitar challenges later?"

"Maybe." He shrugged, his shoulders rising and falling in a noncommittal gesture, just as knuckles rapped softly on our door, the sound barely audible over the pounding of my heart. Variant flipped his dagger so that he was holding the hilt, the blade glinting in the dim light. Elena shifted into a massive, snarling cat, her fur standing on end and her teeth bared in a threatening display.

I sat there, unsure of what to do, my hands clenching and unclenching in my lap. I thought about summoning my flames, feeling the heat building in my palms, but I didn't want to put Elena and Variant in danger; I didn't want to risk losing control.

"Elena, it's me." Daris's voice came from the other side of the door, muffled by the thick wood.

I darted to the door and opened it the slightest, the hinges creaking softly. "You're alright," I breathed through the crack, my voice barely above a whisper.

Elena came up behind me to open it further and let him in, her body shifting back to human form as she moved. His eyes were on me as he wrapped Elena in a hug, his arms enveloping her in a tight embrace. I shut the door behind him, the latch clicking into place with a soft snick.

"What's going on?" Elena asked her voice tight with worry.

"I found a body at the Omnipatos, the grand hall where we gather for meals and ceremonies. Burned to a crisp outside and fresh burns inside the chest, like someone had reached in and set fire to her heart." Daris's voice was grim, his eyes dark with a mixture of anger and sadness. "It was made to appear as a fresh kill, but I think it was two or more days old, the body preserved by some sort of magic. They're going door to door right now, inspecting for flame residue, charcoal, any signs of ash, sulfur, or soot they can find in Guild rooms, trying to track down the killer."

"Who was it? Who died?" The question came from Variant; his voice was curious but not excited or concerned, as if he were asking about the weather.

It was the first time Daris noticed his presence, his eyes flicking to the assassin with a hint of surprise. I half expected him to care that an assassin was hiding out with us, to demand that he leave or face the consequences. But he didn't react, his expression remaining carefully neutral. Then I remembered Skia Guild had quite a number of assassins, their skills prized and feared in equal measure.

"I don't know her name. She was from Hecade Guild, the house of healers and herbalists. An Arcane Tertius Apprentice, just starting her training in the magical arts. Just over a year of training. Young, too young to die like that." Daris's voice was heavy with sorrow, the weight of the girl's death hanging in the air like a shroud.

Silence filled the space, thick and heavy, like a physical presence. Daris examined Elena, who hung her head the same way that Variant did, their faces shadowed with grief. I followed their lead, feeling like it was some sort of silent remembrance of the girl, a moment of respect for a life cut short. Even though I didn't know her, my chest hurt for those who did and for the girl herself, for the future that had been stolen from her.

"They think it might be one of us who killed her, then." Variant started fidgeting with his dagger again, the blade flashing as he twirled it between his fingers. "Someone with the power to control fire, to burn her from the inside out."

"Perhaps." Daris studied each of us, his gaze intense and searching. I thought his eyes lingered on me the longest, boring into me like he could see straight into my soul. I wished I was sure of the reason, whether he suspected me of the crime or simply wanted to reassure himself that I was safe.

Burned to a crisp outside and fresh burns inside the chest. The words echoed in my mind, a gruesome reminder of the horror that had taken place. I shuddered, feeling a chill run down my spine despite the warmth of the room. Who could have done such a thing? And why?

DARIS

BOMB

That evening, seven bells chimed, their resonant tones echoing across the campus in an all-clear. The sound meant safety, but it felt like a mistake to me. Some members of the Alliance, felt it was foolish to keep everyone inside, confined to their Guilds like prisoners. My opinion didn't matter to them, and so the bells rang out. I knew they'd mean trouble.

Afterward, Seraphina called the Alliance members and Guildmasters together at the Omnipatos, the grand hall where we gathered for important meetings and ceremonies. The room was vast, with high ceilings and intricate tapestries depicting the history of the Guilds. We concluded our meeting at nine thirty in the evening, the discussions lasting long into the night as we debated the best course of action.

When I exited the building, I found more Apprentices milling around the GOC campus than usual, their voices a low murmur in the cool night air. They moved in small groups, their eyes darting nervously as they made their way across the grounds. The Guilds of Chaos was unique in that it wasn't an academy or university. Apprentices learned and developed their magic arts here, but they were expected to behave as adults. There were no grades, no tests or exams to measure their progress. An Apprentice achieved their skills and ascended to their next level by completing tasks, demonstrating their capabilities, and winning battles—or they did not advance. After two years of remaining at their level, they were graduated, either applying to a position in the Realms or being assigned a position in Guild society commensurate with their skill level.

There were no curfews on the campus, a fact that some saw as a strength and others as a weakness. Curfews encouraged weakness, or so the thinking went. However, there were Guild building rules out of respect for others: Quiet hours after eleven and no outside Guild members in an Apprentice's assigned Guild. These rules were meant to maintain a sense of order and decorum, even in the face of the chaos that threatened to engulf us all.

And then, there were the Incitars, the ancient guardians of the campus who roamed the grounds at night, looking for any sign of trouble. Long ago, Guildmasters upheld that if Apprentices decided to be out in the wee hours, there had to be risks. There didn't have to be a curfew, but there were challenges to face, obstacles to overcome. This kept Apprentices on their toes and encouraged them to travel in groups, to rely on each other for protection and support.

Guildmaster Gauge from Bellator came up behind me and gave me a hearty smack on the back, his hand landing with a resounding thud. "Ho, Daris! When are you gonna take a beating from me in the ring again at the Parabellum?" He wrapped an arm around my shoulders, his voice booming in the quiet of the night. "I haven't had a good scrap in a while."

I raised an eyebrow at him, a small smile playing at the corners of my mouth. "If I recall, Gauge, I handed you your ass last time. You showed up drunk, remember? Then again, so did I. But Sangors clear their alcohol quicker than Slay Orcs. And we're faster. You want a rematch? I'll set up a neutral party to judge. You pick the date and battle form."

Gauge guffawed, his laughter ringing out like a thunder-clap. "I didn't know Sangors could get Mortal Realm dis-eases like Alzheimer's, or perhaps you've had your mem-ory removed. Are they taking you to Lethenthril, my friend? Surely, I've never been defeated by these scrawny things..." His hand circled around one of my biceps, and we both laughed as we jumped each other and tumbled to the ground, our bodies a tangle of limbs and playful punches.

Our fun was short-lived as I spun and dodged a punch that Gauge swung toward me, holding my palm out in apology. The stone in my other palm was glowing a soft pink, a sign that an Apprentice was in trouble. "Got an Apprentice in trouble, my friend." I dashed away with Sangor speed, hearing Gauge laugh loudly, and he bel-lowed, "I knew I was too much of a match for you, blood-sucker! Meet me at the PB soon for a proper fight!"

I grimaced, sad I couldn't continue, but I couldn't be-lieve my eyes as I rounded a corner. After what had just hap-pened, I saw Nix was outside—alone—near the office corri-dors of the Omnipatos. She was obviously drunk, her body swaying unsteadily as she tried to stay upright. Who the hell had taken her out? Certainly not Elena. My mind flit-ted to the only other person in the room when I visited

Variant.

Was this his doing? Did he encourage this? If so, why? I fumed. The stone in my hand should be turning red instead of pink because that was the color I was feeling in my head as anger welled in me, hot and fierce. Nix didn't even have a Celcom or a Tessar pad yet. No way to call for help if she needed it.

"Nix, what the—what are you doing out here?" I was at a loss for words, as I hurried over to her, picking her up off the ground. She had her trial this evening—her second appearance before the Alliance. This determined if she stayed with us or . . . I couldn't even bring myself to think about the alternative.

My fingertips touched her, and I recoiled at the chill of her skin. Her body was cold, too cold for the light clothing she wore. She had on a pair of green pants and a golden blouse with a green print but no jacket to ward off the night air, and the heels of her brown ankle boots were too high for her to walk in, especially in her inebriated state. I ran my hands rapidly up and down her shoulders once she was standing, using friction to warm her, to bring some color back to her pale cheeks.

Her cheeks flushed, and she slurred her words, the alcohol making her tongue thick and clumsy. "I shst went out wif shome friensds."

I caught her as she wobbled, her face getting closer and then farther from mine, and the smell of Ulnarthi alcohol blasted me, strong and cloying. This was a disaster. She'd need an antidote, and quickly, if she was going to make it to her trial in any kind of presentable state.

"Are you serious?" I let go of her and stepped back. Chastising her was pointless, but I couldn't stop myself. "You do understand that someone died today, right? That there's a killer on the loose?"

"Daris, . . . " She was still shivering, her arms crossed over her chest, her teeth chattering. "It was—" Sparks flew around her body, little flashes of light that danced across her skin. I jumped back, surprised, then tried to pat them out, but they burned little holes in her clothing, singeing the fabric.

"Magisar Ravencroft," I corrected, my voice stern. "You need to remember. You must call me Magisar Ravencroft. And you, Nix, need an antidote for what you drank. Then you need to get ready for your appearance with the Alliance. Do you understand? You see them tonight!"

Her eyes widened as if she'd only just realized this, and was she genuinely surprised, like the knowledge had been lost in the haze of alcohol. "I'm not sure what happened. I . . ."

It wasn't too late to fix this, to get her sobered up and presentable. "Alright, let's—"

Nearby, a door opened, and a golden light flooded the ground beside us, casting long shadows across the grass. "Is someone out here?" My heart quickened as I recognized Devereux's goaty voice, the sound grating on my nerves.

Without much thought, I grabbed Nix and moved her against the side of the building, covering her lips. I pressed closer to her as Devereux approached where we'd just been. Nix stared into my eyes, and I felt her smile beneath my palm.

I prayed to the Celestials that her sparks didn't make an appearance again now. Then an ember released, dropping down on my foot and burning through my shoe. I gritted my teeth. More fiery sparks rained from her fingers, and I scooped both her hands with my other hand and pushed them into my chest. Chaos, how they burned. It was a good thing I healed quickly.

I could have removed my other hand from her mouth to help me, but I worried I wouldn't be able to keep from kissing her if I did. What would probably happen first is she would giggle in her current state, and we'd be done for.

I heard Devereux sniff the air. Thankfully, he was carrying on a conversation on his Celcom, obviously engaged elsewhere.

I didn't move. I couldn't. I was trapped in a gaze with Nix, our bodies in a twisted knot, as I tried to keep her sparks from betraying us. After an agonizing moment, Devereux turned, continuing his conversation, closing the door behind him. We both relaxed. I healed my chest, almost wanting Devereux to come back and search a little harder so that I had another reason to press my body against Nix again. Ah, but by Chaos and all the Celestials—the scent of her blood . . .

I tore myself away. I'd have to visit a blood bar very soon to satisfy my need, or I'd do something vile. She was drunk, not to mention my Apprentice, and I didn't particularly feel like losing my job and having us both suffer. My bond with her protected her from me unless she gave me consent, but others, not so much.

"I'm taking you to my office, Nix. You need an antidote for what you drank. It's powerful alcohol. It won't wear off in time. You appear before the Alliance at eleven. And Elena told you about the Incitars, right? She'll be going back with you, so you won't have to worry."

Nix raised an eyebrow, almost as if she didn't know about Incitars, but said, "Yes, shir," and saluted me with the wrong hand. We couldn't waste time. I swept her into my arms and raced to the Skia Guild with Sangor speed. That's a benefit. At full speed, almost no one could see me or anyone with me. We're fast as Agons—faster.

I whisked her inside, burning with desire for her. I burned to drink her—and I couldn't—and knowing that drove me mad. And I couldn't tell anyone. We were bonded, but as far as anyone would know after tonight, it was for protection only.

I decided to take Nix to my quarters instead. I had the supplies I needed there and I was missing one item my office didn't have. Luckily, my Guildmaster quarters was in a secluded area of the Skia Guild, and I had wards in place to ensure Apprentices didn't wander there. I entered and placed Nix into a comfy chair by my small kitchen and opened my apothecary cabinet. I kept everything I needed there, just in case. Apprentices, as well as Magisars and even Guildmasters, were well known to get into scrapes.

I brewed the potion quickly—I knew the concoction by heart due to so many years of Apprentices taking the Ulnarthi

Bomb challenge—and lifted the silver cup to Nix's lips. Three generous sips would do the trick.

"Drink."

She sipped and shuddered, pushing it away. "No way. This is terrible."

I brought the cup back up to her lips. "Yes, way. It's the only way."

She started to push it away again, and I sighed, seeing how this was going to go. I hoped the Celestial stone in my palm would understand I was protecting her.

With Sangor speed, I zipped the cup to her mouth, tilted it, opened her jaw, held her nose, and made her swallow. Instead of three sips, she accidentally downed half the cup. If I were Nix and tried to say I felt bad about that, I'd have turned five shades of scarlet.

She spluttered. Gagged. I hoped she wouldn't throw up because I didn't want to do it again. She kept it down, but her eyes lit with that red and blue fire in her iris, and I backed away when, for the first time, I saw a blast of fire fly from her fingertips.

She peered up at me balefully. Instead of commenting on the fire—she surprised me.

"And just when were you going to mention to me that you were a Sangor?" The hurt and anger in her voice was palpable. I understood now. This was part of what had prompted her to go out tonight.

Alarm bells sounded in my head. The mention of heritage—of what I'd become—and what I needed made me crave blood even more. Her blood.

"Who told you?" As the words left my lips, I already knew. Nix had limited contact with anyone right now. There was only one person who would feel comfortable enough talking with her about who I was. One person who might assume I'd told her already or that she'd put it together.

"It's not a big deal." Nix said, looking off into space like she imagined she was elsewhere. I might have wondered if she was lying, but her skin hadn't changed color. "I was just surprised. And then I wondered . . ."

I pulled up a chair to sit near her, leaning forward with my elbows on my knees and my head in my hands. I was getting tired. I hadn't recharged—hadn't had a blood meal in two days.

I'd been up doing research on breaches of Guilds of Chaos security and recent infiltrations, trying to find any sort of clue as to who had killed the Hecade girl. I'd found nothing. I needed a break, and Nix was giving me one. "What did you wonder, Nix?"

My pulse started to beat faster. Sangor physiology is extremely complex. In some ways, it is similar to that of a hummingbird. We have two stomachs. One for blood, which gives us quick strength and energy and adds to our magical power. And then we have our basic physiology, which allows us to consume proteins and fluids—crude foods to function. But the blood—that is what we crave, what we need the most.

The world around me spun as Nix turned her eyes to mine and poured her entire soul into them. Heat rose inside me. My breath deepened. I knew. I KNEW what she was going to ask me, and as much as I wanted it, as much as I desired her beyond all comprehension, now was not the time. There would be time. And I wanted it to be the right time. I found it odd that the stone in my palm was quiet. It should be raging!

"I wondered . . ." she breathed, leaning in toward me.

I brought my finger to her lips. "No. Not now." My words were so thick with hunger that I could barely get them out. I exhaled and made myself smile, then leaned back. She did the same. Thankfully.

"Let me ask you another question. Who was with you when you were out?"

"Well, after the seven bells, Variant suggested we go blow off some steam. He asked if I'd ever seen any of the Taverns just off the GOC campus. I said 'no.' Elena said she was coming with us, so they showed me how Apprentices have to portal with three together. We went to the Dancing Dirks."

"I see." Variant was Oscuro Guild. They held knife-throwing competitions there. Of course, he'd suggest that.

"Variant bought all the drinks. And, well, Elena started telling everyone about me after a while. How I was from the Mortal Realm, but pure Orphic blood. And how I was Skia Guild now, and we were friends."

Great. Hopefully, you will be Skia Guild, Nix, I thought, *after tonight.*

I thought about how being in the Skia Guild would ensure we'd have to be apart. I wanted to tell her to choose any other Guild. That way, I wouldn't be her Guildmaster or her Magisar. But how could I? To do that meant I'd hardly see her. And there were other factors in play.

"Well, Elena gets a loud mouth when she drinks. And she doesn't get out much." I chuckled. "So, how did you get back to the GOC? How did you end up at the Omnipatos?"

Nix's face twisted, a mass of confusion and uncertainty. It was clear she remembered they had to portal using three Apprentices. That was their limitation. If they didn't portal, they had to walk back, and it would have been a three-mile walk.

"I . . . I can't remember," she admitted. "I was watching a knife competition with Elena beside me and holding a drink, and then, poof! There you were!"

"Was Elena drinking the same thing as you?"

Nix nodded.

I set to brewing another batch of the same potion.

I glanced at Nix. She'd curled up in the chair, her head leaning back against the headrest, and her deep breaths told me she'd fallen asleep. Good. She'd wake somewhat refreshed.

My lungs were shaky in my chest at the thought of Nix possibly being banished. She could not go to Lethenthril. We were bound now, and I knew I would risk my job, my entire livelihood, for this Apprentice I'd barely known for only a couple of days. There was a reason I'd bound myself to her–and so quickly—but that reason was beyond my grasp right now.

I placed the potion into a silver-lined bottle and gathered Nix in my arms. We arrived at Elena's corridor to find two shadows entangled in the alcove nearby. I kept walking, averting my gaze and hoping I wouldn't be recognized in the dark. A strange feeling of jealousy tinged my chest. I imagined myself wrapped up in Nix like that, trailing my lips down her delicate chin . . .

"Magisar?" a voice called behind me.

I braced myself and turned as I met Elias' eyes. Whoever he'd been with had vanished in a flash. He glanced back, incredulous that the person was gone as well. His eyes flitted to my arms.

I tried to keep my voice smooth, though I had a feeling it wasn't. "Yes. Nix—Ms. Emberwind . . . I found her outside. I wanted to get her back safe." He didn't need to know more than that.

"I understand," Elias murmured, though a smirk was sliding across his face. I wanted to smack it off. And if I weren't carrying Nix right now, I'd put Sangor speed to the test and do a "sip-by" on him to get me through the night.

"Don't you need to clean up, Mr. Incinder?" He looked down at his arms and hands. Fresh blood stains. The question didn't faze him. He just regarded me through slitted eyes.

"I guess we've both got dirt under our nails." He shot Nix one more glance before heading off toward his room or after whoever had just disappeared so quickly.

Elias was a troubled kid, but he wouldn't tell anyone about this, not after everything I had done for him. Trust didn't come easy for either of us. I was sure he simply felt better knowing a secret of mine the same way I knew many of his. He was a monster, and a hunter, but sworn not to take any lives within the Guilds of Chaos within any of the Realms.

I knocked softly on Elena's door and earned a garbled moan that opened the door. I slid Nix into bed, then I broke away to eye Elena critically. "I heard you *three* had a fun night at the Dancing Dirk."

"Looks like you added to it," Elena grumbled, peeking from under her blankets. Her hair was a tangled mess across her pillow. She turned her gaze upward and moaned. "Okay. I went to look for her, but I couldn't find her. I was frantic, but I was wasted. Variant was gone too. I had to hitch a ride back with some crazy Lupines. I swear, I didn't look, but it's gotta be a full moon tonight. Anyway. What were you two doing?"

Reaching into my pocket, I pulled out a purple bottle and uncorked it. "For you. Nix told me—Ulnarthi Bombs? Really, Elena?"

"It was absolutely not like that . . ."

Before she could launch into her usual excuses and lengthy verbosities, I put the bottle to her lips and upended it. I seemed to be doing a lot of that tonight. This had better be the last one. Two was enough.

"Elena, I need you." I wanted to explain to her everything that had changed. She was my family. I loved her. She was, in many ways, my best friend, too. But there wasn't time. We had thirty minutes until we all had to be at the Omnipatos, and we had to be alert, shining, and at our best. My gaze swept over both of them sprawled over their beds.

Chaos, help me—this was NOT me. It was not my approach. It was Elena's. But it worked on the Apprentices, and I needed Elena because I needed Nix, like the air I breathed and the blood I drank.

I conjured the brightest light I could overhead while still making it pleasant. Both girls threw their arms over their heads. With my fingers, I made the signs and conjured Elena's famous gong. I suspended it from the air along with the mallet and placed a particular spell in place. The gong sounded and shook the inside of the room. Both girls sat up straight, Elena's eyes fixed on me.

"You have thirty minutes to get Nix to the Alliance, Elena. Looking sharp and ready to go. The gong will stop when you are ready." With that, I fled, knowing that both girls were probably throwing curses my way. But I didn't care. I was being selfish, and I was protecting the one I was bonded to.

I stopped at the door at my Guildmaster's quarters. It was impossible. But I caught the sound of a footstep inside. Who would *dare* enter my quarters without my authorization? I elected to use my Guildmaster portal spell and portaled inside instead.

Devereux's goaty ass was sitting where Nix had sat only thirty minutes ago. He was sipping some of my Abssynian tea.

I eyed him calmly and pulled up a chair. No point in any display of anger. Devereux did nothing by chance. So, I waited.

He sipped. Then he set down his cup and leveled his gaze at me.

"I thought you should know. The girl's parents and her brother are dead."

NIX

PRIMAL

The gong kept going off every five minutes, and so did my head. The alcohol was gone, but I pressed my hands to my face. What had I done?

<<BAROWUNGGGG!>>

Elena's voice kept hitting the air like a secondary alarm, and my nerves were getting frazzled. I couldn't shut off the gong—or Elena—or even put them on snooze!

<<BAROWUNGGGG!>>

It wasn't clear if the bright light filling our room was helping or not, though at least Elena had no trouble finding the clothes she'd picked out for me tonight. What would I have done without her? They were a smart combination of fashionable clothes and ankle-high boots. All black with a red belt and a red necklace and earrings.

<<BAROWUNGGGG!>>

I glanced over at Elena to thank her and stopped. She was sitting back in the bed, hugging her knees against her chest. Her face drooped and her eyes held a pained expression in them as her brows knit together with a combination of a question and concern. She stared at my palm, at the protection knot there.

"Daris," she whispered. "Daris had one too. With a Celestial stone. I noticed before he left."

A groan escaped my lips, and that's when the sparks flew from my fingertips. My gaze flew toward her as I tried to shake the sparks away, only making them worse. Now my fingertips were on fire.

"Oh, shit. Shit!" I wanted to cover my face with my hands, but I didn't know what that would do.

"'Oh shit' is right. You have half an hour until your trial. Now what are you going to do?" Elena headed toward the door. I'd never seen her like this. Elena, the light-hearted. Elena, the friendly. Elena, the happy. Now, Elena the bitter and surly?

"Elena, wait. What's your deal?"

She spun like she'd been waiting for me to ask, waved her hand, and stopped the gong. Her hair was a storm around her shoulders. "I just wanted to have a good night with you last night, but you disappeared! I had to find my way home with a couple of drunk Lupines. And my brother of all people had to carry you back to our room. And now," she gestured toward my hand accusingly, "NOW I see you have a protection bond with him? My brother and I are close. He didn't even tell me. I have to find out by just looking at you two. What is going on, Nix?"

I was caught. Half of it, I didn't remember, and the other half... I'd have to tell her. At least some of it—or I'd turn scarlet red. Thankfully, the fire at the tips of my fingers died down. No more sparks, but they still glowed fire-hot. I couldn't get dressed yet, and we only had fifteen minutes.

"El, after the death today, Daris realized he needed to protect me. I told him where I was from and about my inability to control fire. I'm new here and at risk for being sentenced to

Lethentril. He felt responsible for me as his student and wanted to show me he'd do anything to protect me. " As I blurted out the words, the half-truth burned in my veins, but my skin stayed clear. "And I'm sorry I left you, but I honestly don't remember what happened. One minute we were drinking and watching the knife competition, and the next I was stumbling near the Omnipatos. Daris found me."

Her eyes widened. "That's why you left?"

I shrugged and glanced down at my lap. "I want to fit in here. I don't want people to see me as an outcast. It's bad enough that I'm from an Outskirt Realm. I'll tell everyone where tonight. We have magic offenders everywhere. The town is –"

I wanted to say 'nearly fifty percent inhabited with arcane creatures and law-breakers,' but I stopped short of it. The wards some of our townsfolk had set around the perimeter of the county kept magic in and kept riffraff out. For the most part, it worked.

But not always. I shook the thought away.

"I'm sorry, too." Elena crossed the room and sat down at the edge of my bed. "I hope I didn't embarrass you. I don't make friends easily. Guildmaster's sister is a position that acts like a warning label to everyone. It's a double whammy since we're Bloodwraith. I wanted to show you off in my own weird way. Show the others that I'm not so bad." She smiled a little. I did, too. "And I wanted people to know you're my person."

I moved beside her and leaned my head on her shoulder. "I've never been great at the friend thing, either. Thanks, El."

We stayed like that for a couple of seconds. My eyes went to Elena's round black clock on the wall, the Roman numerals glowing like a warning sign.

"Crap! The trial . . ."

We both leaped up, Elena helping me get ready. I didn't have time for a shower.

Washcloth wipedown it is.

As I wiped myself down, brushed my teeth (spitting into the bucket), and made my hair presentable, my eyes swept over our shared room. I couldn't bear the thought of leaving. I supposed I could search for my parents, but until I learned to control the raging fires I created, I had nowhere else to go. And it wasn't as if they didn't know where I'd gone. Dad would know and tell Mom.

I knew he wanted me to enter the Skia Guild. He'd said he came here to learn too, becoming a top Apprentice before he left. I wanted to make him proud—finish my education here with Bloodwraith. If this trial went south and they banished me to Lethenthril, I didn't know what I would do. I'd have to run.

"Time to go!" Elena pointed at the clock, and I did a check. My black shirt was clean and pressed, and my black trousers hugged my ass and thighs, complementing the shape of my body. Black ankle boots. Red accessories. Elena grabbed my arm and pulled me out the door.

Part of me wanted to tell the Alliance, "Fuck you," when they started their questioning. I was still pissed at how they'd treated me the first time.

Despite the antidote, the nap, and the adrenaline, my head still pounded when we stepped outside under the full moon. As we dashed toward the Omnipatos, I wanted to turn back, but my mind flitted to thoughts of Daris. No, I needed to get through this. I belonged here. And I knew in my heart I belonged with him.

We stepped through the main entrance, and a small figure approached us. He was a tiny man with a lot of hair on his head, face, and hands. He had large ears that swept toward his back. He wore a fancy three-piece suit with a pink vest and white fluffy collar, but his feet were bare, wide, and hairy as well. "Excuse me. Ms. Nix?"

I nodded.

"Guildmaster Ravencroft needs to speak with you. At the side chamber." He indicated a small and barely-noticeable door at the end of the hall.

Elena nodded toward it, and I followed her lead.

But, before I could place my hand on the door, a voice called out to me. A tall man in black who had the look of an Immaru held a watch in his hand and stood by Elena, regarding me balefully. "Ms. Emberwind. You are almost late. Please step inside and take your place."

I glanced once more at the door, sending a mental *I'm sorry* to Daris. Whatever it was he had to tell me would just have to wait.

I entered the courtroom last with Elena. All eyes turned to me as Elena whispered, "Good luck," and slipped into one of the gallery seats.

Daris was sitting among the Alliance members, as if he'd been there all along. He didn't even look at me. As I moved to stand in the middle of the room, I felt the gaze of the Arcane Alliance members upon me, some disapproving, others ambivalent. Not many seemed as if they would advocate for me. Not even Daris.

I thought of how Elena had mentioned him carrying me last night, and seeing her crushed expression when she described noticing the bonding knot between me, and Daris twisted my heart. Unbidden, the image of the Immaru, Leander, appeared in my mind again. I thought of him soothing me, helping me to breathe. Strange, but I was grateful. It was hard to think of anything but the trial, but I liked the idea of paying him a visit.

Seraphina waved her hand, and the lights dimmed, then brightened, the sound of a strong chime signaling the start of the proceeding. The court's administrator, Uli Umber, stepped forward like before. This time, he was attired in bright blue with gold brocade. He looked better-dressed than he had before.

"Maestra. Alliance Members. The case of Ms. Phoenix Emberwind continues. Today we determine if she shall have a full Orphic awakening by igniting her magic with the Blaze Ceremony—if she is to remain at the Guilds of Chaos and Apprentice with a Guild."

High Inquisitor Devereux rose from his chair. Elena had told me that today would be different. My job was to answer questions truthfully, and theirs was to deliberate and arrive at a final decision.

"Ms. Emberwind, if you will approach the stand, please."

A half-circular golden gate, waist high, appeared in front of me. I tentatively grasped the bar, taken aback when it automatically cuffed my wrists in place. Devereux seemed pleased.

"Ah, our apologies for not explaining. Sometimes, the conclusion of our procedures is not to the liking of the person on trial, and they are—disagreeable. This precaution minimizes that outcome. You understand, of course."

I nodded curtly, trying to keep the sarcasm out of my voice. "Of course."

"Now, first, Ms. Phoenix Emberwind, we've established that you like to be called 'Nix,' by your friends. Is this correct?" Devereux arched a brow.

"Yes."

"And we've established that you cannot lie, is that correct?" There was a pause here.

I decided to demonstrate. "No." My skin turned a brilliant shade of scarlet. To my surprise, Devereux laughed, and so did everyone else. I smiled.

"Thank you for that demonstration, Ms. Emberwind. It will be helpful as we proceed. Now, Ms. Emberwind, as agreed two evenings ago, we are here tonight to learn the answers to your background.

"When our Apprentices are accepted here, we are at least familiar with where they come from. Their backgrounds, and their families. You understand this by now. If you answer my questions, you may be granted a place at the Guilds of Chaos, pending the Alliance decision. Refuse, and there will no longer be a place for you here. I gather you understand the repercussions of that decision." He was matter-of-fact, but I could hear the implied threat.

"I do understand. I will answer your questions." I felt as if a piece of my soul was being stripped away. What was I doing? Putting my family and the entire town at risk? But there was no alternative. According to Daris, and from what I'd learned so far, they'd find out who I was and where I was from no matter what. What mattered was *how* they learned—*how* I told them.

Tonight, High Inquisitor Devereux wore a golden suit with a red shirt, embellished with a pattern of snakes that slithered every time he moved. I thought about how unsafe I'd felt in Drade my whole life. And how my parents, probably even my brother, had known and maybe even used magic. I'd been ignorant of it all. I'd been an imbecile not to see it. Not to understand.

I'd worried about their safety all this time, but should I have worried? They'd seemed more concerned about me, and I'd thought they were silly because it was my fire that was a threat to them. They'd never once seen me harmed by it. Now, I wasn't sure of anything anymore.

"Ms. Emberwind, what Realm are you from?"

I started to bite my lip but stopped myself. I did not want to appear hesitant. "The Mortal Realm."

There were a few sharp intakes of breath. The room became quieter.

"I see. And, as I understand, your inability to lie is not the only magical trait you are aware of. Is that correct? You have had this other magical ability since you were a child?"

How did he know that? I thought of Daris. If Sangors were anything like vampires in my world—if Daris had the ability to hear my heartbeat—then he heard mine pounding like a racehorse right now.

"Yes," I confirmed. "When I was a child, maybe six or eight years old—I can't remember what age exactly—my parents found my bed burning after they had an argument. Since then, sometimes I've had outbreaks of fire I couldn't control. Magic is forbidden in the Mortal Realm, and so my parents tried to work with me to suppress it. My dad was the one who gave me the spell to come here if I should ever need to get away."

"And you had to get away?" Deveraux eyed me as if he knew the answer to the question.

"Yes," I responded. "I . . . " Here was the worst of it. What I had to admit in front of everyone. "I knew that magic was illegal, but I was afraid that if I didn't learn to control my flames, I'd hurt someone—accidentally display it—getting my whole family in trouble. I'd have episodes sometimes where fire would just explode from my hands. I decided to practice a small fire summoning in my room. I couldn't do it outside. If someone saw me, my family could be arrested."

My voice shook, though I tried to keep it steady. "It was fine at first, and then the fire flared. It caught on my bed linens, then my laundry, then . . . " I had to stop. Tears welled in my eyes and rolled down my face.

Shame rose up inside me as I bared my failure to the entire courtroom. "I couldn't stop it. The whole house was burning. I told my family to get out. I knew if I tried to get outside, if I made it out alive, the whole town would know it was me. They'd blame the family, too. I used the spell my dad gave me to bring me here."

Devereux stroked his chin thoughtfully as he passed by me, the snakes on his suit seeming to coil. "Can you summon your flames for us now, Ms. Emberwind?"

I tensed, looking from him to Daris, but Daris only sent me a tight, pained expression I did not understand. He gave me no indication if I should or shouldn't. I had no idea what to do.

"I don't want to hurt anyone. I don't want to burn anything."

"I assure you: the Alliance is quite capable of handling all manner of flames, Ms. Emberwind."

The cuffs dropped from my wrists and hung loose from the golden rail.

I considered my failures when I'd tried summoning the flames before. Then there were times my sparks had also come against my will, summoned by my concentrated emotion.

Perhaps any strong emotion could leap from my body as fire? I concentrated on the heat I felt for Daris, already crawling under my skin, and I felt myself warm.

I thought of how badly I'd wanted him to touch my skin last night, how I melted from the way he looked at me. He consumed my every waking moment. My eyes found him sitting in his Alliance seat before me, and as I caught his gaze, I held my palms out, letting my mind break free of my self-imposed chains.

The first sparks darted around my wrists. Others quickly followed, running like mad spirals down to my nailbeds and fingertips. The strength of my emotions seemed to make them brighter and more intense. Flames burst around me, and I screamed, realizing my body was literally on fire. But the fire didn't burn me.

My feelings for Daris—those licked my skin and my mind. Power welled in me, needing release, and I realized as it built inside me that it had nowhere to go. I had to aim this slingshot of energy at something.

With each spark that flew from me, I felt my desire for Daris increase. I tore my gaze away from him, searching for an object to take the brunt of my flames. There was a giant marble statue of a woman in flowing purple robes and an enormous metal cauldron in front of her. I aimed my palms at that, blasting it with fire that turned from yellow to orange and then dark neon blue. I'd never felt this kind of power, never felt so good! The neon blue flames poured in giant waves from me like a tornado gone wild.

The caldron glowed red with the force of my heat. I watched one side of it dip, almost as if it had started to melt. A primal yell filled my throat, and I let my cry rip through the Universe. Then, like snuffing a candle, my flame was extinguished. I dropped to the ground, trembling, vaguely aware that I was naked.

Silence filled the room. Then Daris was beside me, wrapping me in a curtain, and Elena was there next to me, casting clothing onto my body.

Devereux approached me with a bottle of Aphrodite's Gold juice and a bottle of something called Hera's Shake—Vanilla.

"Drink these." He pursed his lips, and I thought I detected a quiver in his hands as he passed the bottles to me. "They'll help you regain some of your energy."

To the Alliance members and the gallery, he announced, "Ms. Emberwind did indeed present a powerful display just now, and I submit to the Alliance that she has willingly answered our questions and demonstrated her openness to us all. I, for one, believe her heart is true and that she deserves a place among us. I do have one more question, though, for you and your potential Guildmaster, Ms. Emberwind and Guildmaster Ravencroft."

While Devereux was speaking, I'd swallowed down both the juice and the shake. My strength was coming back to me. Daris and Elena helped me to my feet.

"Ms. Emberwind, I noted you have a Celestial protection knot on your right palm. To whom are you bound?" Devereux spun on his heel toward Daris before I even answered.

I was careful to answer appropriately, though my voice shook. "It is with Guildmaster Ravencroft, High Inquisitor."

Before Deveraux could ask any more questions, Daris addressed Seraphina and the rest of the Alliance members. "Maestra and Alliance Members, tonight an Apprentice's body was discovered on the steps of this very Omnipatos. It is clear she was murdered, though the exact time and manner are under investigation. When we last met over Ms. Emberwind's case, I was charged with her protection.

"I made the choice to bind with Ms. Emberwind using a Celestial Stone protection knot to ensure no harm would come to her. She has not had an official Blaze Ceremony, something I look forward to in a moment. But as my assigned Apprentice, staying under the roof of the Skia Guild, and given certain circumstances recently come to light, I saw, and still see, Ms. Emberwind as my sole responsibility." Daris's strong voice brooked no discussion.

Devereux inclined his head and then tilted it toward Seraphina. She stared coolly at Daris for a long moment and then nodded. Daris's gaze swept over the rest of the Alliance. Each member also nodded. Devereux faced me.

"The Arcane Alliance officially admits you, Ms. Phoenix 'Nix'" Emberwind, to the Guilds of Chaos. From this point on, you are an Apprentice at Skia Guild, an official Bloodwraith. Your Blaze Ceremony must occur before we conclude our meeting tonight. If you decide to choose another Guild during the Blaze Ceremony, that is your right. Gallery members are free to depart."

"Thank you!" The words of gratitude rushed from me, and I would have lunged forward and embraced Devereux if Daris hadn't stopped me by gripping my hand. A great smile bloomed across my face. Elena yelped excitedly and gave me a hug. It felt so good to have her arms wrapped around me.

Devereux smiled at me, though I saw no joy in his eyes. He strode solemnly toward me and placed a hand on my shoulder. "And I wanted to tell you, I'm so sorry, dear. I'm so sorry for your loss."

DARIS

STRATEGY

M y heart plummeted to the depths of Carnsth's Chasm the moment I heard Devereux utter those words to Nix. *"I'm so sorry for your loss."* The words hung in the air, heavy and oppressive, like a thick fog that threatened to suffocate us all.

Nix's eyes slid to mine, seeking confirmation of the truth, and I saw the realization dawn on her face, the color draining from her cheeks as she understood the implications of Devereux's words. That son of a putrid, rotting, curse-riddled, Zeel-core just had to drop that Goyle bomb before I had the chance to tell her myself. Any fool would know she wasn't aware yet. Her demeanor said it all, the confusion and shock written plainly on her features.

I couldn't say anything to Nix right now because I didn't know the specifics. I didn't know how Devereux had found out they were dead, who had told him, or what the circumstances were. Nothing. And he'd zipped out of my quarters before I could ask him, leaving me with more questions than answers.

So, all I could do was stare at Nix with a look that said, 'We'll figure this out.' But she had no idea what I was saying with my eyes, the message lost in translation as she struggled to process the news. I watched as the world dropped beneath her feet, as if the ground had suddenly given way, and she was falling, falling, falling into an abyss of grief and despair.

If ever I wanted to use my Sangor Seduction voice, it was now. I considered it, the temptation strong, but even with the consideration, my palm started to burn. I turned my hand slightly and stared at the stone in the center of the protection knot. It was turning color, a clear 'no' from the powers that be.

Nix's eyes were still glued to me, one of her ears still turned toward Devereux. "M-my . . . l-loss?" she stammered, the words catching in her throat as if she couldn't quite believe what she was hearing.

If Devereux could have been a peacock preening under the sun, uttering knowledge that I hadn't been able to offer my Apprentice and the girl I felt affection for, he would have been the best damn peacock the Mortal Realm had ever seen. Right up until I ripped his throat out, my fingers itching to squeeze the life out of him.

Usually, we were amicable adversaries, our banter and rivalry a familiar dance that we both enjoyed. But this time, he'd stepped over the line, deliberately hurting my girl for no good reason, and I didn't understand why. This wasn't like him.

I thanked Chaos that Elena was still holding on to her, providing some measure of comfort and support. I wanted to scoop her up and run her out of here, to take her somewhere safe and quiet where she could grieve in peace. By all the Celestials, the

FATEs, and Erinyes—I swore Devereux would pay for this one, my anger burning hot and fierce in my veins.

Still, my Sangor speed was faster than my brain this time. My fingers latched around his silky throat, and I dug my nails into his squishy center as I squeezed tight, hissing in his ear. "She didn't know, you ass, and you knew it! Back off—now."

Grand Guildmaster Seraphina sighed and cleared her throat, the sound cutting through the tension like a knife. She was clearly bored with our theatrics and unappreciative of what amounted to our display of her lack of discipline under the dome. "That will be ENOUGH." The word 'enough' was amplified, shaking my insides violently. Both Dev and I doubled over, the force of her words hitting us like a physical blow. Slowly, we stood, our bodies aching and sore. I glanced around. Just Dev and I seemed affected, a testament to Seraphina's power and control.

Seraphina called out, her voice ringing through the room. "Bring The Reflection of Chaos. Everyone else, clear the floor except Ms. Emberwind." The room hushed once more, the silence broken only by the shuffling of feet as people moved to obey her commands. Some seats were vacant now, but most of the people in the gallery had elected to stay, their curiosity piqued by the promise of seeing what other magic types the newest Apprentice might have, if any.

It took a few moments, but our senior historian, Master Coeus, finally appeared on the Court Arena, his movements slow and deliberate, as if he were moving through water instead of air. His robes seemed to flutter in slow motion with him, the pale, luminescent blue fabric shimmering in the light. With his flowing beard and age, he appeared quite regal, the octagonal tam upon his head looking almost like an arctic landscape with the map of several solar systems plotted along the top of it.

Behind him followed his Apprentice, Reed Marsh, carrying with him the Obsidian Mirror—at least, that was what it had been called until Reed found an ancient text. Now it was the Reflection of Chaos, and I was still getting used to the change. Passed down from the ancients, it was a slightly concave piece of polished volcanic glass, at least thirty-five centimeters in diameter. Not huge, but powerful, the surface seeming to shimmer and shift in the light.

As they neared Nix, a gleaming wooden table rose from the floor of the Arena, the wood polished to a high shine. Reed beckoned Nix over, and she strode to him, her movements stiff and jerky, as if her body was moving on autopilot. Still, her jaw was set, her eyes focused, a determination in her gaze that belied the grief and shock that must have been coursing through her.

"Your finger," Reed coaxed, warm and overly excited. As always.

Nix offered her index finger, and Reed noted the protection bond on her palm, frowning slightly before opening a long case and removing a needle. In a flash, he pierced her skin, a single drop of blood welling up on the tip of her finger. He held it over the mirror, the blood hanging in the air for a moment before splashing onto the surface.

A mist rose into the air, circling around the center of the mirror, the tendrils of vapor twisting and turning in an intricate dance.

Another block rose under Master Coeus' feet, and he gazed into the mist and the Mirror, his eyes distant and unfocused, as if he were seeing something beyond the physical world. He coaxed Nix to come beside him, and together they gazed down, their faces bathed in the eerie glow of the mist.

I don't know what they saw together. Each Apprentice received a power based on their innate traits—their character power based on their strongest good combined with what they must overcome. But Nix had not one but several tears streaming down her face, the droplets glistening on her cheeks like diamonds in the light.

I wished more than anything I'd been gifted with the Sangor power to read minds, to know what she was thinking and feeling at that moment. But that one wasn't mine. My powers were useful in their own way, but they couldn't help me now.

Grand Guildmaster Seraphina appeared at Nix's side in a blink, moving with a speed and grace that was almost uncanny. She brought her to the center of the room, drawing a crystal wand, and started a small crackling fire before the two of them, the flames dancing and leaping in the air.

"Apprentice Emberwind, you are accepted by the Guilds of Chaos. You have gazed into the Reflection of Chaos and discovered a power that you now possess. You and your Guildmaster must ensure you develop it well. Are you sure of your Guild?"

Nix nodded, her face set in determination, even as tears welled in her eyes and threatened to fall.

What if she chose another Guild? I wouldn't blame her. I could still protect her from a distance, and I would, my resolve unwavering. I wanted to explain that I didn't have time to tell her about her parents and brother, the words stuck in my throat, unable to find their way out.

"Skia Guild." Nix's voice rang out firm and strong.

"Well done," Grand Guildmaster Seraphina intoned, her voice rich and melodious. "And now, we know of your inability to lie, though that may be more of a curse than a magic. Time will tell."

Everyone smiled, and a few chuckled, the sounds echoing off the walls.

"And your display of fire magic, what we call Ignitor, however unrestrained and untrained, was impressive. Under this Blaze Ceremony, let us see if your Orphic blood, Chaos, and the Celestials hold any more gifts for you."

This part coming up would be hard for me to watch, my stomach twisting in knots at the thought of what was to come. No one was allowed to tell any Apprentice about this part, the secrecy shrouding the ceremony in mystery. Even most observers could not remember anyway, their memories wiped clean by the ceremony's deep-rooted magic that left only vague impressions and fleeting images.

There were rare exceptions, the magic allowing the Grand Guildmaster and the Guildmasters to remember until they no longer held those positions, the knowledge a burden they carried with them. Seraphina didn't know it, but one of my Sangor gifts was the inability to forget, my mind a steel trap that held onto every detail, every moment, with perfect clarity. No potion, no spell—nothing could ever block my memory, the curse of perfect recall. I'd let her assume it was possible in the past, the deception serving me well.

Grand Guildmaster Seraphina stepped away from Nix, moving her hands in a fluid circle. Her spell swathed Nix in something that looked like cellophane, the material clinging to her like a second skin. I'd seen this before, but it hurt to see it happen to her, and my heart ached with every labored breath she took—until the wrap covered her mouth and her nose, cutting off her air supply.

Moments passed, each one feeling like an eternity before the scent of clean air after a storm filled the room, the freshness cutting through the tension like a knife. A wild wind whipped at her body, the gusts tearing at her clothes and hair, and we all watched in amazement as birds of every kind flew into the courtroom through whatever entrance they could find, their wings beating a frantic rhythm in the air. They tore at the plastic around her, their beaks and talons ripping the material away from her airway and freeing her from the suffocating prison.

The wind held her aloft as the birds disappeared, their job done, and although it was night, a cloud of red and blue butterflies circled around her, their wings shimmering in the light. They landed on her, their delicate bodies resting on her skin for a moment before gently flying away, their departure as sudden as their arrival. The winds deposited her gently on the floor as they dissipated, the room falling silent once more.

Seraphina pursed her lips, seeming unimpressed but satisfied with the result, her expression carefully neutral. "Cielo," she announced, her voice ringing out in the silence. And Reed Marsh typed it in on his Tessar Pad, his fingers flying over the keys. Along with the power of air, Cielo embraced love and healing powers, which was good for someone with the destructive Ignitor or fire forces.

Waving her hand, Seraphina now encased Nix inside a block of tightly packed earth, the soil pressing in on her from all sides, suffocating and heavy. I felt her body as it was compressed, the sensation of being crushed almost overwhelming, and the stone in my hand burned fire hot, the pain searing through my flesh. I gritted my teeth, the effort of remaining still and silent almost too much to bear. I could not interfere with this one, the stone's warning clear. The stone had to know, too, because it wasn't killing me, the pain a reminder of my place in all of this.

The requisite moments ticked by slowly, and nothing happened, the earth remaining solid and unyielding around her. Seraphina made the earth vanish, the block disappearing as suddenly as it had appeared. No Teragos power, the earth rejecting her.

Next, Nix was presented to us in a clear box, the walls transparent and gleaming, but under a light that I knew to be hot, the heat rising in waves from the floor. The inner temperature rose, as likely did her core temperature. The heat had to be dehydrating her body and increasing her thirst, making the need for water overwhelming. She banged on the walls, her fists pounding against the unyielding surface, and sweat poured out of her skin until there was no more, her body wrung dry by the relentless heat. Her eyes rolled back, the whites showing, and I knew that Aquane power was not hers either, the water rejecting her as the earth had.

Seraphina seemed disappointed, but two Elemental powers were good by any standard, the combination rare and powerful. She banished the box with a wave of her hand, and Reed brought Nix water, the liquid sloshing in the glass as he hurried to her side. The girl drank as if in a trance, the water disappearing down her throat in huge gulps, her thirst unquenchable.

The other powers were next, the Ariparz powers, which were so difficult to assess. Osculos, Umbrani, Luxan, and Apparlusio, each one a mystery waiting to be unveiled.

"Master Coeus," Seraphina called, her voice cutting through the silence like a blade.

The old historian made his way toward Nix, his steps slow and measured, and conjured a chair for both of them in the middle of the Arena, the furniture appearing out of thin air. The room went pitch black, the darkness so complete that it was almost tangible. Only Nix and Master Cocus remained illuminated by an unseen light source.

The Master grew a table between them from the floor, the wood twisting and warping into shape, the surface smooth and polished. He then conjured a generously sized glass ball, the surface of it clear and flawless, and placed it on the table. The ball was filled with a mist that swirled in several directions, the tendrils of vapor twisting and turning in an intricate dance, hypnotic and mesmerizing.

Master Coeus gave Nix directions. "Ms Emberwind, please place your hands on the ball. Clear your mind. Take a breath. Now, look into my past and tell me if I ever had brothers or sisters."

I didn't have much hope for this. Nix was from the Mortal Realm, and even if her family originally came from Arnexis, I didn't know her parents. Emberwind was not a name I recognized. I stared at the swirling mists, waiting for Seraphina to halt this part of the test when Nix spoke. "You had a twin brother. You both Apprenticed together in the Magus Guild because of your many gifts. You found a spell in the Archives. One that could take you—"

"Do not speak the place, Ms. Emberwind." Master Coeus' fingers signed the Compulsion spell, enforcing his words.

"Your brother never made it back alive," she finished.

If I were asked to say something right now, I'd be speechless. Osculus magic. Nix?

"Osculus!" Grand Guildmaster Seraphina shouted the word, and in the dark, it seemed extra loud.

"Do you know my brother's name, Nix? What was it?" The old man's voice was almost a whisper at this point, and I thanked my Sangor ears for their abilities.

"Sutrh," Nix whispered.

"And my name?"

"Aesirh."

I heard Master Coeus swallow. The darkness pushed in while the light Master Coeus had generated dimmed.

"What message does my brother have for me, Nix? Can you find him?"

The silence was nearly deafening around me. I was one of the unfortunate left to hear the thrum of every heartbeat in the courtroom while everyone else sat perched on the edge of their seat.

Nix's head jutted back, her chin thrust toward the ceiling, and her voice low and deep—not her voice at all—spoke: "I am waiting for you, BROTHER. Your time is SOON!" Her head dropped, her chin falling against her chest.

I wasn't sure why the Grand Guildmaster deliberated. Nix's experience was not a performance. But maybe—

"She's Umbrani, Reed—write down Umbrani!" Seraphina said quickly like she was losing her place.

Watching the scene unfold, I felt like I was losing *my* place.

Guildmaster   Coeus was obviously shaken. And his light was waning. Yet, Nix seemed uninclined to help him. I wanted to call out to her, to tell her that he needed her.

"Ms. Emberwind," Seraphina prompted. "It's dark in here, and I think Master Coeus could use your help. Talking with his brother took a toll."

Nix studied her blankly and then only half considered him. I could tell part of her was somewhat aware of what they'd done to her so far, and she wasn't pleased. But she sighed, shaking her head, probably figuring all she'd do was conjure her fire. Nothing happened. She shrugged her shoulders at the darkness as if to say, "See?"

Master Coeus vanished before her, along with the ball of swirling mist and the table. His chair remained.

"Nix," Seraphina's voice echoed everywhere. "Can you hear me?"

She nodded very slightly—it was almost imperceptible.

"There's one last portion of the Blaze Ceremony that we must complete to know the full extent of your magic. We are so close to the end, and you've done incredibly well. This part is extremely hard, and sometimes we don't discover Apprentices have this skill until much later, but I feel you are up to this task. Will you try?"

'Up to the task.' Did Seraphina realize Nix had just found out her parents and her brother were dead? That she'd killed them? Of course, she did. She didn't care. This was another Apprentice to test to be done with. My Sangor blood boiled.

Again, the dull, almost dreamlike, tiny nod from Nix.

"Look at the chair in front of you," Seraphina directed. "Think of someone you'd like to see *right now* and make that person real in your mind. Make them so real you could reach out and touch them, feel them."

I watched Nix's breath increase. Darkness still surrounded her except for the light on the chair. A fuzzy outline started to form on the seat. I couldn't tell what it was at first, but then it dawned on me as it started to take form.

It was a man. Probably her brother or her father. It wasn't fully formed. I didn't see the likeness, but as she reached out toward the figure, it mirrored her movement.

"I'm so, so sorry," she choked. "I'm sorry I couldn't . . . "

Nix stood, tears streaming down her face. The figure vanished. As it did, an eerie blue light encased her forearms. I watched as the Celestial forces drew their marks on her. A gentle swirl from her elbow on each side to the center of her forearms, around her wrists, and then spiraling around her fingers. Her blank palm carried a design. Her right palm maintained our Celestial bond.

Nix's eyes flew wide, and she became instantly decisive. She started to mutter a chant—one I'd never heard before—and in an instant, she was gone.

The courtroom brightened as the light nearly blinded all of us. I watched everyone rub their eyes.

"Apparlusio!" Seraphina said in a loud but firm voice to Reed. "And make sure to mark her as Myrocans."

I prepared to leave, but Grand Guildmaster Seraphina called out to me before I could zip away with Sangor speed. I expected a reprimand for Nix.

Seraphina approached me with a half-smile. "It was unusual to have a new Apprentice exit a Blaze Ceremony in such a manner, but it was understandable given Apprentice Emberwind's circumstances. She has powerful potential but an unbridled start. You have your work cut out for you, Daris. Good luck, and well done." She gave me a nod.

I pressed my lips and tilted my head in acknowledgment. "It is late notice, I know. But I need you to come to my office tomorrow, Maestra. I'm free at one in the afternoon, and I believe your schedule is open, too. Someone in admin told me."

When she opened her mouth to argue, I shook my head to stop her. "No. This is important."

I turned and flashed out of there, thinking, 'Well done?' How could she tell me 'Well done' over something like that? Like I had anything to do with Nix's outcome? What had happened to her was a travesty, and I hadn't even had the opportunity to break the news to her gently.

But then, I was sure now that the timing was Seraphina's doing. I thought about the Blaze Ceremony. It was always a challenge to read an Apprentice's Ariparz gifts. Seraphina took advantage of the situation.

The four Ariparz powers didn't depend on the Elementals. They were occult and mystical, spiritual and psychological. They dealt with the forces of dark and light. What Seraphina had done was harness Nix's grief, forcing her to demonstrate those aspects right away.

Often, an Apprentice had nothing pushing them toward revealing those particular gifts, but Seraphina had used Nix's horror at losing her family, her recent tragedy, and awareness that she played a part in their deaths to draw those aspects out. It was heartless. It was brilliant. I hated her for it, and yet I understood why she did it.

I thought I understood Devereux's confusing behavior now. While he probably hadn't objected to doing what he did, I was guessing that Seraphina had told him. Since he led the Magus Guild, he would benefit if Nix ever elected to change Guilds. Nix and her multiple magic gifts would be a huge asset to his Guild. More than he even realized.

My bet was no one had explained to Nix yet that since she'd lived in the Mortal Realm all this time, her species' genetic code remained unawakened. Before, she would have called herself Mortal or human. Now, since she had pure Orphic blood, everyone assumed she was solely Arnexin. But what flavor of Arnexin? Many species inhabited this Realm now. And Nix's parents had fled to the Mortal Realm. That meant—they'd had secrets. What kind of secrets... those remained to be seen.

I didn't sleep well, so around three in the morning, I left to visit a blood bar. I hit Hemere up on my Celcom to see if he wanted to hang. He lived in the Magisar wing, though some Magisars elected to live off GOC grounds. He was solo, like me, and preferred the company of others and being available to Apprentices. I didn't much approve of his definition of 'company of others' since he'd managed to seduce quite a few of the other Magisars in the area. It was a game to him, but that was his affair.

"I'm ready for something hot and wet," Hemere winked at me when I knocked on his door.

I grinned. "You never stop, do you?" I shook my head. "Let's go. I need a pick-up after today. Watching my Apprentice at her Blaze—it was a tough one."

We didn't bother with a portal, racing the five miles to Oneg's Run. Our favorite bloodtender, Art, was on shift. He hooked us up, and we did what none of us were supposed to do. We talked Blaze Ceremony. I told them how Seraphina ran it this time with Nix.

Art and Hemere sipped on warm, frothy mugs, finishing three by the time I'd cleared two.

Seraphina's methods didn't seem to bother them much. They were more impressed with the fact that Nix had two Elemental gifts and three Ari-parz. I still didn't know what she'd seen in the Reflection of Chaos, and I said as much. And I let them know that Nix still hadn't had her genetic code awakened.

Art was blond, with crystal blue eyes that were almost white. He was well preserved—like he hadn't aged a day in the six hundred years I'd known him. Maybe a little crease on his brow, but I wasn't sure. He grinned. "Dude, do you really want to risk spikin' up that code? Do you know what you're gonna get?"

I didn't tell him what I suspected. After drinking Nix's blood, I was almost certain of what would happen if she went through the Eye of Chaos. I had a taste of what she might become. And I had to make sure no one else tasted her—that was part of why I put the Celestial bond in place.

Hemere nodded. "He's correct, you know. She could become a full-on monster after she goes through the Eye. You could find yourself Celestial bound to a Gorgon—Medusa snakes swinging around you everywhere. I'm open-minded, but say you guys end up hitting it off after Apprenticeship . . . "

"There'll be none of that," I said, shutting them down. "She's my Apprentice. I'm her Magisar. There's no relationship beyond that."

Then they both did something I'd never seen a Sangor do in a thousand of my blood-drinking years. They dropped their toasty mugs of blood.

Both of them stared at me. I stared back.

"What's your problem?"

Art did a double take. He slid a glance at Hemere. "You saw it, too, right?"

Hemere nodded. "Say it again. What you just said."

I thought. What did I just say? Ah, about me and Nix. "She's my Apprentice. I'm her Magisar. There's no relationship beyond that."

Their eyes got big as Harvest Moons in the Barno Realm. "Dude," Art laughed out loud and pointed, "Quick, look at your skin!"

I gaped in the mirror across from the bar instead and dropped my own mug. My skin had turned a blaring shade of scarlet.

A day for a Sangor usually flies by. Seconds are faster than any living being can imagine. Hours are like minutes, and so on. This morning, time moved in slow motion as I considered my Celestial Protection Bond with Nix. Somehow, it now connected her inability to tell a lie with *me*.

I cast an accusing eye at the Celestial stone in my palm. There was a phrase in the Mortal Realm that I never understood until now: '*Good deeds never go unpunished.*'

If I'd followed the Slay Orc phrase, "Selfless deeds die for self," my circumstances would be very different. But then, I couldn't imagine not being bonded to Nix. She was in my mind every moment. It was a simple fact that I'd have done anything to protect her, Celestial bond or not.

I stared at my face in the mirror and ran my hands over my eyes and nose, pausing to peer between my fingers. This *thing* hadn't happened right away. But once Nix's Blaze Ceremony concluded—once her magic was fully awakened—it was done.

Maybe I could fix this. Or maybe it was just a residual thing that happened for the rest of the night, and then it was done. I tried it out.

"It's okay, really. I don't mind not being able to lie at all." Even though I was alone, I was embarrassed at how red my skin turned. How was I ever going to leave my Guildmaster quarters?

I thought about how often I lied. Lying was an art. It was part of keeping secrets. It was my currency, and I survived and thrived off my ability to misdirect, imply, or say any number of words that were not exactly the truth.

Perhaps I'll write a note to everyone and tell them that I'm taking a vow of silence.

And Hemere and Art. They knew now. They were fellow Sangors, though. We shared some of the most secret information related to the GOC. They wouldn't say anything, so . . .

A knock at my door interrupted my thoughts. Only a few people had permission to cross my wards. Hemere. Elise. I opened the door.

Hemere appeared quite dapper, though I didn't expect to see him up so early. He wasn't usually out and about till noon or so. I let him in.

"I don't know what I'm going to do about this, Hemere," I grumbled. "I don't think I can make it through the day without telling a lie. I mean, just a slip—"

"So it's TRUE!" Elise shifted from Hemere into her normal form. She was dressed for her morning training in Alchemy, her eyes bright, almost laughing.

I stood there, dumbfounded at first, and then anger started sparking inside me. "Who told you?" I bellowed. I had to know who else knew. Did all of the GOC know now? Elise tried to put me at ease, but her smile wasn't helping. She hadn't done anything like that in a long time.

"Sorry about that. Hemere told me. obviously. Yes, I know, Sangor brothers to the end and all, but he was worried about you." She lunged in to hug me. I wasn't feeling it and rolled my eyes, taking the sisterly embrace as much as I could endure. She pulled away, examining me like I was an Apprentice project. "And since I'm your sister, and Nix lives with me, it made sense to tell me. She needs to know about this, Daris. This way, we'll all work together to help each other. You need to tell her, though."

I swallowed, pushing my anger down. In my thousand years, nothing so inconvenient and humiliating had ever happened to me like this. I'd seen others debased and suffer humiliations and embarrassments and thought nothing of it. Now that I was in their shoes and held a position of leadership, I saw the wisdom of her words.

"There's one more thing," she added. "I haven't told Nix this yet. I've been waiting for the right time. When we brought her to the infirmary and cleaned her up. When I got rid of her burned clothes. I emptied her pockets. She had a note in one of them." Elena reached into her pocket and pulled out a crisp, clean scrap of paper. I read the words:

You will See
When You Pass Through The Eye
And Turn for Blood
Eternal Love
Ascend as You were Meant to Be.

"This makes no sense," I quipped.

Elena laughed and pointed. "Oh dear brother, you are going to have to learn to think before you talk. This obviously means something to you."

"I guess I'm flaming red, aren't I? Damn." This was a problem. But *maybe,* I gritted my teeth at the thought, *maybe I'll learn something useful from this.*

My eyes drifted over Elise's clothes, and I thought about her Alchemy class, which led me to consider the entire topic of Alchemy. Alchemy could be a way out of this mess.

For me and for Nix.

After an intense battle training session at the Parabellum Land Arena, I used a transport spell to retrieve some basic sustenance and bring it back to my office. The scent of the simple meal wafted through the air, a welcome respite from the sweat and grime of the training grounds. The Apprentices had performed adequately overall, though Nix still refused to unleash her flames, and I understood her reluctance. She was still reeling from the shocking news, and the weight of her new magic hung heavy on her shoulders.

I hadn't had any time to see her yet, and I knew she must be wondering why I hadn't been by. I hoped that Elena had taken the time to explain some of the situation to her. In Nix's absence, I had paired her with an advanced Apprentice named Nika. Nika was a unique cross-species water child, born to a Naiad mother and a Mervi father. They called themselves Naimer and wore their mixed heritage with pride. Naimer excelled at both ocean and freshwater skills, their dual nature granting them increased power and versatility in both domains.

Since Nix wouldn't demonstrate her fire abilities and couldn't swim, I assigned Nika the responsibility of taking her to the water arena and beginning some basic swimming lessons. Nix glared at me as Nika attempted to lure her away with an enchanting song, but the melody seemed to fall flat, its magic ineffective.

I pushed my thoughts aside. As long as my stone didn't turn red in, I didn't need to worry about Nix. When the girls returned, neither wore particularly happy faces, and I decided it was best not to pry into what had transpired. Not yet.

I ate my food in contemplative silence, waiting for Seraphina to arrive. She was late, a fact that I found irksome and disrespectful. Fifteen minutes after our appointed time, she finally graced me with her presence.

When she arrived, I was ready, sitting in my chair with documents prepared as needed. I had decided it was time to start taking some matters into my own hands. "Thank you for showing up, Seraphina," I began, my tone measured but firm. "You need to know that I called an Alliance meeting tonight to discuss the murder that took place on GOC grounds. As I said, I believe it was very different from the usual fare. Something needs to be done about it, and we need to address it before more Apprentices are killed."

"I am a very busy woman, Guildmaster." Seraphina paced around my office space, her fingers trailing over various items that caught her curiosity. "I cannot come and go as I please, contrary to popular belief. My calendar will not allow for this. I have other items to attend to."

I stood up, refusing to let her talk down to me. "The Alliance was designed so that we would be able to meet during emergencies like this." I pointed to our Realm and Guild Treaties and our Charter, the documents laid out before her. "Make time, or step down."

Seraphina's eyes widened in surprise, a flicker of anger passing over her features. "That is no way to talk to me."

"Break the treaties and step down—or attend the meeting and keep your title. The choice is yours. Now, if you'll excuse me, I have a lot to do prior to tonight." I swept around my office and opened the door for her, a clear indication that our meeting had concluded. She was pure rage; I could see it in the tension that radiated from her body. I gestured for her to leave, unwavering in my resolve.

As she passed me, she paused to whisper, her voice low and threatening. "Watch yourself, Guildmaster. I have more power than you think."

When she was gone, I bellowed in frustration, the sound echoing through the empty office. No one was around to hear me, but the release of tension from my chest was a welcome relief. After what she did to Nix, after witnessing her manipulations, I was done tolerating the way things were run at the GOC. After seeing how Devereux was so cavalier about the Apprentice's death and then not hearing about a report, I shook my head, knowing I needed to have a clear mind for the meeting tonight. I would be the one addressing everyone.

I still needed to see Nix. To explain what had happened and why I had been absent. I hated being away from her for so long, and the guilt gnawed at me. As soon as this meeting was over, I'd go to her, determined to make things right.

The meeting tonight would be held in a secret space, one that could only be reached from a portal inside the Cave of Secrets in the Mountains. This portal took the traveler to *'Cor,'* the one central meeting space that had existed since time immemorial, known only to the Alliance members. It existed in a place between Realms, between time and space, a hidden sanctuary.

In this place, the *Eye of Chaos* existed as well. This was where Apprentices who had not had their genetic sequence ignited came to have it done, should they decide it was what they wanted. Some Apprentices never came, fearing they'd become a monster or something else so reprehensible it was beyond description.

Our meeting was scheduled to begin at three in the afternoon. I struck out toward the Cave of Secrets. As I headed around the side of the mountain, two tiny blue stars darted up from the ground, alerting me that someone else had already entered. They stuck themselves to my wrist with a sting, a reminder that they'd disappear when whoever had entered the meeting room left. It was my way of keeping an eye on things, a precautionary measure.

I found the Daphins tree tucked against the darker part of the Carlith mountain, its massive roots wider than my body. The deep green leaves fluttered in the wind, silver-green and never falling, always bright and glistening. It was there and only there, that a portal to the Cor could be opened.

Usually, I would have stationed two guards outside, but I hadn't had the time in all the pandemonium. I plucked a twig from a hole in the trunk and drew blood from my wrist, the crimson droplets staining the bark. Painting the tip of the twig red, I waved it in the sky before me like a wand until golden mist began to swirl, then tucked it into a pocket, the magic complete.

Stepping through the mist, I emerged into an immense, golden space. In the center, a spectacular fountain of water splashed down while rising up on the other side to splash above, a mesmerizing display of perpetual motion. Two massive koi fish, one gold and one silver, circled below, their scales shimmering in the ethereal light. Above, in a pool suspended over our heads, a black and a white koi fish circled as well, a perfect balance of light and dark.

No one knew where they had come from nor how they had survived for so long. Even the most learned Guild-masters weren't sure what they were. They'd been there since I was a boy, when my Guildmaster of Blood-wraith had brought me here as his Apprentice. When I came to pass through *The Eye*. The day I became a Sangor.

Whatever the case, they only deviated from their path if the Guilds were in danger. Tonight, I watched their long, silky tails flutter to the left, then the right. Their bodies brushed one side of the fountain, then the other. It wasn't a good sign.

The woman who was so busy—Seraphina—had been the first to arrive. She was sprawled in a plush chair, relaxed, her eyes fixed on the fish above. Only when I cleared my throat did she look up.

She inclined her chin, but we didn't speak. Instead, she led the way from the fountain to the adjoining chamber, where sizable chairs were evenly spaced in a circle. As the Maestra, hers was centermost and tallest. She pointedly fixed her gaze on me as she settled into it.

Seraphina didn't have a Second, since Devereux was Magus Guildmaster in her stead. But, a figure cloaked in black lurked near the wall behind her. I wanted to ask, but others began to arrive.

Hemere, my Second for tonight, stepped through my portal next and took a seat in the slightly shorter chair next to mine. I squinted my eyes at him with a 'Thanks for telling my sister about last night' look, and he responded with wide, 'I have no idea what you are talking about' eyes. Oh yeah. We were definitely going to have a one-on-one Parabellum meeting later.

Soon, all eight Guildmasters and their Seconds, in total, were present. It was my responsibility to record the meeting. I pulled out my Tessar Pad and listed the Guildmasters seated at the table: Leander from Immaru, Devereux from Magus, Gauge from Bellator, Omani from Mernai, Myst from Hecade, Gissu from Oscuro, Ur from Terra and Daris from Skia. Grand Guildmaster Seraphina was recorded as present, and all Seconds were listed. I eyed my arm. Bright blue stars had taken up most of the skin on my wrist, accounting for everyone here.

Grand Guildmaster Seraphina clapped her hands, amplifying them and making them sound like a loud chime. "This meeting is called to order. I called this meeting at the Cor to discuss a rather troubling prophecy made known to me by Guildmaster Myst Rivers of Hecade Guild. Before I bring that to light, Guildmaster Daris Ravencroft of the Skia Guild wishes to speak."

All eyes fell on me as I stood. Anger still fueled me on this topic, as well as what I deemed poor leadership overall, and so I felt very glad to step up and bring this issue to my Guildmasters. They needed to see. To understand. Few of them had lived as long as I had.

"Fellow Guildmasters, A recent tragedy took place on our campus, on the very steps of the Omnipatos. An Apprentice was found murdered at night, with extensive gashes in her torso and chest—a fire blazing in the center of her chest." I paused, allowing the murmurs to die down. "I am calling for increased security measures on the GOC campus until the murderer is found."

"Skia Guild takes in the most assassins," said Gissu from Oscuro. "Seems like you should look in your own backyard first." Gissu was a round man, almost too old for Oscuro Guildmaster now. His was a Guild of stealth, spies, and secrets. His Apprentices drew on several magic arts, but they practiced physical arts as well, including acrobatics, sleight of hand magic, and other things—never relying solely on magic alone. Gissu didn't bother to hone those skills anymore and worked less to remember them.

I met his lazy stare. "We don't know that it was an assassin. Gouge marks in a chest are not an assassin's style, and the Apprentice did not die on the steps. My nose detected decay. At least two days' worth. This Apprentice was from Hecade Guild. It could be one of your Apprentices next. Or what if it kills outside the GOC? Not everyone has magic skills."

I'd planned to say more, but questions and concerns kept arising. The skeleton of a plan came to light, too; Gauge offered to station Bellator's best Apprentices at each Guild for a time. The Terra and the Hecade discussed spells for plants and animals recognizing malicious intent and attacking and holding an offender until security arrived. They wanted only to enforce that if the killer tried to kill again. Devereux said he could increase the level of Incitar attack after eleven in the evening to discourage anyone being out at that time, and to discourage attackers.

The gargoyles were supposed to protect Apprentices from the inside. I didn't want to wait, but Seraphina and some other Guildmasters took her side.

"For now, I propose we restrict rather than mandate." She spoke only once everyone had quieted. Her guest stood silently at her shoulder. "We should not station Hammerfists at everyone's Guilds unless we fail again to catch the killer. That's too much to ask for Bellator Guild. They have warriors to train.

I recommend leaving it up to each Guild to take their own protective measures and accountability for their Apprentices. Each Guild's gargoyles can sound their alarms, but overall, each Guildmaster is always responsible for the coming and going of personnel. If something becomes suspicious, no matter how doubtful you are, you can bring it to my attention immediately."

The Alliance voted. The majority ruled, and they sided with Seraphina's approach. Her words, " . . . unless we fail again to catch the killer" made me ill. In my lifetime, I'd killed. And I'd learned how not to kill. Her approach was 'waiting for someone to kill again' to see if we would fail again when we had no leads, not understanding much about who the killer was. This made no sense.

"The next order of business, "Seraphina intoned," concerns the prophecy I received from Hecade Guild. I will read it word for word and ask for your thoughts." Seraphina unrolled a small tan scroll her guest handed to her. It bothered me that I couldn't see the figure's face, but the hands were familiar. She cleared her throat before reading:

"Tooth, Claw, and Staff will merge
Each of secret, each unknown

Together power, great the surge
To die or wait till seeds are sown.
Tooth, Claw, and Staff will fight
Friends and enemies the same
Sides they turn, and blood for right
Shadows call. Embrace the name."

Before any of us could express our thoughts, a crash came from behind me. I spun around and witnessed a commotion outside of our circle, beyond the archway that led to the fountain. Others rose from their seats, but I beat them to the source with my Sangor speed, rage filling my blood.

Nix was a mess on the floor, trying to gather a decorative column she'd managed to knock over along with shards of an Athena statue. Movement to my left caught my eye. Elias and Elena, of all people, were here, too. They were standing near the portal I'd come through. Nix looked back at them with wide eyes, shooing them back through it. Relief lightened my chest once the two disappeared, but Nix remained, looking up at me.

Then, Seraphina strode into the room.

It was too late for her to flee.

PROPHECY

This—this was not supposed to have happened. Elena had told me the Alliance was having a secret meeting that afternoon and that it had something to do with the campus murder. Elias had been there when we grabbed snacks in the common room at the same time. He let us know there was a rumor about me now—that I might have something to do with the murder since I had such a powerful display of uncontrollable fire magic last night.

"They're saying maybe you tried to cover it up." He shrugged. "It's ridiculous, I know. Like you'd have any idea how to do something like that *here* before you had your powers ignited."

I didn't volunteer that I'd actually burned down several trees, a cabin, barn and set a field on fire before I came to Arnexis. It was true I hadn't set any *people* on fire.

Elena asked me if Daris had mentioned the note she'd found in my pocket that night I came to Arnexis.

"What note?" I had no idea what she was talking about. My pockets had been empty.

"I wanted Daris to tell you, but with you being a potential suspect and Daris so busy . . . He has a protection bond with you anyway, and I am your Guild sister, so here goes." She pulled the note out of her pocket. We all read it.

"It reads like a prophecy," Elias said.

"Or at least a riddle," I thought. "But I can't think of where it would have come from. Seriously."

We'd sat in silence for a few moments, and then Elena suggested we go sneak into the Alliance meeting. "I know where they go. I've followed Daris a ton of times."

"If he wasn't your brother, I'd say you were some kind of weird, creepy stalker," Elias ran his fingers through his blond hair and then drank down a bottle of Circe's Crystal Tears. He pulled out his Celcom. "Dudes. It's blowing up on Nix." He showed us the Chatbox. 'Murder on campus #newapprenticeonfire #nixthenix #fingersoffury #smothertheflames.'

Elena rolled her eyes. Everyone's just scared. I say we go after Daris and Hemere leave. The Alliance will meet in the far room. We'll go in while they are meeting, hang by the fountain, and zip out before they're done.

Elias winked at me. "I did ask you if you wanted to get into a little trouble . . ."

And now—now, I was in trouble.

I heard the   shouts   behind   Daris,   but   all I could do was look helplessly up at him. His lips turned down like I'd just slapped him across the face.

I imagine I practically had. I'd just been accepted to the Guilds of Chaos. I'd had my Blaze Ceremony, and I was his Apprentice now. *His.*

"What in the Realms are you doing here, Ms. Ember-wind?" Seraphina stalked over to me, her silver heels echoing loudly against the golden floor.

"I—I . . . " My mouth gaped open. I licked my lips, realizing I didn't know what to say. I certainly couldn't tell them that the three of us decided to come spy on them and that upon hearing the prophecy, Elias had stumbled backward into the column and knocked over the Athena statue. It had looked like a part of the wall. We'd found out the hard way it was not.

"I do apologize for my bumbling new Apprentice, Maestra." Daris's jaw was clenched as he addressed Seraphina, turning toward her like I wasn't there at all. "She . . . "He paused as if realizing something. "She is my Apprentice now, and she is arriving late to this meeting, which is a rare opportunity to attend."

I found it odd that he peered at his skin when he spoke those words, but he seemed relieved for a second. I didn't have time to think about what he was saying or why. I just nodded vigorously. "My sincere apologies, Maestra. It won't happen again. I hope the statue can be replaced. "As soon as the words were out of my mouth, I wanted to wince. I lived in a world of magic now. Probably every single person in this room could create a new one. The heat of extreme embarrassment rose to my cheeks.

Daris offered me a hand. His eyes threatened murder as they fell on me. I stood as Seraphina spoke. "Well, I'm glad you made it, though it is unusual for such a brand-new Apprentice to attend something like this—but you are Grandmaster Ravencroft's Apprentice after all. Officially assigned to him, as I recall."

I nodded.

"In any case, let us continue with the meeting. Daris, you are welcome to fill her in quietly. I expect no further interruptions from either of you. Now, everyone, back to your places."

Sheepishly, I followed Daris. He led me to a grand chair in which he sat down. Hemere was seated at his right shoulder, an astonished look on his face as he watched me.

"On my left." If Daris wasn't whispering, his words would have been a bark. The anger he felt toward me was palpable as I stood, rigid as a statue, mimicking the other Apprentices around the room.

I expected Seraphina to start speaking. Instead, she focused her attention on the fountain, watching the two massive gold and silver koi fish swim in a circle. My breath hitched: they were stunning.

"Apprentice Emberwind." My head shot to attention when Seraphina addressed me. "Come here, please." She rose again and walked to the fountain.

Daris leaned forward slightly. My glance flicked to him for guidance, but I got nothing. I swallowed and padded toward the fountain with her, then stood beside Seraphina.

"What do you notice about these fish here?"

I tilted my head. Was this some sort of test? If so, I didn't know the right answer. I observed them in silence for a long moment. They were koi fish. Big ones. "They're . . . enormous." A few Guildmasters and Seconds laughed. I swallowed my embarrassment. "They're stunning. They don't ever stop moving, do they? Are they a special kind of koi?"

She ignored my questions. "What else?"

"They've barely moved their fins. They move as if they're streamlined. Their paths are in perfect harmony with each other."

"Yes." Seraphina turned in a circle and brought me back in, addressing everyone in the room. "Moments ago, the koi were swaying against each other. Now, in Nix Emberwind's presence, they are steady—calm—again. I believe she is the one destined to discover who our prophesied subjects are. The Koi of Knowledge have given us a sign."

When the Guildmasters started murmuring to each other, Seraphina stepped close enough to me to whisper in my ear without anyone hearing, though Daris watched us closely. She bent her head down, away from view. "Their erratic movements stopped when you and your . . . friends arrived. Yes, I know about them, as I know you are *not* Daris's assigned Apprentice for this evening. You didn't exactly lie—part of what you said is true. All of you are involved in this now. Assist me, and the others don't need to know about your friends sneaking in here—and how incompetent your Guildmaster is for allowing this."

She stepped away, resuming her speech like nothing had happened and leaving me reeling. My gaze. slid to Daris. I wouldn't get him in trouble or even have him look less than magnanimous for all the world.

Grand Guildmaster Seraphina spoke so the others at the table could hear. "Daris Ravencroft, Guildmaster of Bloodwraith and Magisar of Apprentice Emberwind, it is the decision of this table that you will accompany Apprentice Emberwind on the quest to find the representatives of this prophecy, along with my own Apprentice, Variant Darkthorn."

A shadow stepped forward at the table. The figure was cloaked, but I recognized his face from when he'd hid out in my and Elena's room during the murder lockdown. He dropped his hood, not even looking around. He wore his typical bored expression.

My eyes shifted to Daris. If he was seething before, he seemed nearly explosive now. He stood up to protest, but Hemere placed a hand on his shoulder. Daris's nostrils flared, but he remained silent.

Seraphina measured me with her eyes as we all made our way back to the table. "You and I will discuss the details of the mission with Guildmaster Ravencroft and Variant. You will need a team to assist you. Daris is proficient at battle and team strategy. I trust that you all will choose your team wisely."

After regaining her seat, Seraphina addressed the Guildmasters around her. "As for the rest of you, discuss the prophecy among yourselves, and bring any ideas or anything you discover to me so I can present our collective thoughts at our next meeting. This Alliance meeting at the Cor is concluded. Everyone is dismissed."

Something drew me toward the fish again, and as I watched them and peeked up, I was startled to see the black and white koi swimming above me. The water defied gravity here.

Variant swept toward me as the Guildmasters, their Seconds, and Apprentices filed out to leave through the portal. Seraphina ushered the two of us a few steps away from the fountain, though her eyes were trained on the ever-moving fish. Daris had the look of a man who wanted to strangle me.

I thought he had nerve. I felt the same way. I was still shocked at having to find out my parents died in the courtroom yesterday. I still hadn't processed it. Hadn't had time to grieve.

Why hadn't Daris found a way to tell me? After High Inquisitor—Guildmaster Devereux—told me my parents and my brother were dead, I think I was nearly catatonic.

I didn't remember much about my Blaze ceremony at all, but I remembered looking into the Reflection of Chaos, sitting with Master Coeus, and speaking with his brother. I also remembered trying to conjure an image of my dad and how much pain it caused me.

In the end, I used the 'Anywhere Spell' and had it whisk me away to my room. It had worked perfectly—no bumps, bruises, or split skull. And no more prying eyes.

I swore I was keeping that spell in my head forever. That thing was going to be handy.

"Now, first and foremost, I am no fool, Daris. I know Nix was not assigned as your official Apprentice for this meeting. And I know as well as you that she did not come here alone. The two that were here with her will be part of your team now. They know too much. I don't care if one of them is your sister."

"Yes, Maestra."

Seraphina stared at him for a long time. Surprise bubbled under my skin. Why didn't Daris didn't fight her about this? Then again, what purpose would it serve to do that? Maybe he wanted Elena with him. There was so much I didn't understand.

I nearly jumped off the floor when a deep voice spoke to me:

Come.

I glimpsed around. Had anyone else heard it? Daris and Seraphina were still talking. They didn't pause in their conversation.

Come.

There it was again! The voice shook inside my head—it moved across my skin. It filled the room. It was deep, like the depths of the greatest tunnels in the ground, like the fathoms of the ocean. It was like what I imagined a black hole in space would be like . . . it pierced my heart and left a gateway inside it.

"Nix? Nix!" Someone was shaking my shoulder. Daris. "You okay there? You paying attention?"

"I thought I heard," and then I saw them both eyeing me like I was a time bomb or something. "Never mind. I'm . . . tired." That was true.

Seraphina didn't give it up that easy. "You thought you heard what, exactly?"

There was no help for it. Evasion wasn't going to save me. It never did. "I—I thought I heard someone else. Someone else's voice."

They both glanced at each other. I changed the subject, hoping that would work. "What about the prophecy?"

Seraphina eyed Daris before moving on. I got the feeling they knew something I didn't. Seraphina repeated the prophecy for me.

Hearing her recite the lines again, other Guildmasters who hadn't left yet approached her and offered their own insight. After some discussion, the thought was that the first three objects mentioned – tooth, claw, and staff – represented three groups of species—Sangor, Lupine, and Meta, as well as Arnexin, Elsh, and Abyssoul.

Daris wanted us to start our quest in the Zeleel Realm. He said it was one of the first Realms Chaos created, where the Ancient Celestials settled and ruled for eons, creating creatures of their own. The forests were massive, the waters full of impossible monsters, and the mountains so immense that most species without magic could never climb them.

Despite the loss of my family and the shock of obtaining my new magic gifts—which I had no idea how to use—the excitement of going on this quest pulsed through my veins. Going on this mission meant I didn't have to be at the GOC, at Skia Guild right away as Daris's Apprentice. Sure, Variant would be there, but when he wasn't around, maybe Daris and I could be alone together. Maybe we'd find time to be close.

I wanted to leave right then. My fears of Daris's repercussions faded away until Seraphina left, leaving just me, Variant, and Daris. Daris turned his eyes on me, deadly serious.

"You need to understand. This is a sacred place. You've risked more than you know—more than you understand, coming here unprepared."

His gaze cut to Variant, and I understood there were things he wanted to say that he couldn't. His lips pressed together. "Go with Variant now. Leave the way you came. As my *Apprentice*, you have the duty of letting Elena and Elias know their schedules are changing and they need to pack. We leave tonight."

I followed in Variant's footsteps, emerging at the base of the tree where Elena, Elias, and I had entered. I was grateful Elena and Elias were waiting for me between two rocks nearby. They jumped out to greet me as soon as I was through, surprised to see Variant as well.

Storm clouds rolled down the mountains, and high winds whipped the trees. Lighting slashed through the sky, and as the large, freezing raindrops started to pelt us on the way back, I was thankful for the practical clothing Elena had provided earlier.

"Is everything okay?" Elena placed her hands on my shoulders, her eyes searching mine. I smelled pines and cedar on the wind, making me wish for the scent of Daris.

"What happened to you? Tell me you're still allowed to stay, Sparks."

I hardly knew Elias and hadn't expected so much concern from him. I didn't mind it, though. It was odd—I'd been here less than a handful of days, and I was having deeper relationships than I'd had my whole life. I wondered if I'd have the chance to make real friends in time.

Time to break the news.

"Actually, um, the *five* of us—" I gestured to the two of them, Variant, who was flipping a knife around his fingers near the tree, and Daris, who just stepped out of the portal as if on cue— "are going on a fun little field trip."

Daris leaned against a large standing stone while I explained what happened after they left and what we had to do next. Elias shook his head, his skin becoming more pale than I'd ever seen it. "Yeah, I don't want any part in this. Daris—I mean Magisar Ravenscroft—" Elias stressed the name, "knows that I can't go. I have duties."

"Oh, you're going, Elias," Daris said, his voice brooking no argument.

We all paused to watch a flock of Margi birds fly over, their long, streaming pink feathers trailing behind them, rippling, and curling in the wind.

Daris motioned for us to walk as he talked. He seemed in a rush. "I need all of you to pack a good travel pack—plan for two weeks minimum on the road. Travel light. Bring only what you can't conjure. Otherwise, you'll use spells for food, water, spare clothes, weapons, and any magic enhancers you need. And you'll help each other. If one knows a spell for toiletries, help the others, and so on. You all know Nix is just beginning. I expect you to both teach and help her. Skia Guild, meet me outside in our front courtyard—by the east garden—in thirty minutes. Variant—meet us at the Omnipatos portal in forty."

He was gone before we could ask any questions.

I scratched the back of my neck. "This is serious. Does something like this happen often?."

"Never." Elena's eyebrow hitched, and she linked her arm with mine. "He won't ruin our adventure, though. This is unheard of! A quest. Apprentices on a quest! It's gonna be fun!"

"I have better things to do," Variant said. He was all business. "I'm not waiting around. Get your things ready. I don't know about you guys, but I plan to level up to Arcane Quintus this season. By the time we have new Apprentices, I want Arcane Sextus status. Be prepared to battle on the road." He stowed his knives and strode off as if he planned to be the first in line at Daris's office.

Elena widened her eyes at me and giggled. "Geez. Bossy, much?" I smiled, but I felt the edge of a challenge in his words, and I think she did, too.

We raced to our room, and Elias ran toward his. I had to borrow a pack from Elena, and everything I put in it belonged to Elena. The only things I had that were mine to take on the trip were my tattoos on my arms from the Blaze Ceremony, my Celestial bond on my palm, and my own boots. And I was taking my boots. Elena put a charm on them so they would stay comfortable and my feet would never get tired. After that, I decided that, overall, magic could be really useful.

I realized I had so much to learn, and I needed to start getting my stuff when we returned. I had no idea how to go about that either. I had no money. Did I have to get a job? I had so many questions and not enough time to ask them.

An ache settled on my chest for the first time when I thought about this journey we'd be making. How long would it take—days? Weeks? Months? What would happen if we failed? I ran my hand over the bed I'd been sleeping in and the nice crimson comforter on top. I stared out the window at the lights of the GOC below.

Stress itched along my skin until I realized they were sparks. Elena stared at them, and we both watched in horror as they flared into flames. They shot from my fingers like miniature fireworks. I dropped the cute green bag I was packing and backed away.

It was insane how quickly panic could take over my brain. My martial arts training was useless with this. No matter how I tried to control it, my breathing became erratic. My lungs were convinced I wouldn't be able to take another clean-air breath, so I kept taking them over and over again until I had no air and hyperventilated.

Elena's hands interrupted them. I shook my head at her. "No. Don't."

Too late. My sparks exploded in front of her, and fire seared her skin. She winced and flailed her hand. I'd burned her. I'd hurt my own friend.

My clothes were on fire again. In the back of my mind, I realized I was going to need a spell to give me fireproof clothing. There had to be one. I was sure Apprentices worked with what they called Ignitor magic all the time. The Magus Guild had a large number of Apprentices with Ignitor magic. And I had Cielo magic as well—powers related to air, healing, and love—whatever that meant.

"Elias," I gasped, pleading to Elena, "Get Elias. I need Elias." My flares were growing into roaring flames. Thankfully, most of the room was stone. As long as I stood far enough away from everything, I couldn't burn the Guild down like I had my house. I aimed my hands at a stone wall.

"I don't want to leave you." Elena shifted nervously near the door.

"Go!"

I didn't know how long I was left in that room, alone with nothing but my fear. I tried to steady my breaths, but the air around me just grew hotter and hotter.

Finally, the door burst open.

DARIS

BY THE STARS

I was immersed in planning our route, using my Tessar Pad to create a four-dimensional visual of the mountain passages, locate any portals, and gauge where the worst weather would occur on Zeleel. It was thunderstorm season, not the ideal time for a visit. If we were searching for people to match this prophecy, we'd have to hit at least four major cities for some leads.

The purpose of the prophecy still eluded me, and I couldn't fathom why Seraphina felt the need for answers so urgently. Nothing in it set a specific time schedule.

My concentration was shattered as Elena barged into my office with Elias at her side, interrupting my planning session. Anger surged through me at the unexpected intrusion.

"It's Nix," Elena's voice was laced with panic. "I tried texting, but you didn't answer."

My anger dissipated, replaced by a sinking feeling of dread. If Nix was injured Elena's wide-eyed expression and frantic demeanor heightened my fear. But the stone in my hand remained calm and cool, indicating that this emergency, while dire, did not pose a direct threat to Nix's life. Still, she needed help.

"Portal there," Elena urged, her tone insistent.

Without hesitation, I spoke the words to summon the mist, a portal spell that allows a Guildmaster or someone proficient in the art to transport one other person with them. I portaled into Nix's room with Elena, my heart pounding in my chest. Elias was already outside her door, waiting. Elena let him in, and we were greeted by a sight that resembled the fires of demon hell.

Nix stood at the center of the room, her body engulfed in dark blue flames. The outer flames lashed out, hungrily devouring her bed posts and reducing her crimson comforter to ashes. I wanted to step forward, to quell the inferno, but I found myself frozen, helpless in the face of her power.

Elias pushed past me, unafraid. He approached Nix, standing as close as the searing heat would allow. "Hey, Sparks. Yo—hey there." He waved his hand in front of her, attempting to capture her attention. "Remember what we talked about that day we met?" He glanced briefly in my direction. "Remember the wind, how good that breeze felt. How cool the ground was under your feet. You're steady, Sparks. You've got friends here who care about you. Deep breath."

For a moment, it seemed as though Nix was transported somewhere else, as if she was recalling a memory. A flicker of recognition crossed her face as she inhaled deeply, as if savoring a particular scent. Visibly, she relaxed, her breaths slowing as she regained control.

Then, she uttered a single, odd word. "Leander." Her flames sputtered and died, leaving her naked and exposed. I quickly turned around, motioning for Elias to do the same. I couldn't bear to look, not because of her vulnerability but because of her breathtaking beauty. Her exotic, wild form, flushed and alluring, called to me. The scent of her blood, her intoxicating essence, beckoned me to wrap my body around hers, to sink my lips into hers, to taste her I had to leave, or I feared I might lose control. The stone in my hand burned, a searing reminder of the myriad reasons for its reaction.

"Elias, time to get packed. Elena, you got it from here," I managed to say, my voice strained.

Elias backed up and called over his shoulder, "You alright there, Sparks?"

I could hear the smile in Nix's voice as she replied, "I'm alright, Goldie."

I realized that Nix had developed a trust and familiarity with Elias that I didn't fully understand, and jealousy twinged inside me.

"Elena? Can you make it in twenty?" I asked. I didn't want to put things off, especially since it was night, and I wanted to get settled. But it was what it was.

"Yes—you guys go. We got this," Elena assured me.

"Twenty minutes," I told Elias before stepping into my mist, my mind reeling.

My pack was already together. That was the luxury of Sangor speed. Everything could be completed in a fraction of the time it took anyone else. In my planning, I'd identified possible potions I'd need to create if certain things occurred and made sure I had Neffar crystals, Menchan moss, and Sevvir serpent venom—the all-purpose supplies that were nearly impossible to get. They also made exceptional bargaining tools.

Sevvir serpent venom was particularly valuable, and I'd hesitated to bring it except that one place we were going, the only cure for a particular curse included this ingredient. Without it, the victim would die in a matter of hours. I'd wrapped a tiny vial of it very carefully with Unbreakable Cloth—the ultimate packing substance—and placed it in a pendant, along with the moss and the crystal, to hang around my neck. Call me superstitious, but it's supposed to bring the wearer good luck.

Sevvir serpents, to my knowledge, were extinct across all of the Realms. There were no substitutes. No magic, no science among any culture, could reproduce their venom.

Once known to exist in the Ur Realm, Sevvir serpents would bite their victims with their shadows. Their venom would paralyze prey while they siphoned their life source away for energy. As victims remained paralyzed, their soul energy would be siphoned as well—leaving the entire body a husk and their soul an empty wasteland. Sevvir serpents were more feared in places where light allowed their shadows to roam.

It was nearly time to leave, so I sent a message to the Magisars and the Skia Guild Apprentices, letting them know that Magisar Hemere Lucyte would be in charge of Skia Guild over the next few weeks while I attended to Arcane Alliance business. I cc'd Grand Guildmaster Seraphina. I then advised that I was taking a team of assistants, and I left it at that.

I'd also read and winced at the rumors that Nix could be behind the recent murder, and my blood boiled. But there was no help for it now. I private messaged Seraphina and Devereux about it and told them I expected the rumors to be put to an end and proper investigations to run their course.

As I entered the Skia Guild courtyard, the waning full moon causing the night frost to glitter all around, I spied Elias's golden hair. At least he was on time. I caught the scent of winter moon flowers—one of the few blooms that tolerated the cold this time of year and released their scent in the dark. The Lupines loved them. The scent did drive them more wild than usual. And it brought out the Cave Moths. Those were huge.

I paused. Someone was next to Elias, and it wasn't Elena. I remembered when I'd seen Elias earlier in Elena's corridor with another figure—someone who'd slipped away before I'd had the chance to focus on them properly. The two seemed to be arguing now—or at least he was.

"You can't be here, Jessamine! He's not going to let you come," Elias growled. "Leave before it's too late."

The figure stepped to the side, exposing her likeness to me. It explained a lot. Now I understood why she'd disappeared so easily. Her long blue hair, small round ears, light blue skin, and slight build were Shadow-Elsh. Shadow-Elsh were often members of the Oscuro Guild. Their invisibility skills made them impressive spies and excellent thieves.

"What's going on?" I raised an eyebrow. I hadn't accounted for this, but part of me was enjoying Elias's discomfort. At the same time, I was also calculating Jessamine's skill level in my head. Depending on what I found out about her, she might be useful.

Elena trundled into the courtyard with Nix in tow. Nix seemed exhausted already. That didn't bode well. This journey was going to take some stamina. Nix was strong, but if she couldn't keep up—well, we'd have to find a way to replenish her energy. Every Apprentice had something that revived them—that fueled them. Nix had two Elementals. Both fueled each other. I'd think about that.

Elena tucked an auburn tress behind her ear, her pack expertly strapped to her all-purpose travel tunic. She had a fantastic belt wrapped around her ample waist. It was made of some kind of substance that resembled green Agon hide, but if it was, I had no idea how she'd obtained it. And there were several charms attached to it. I knew if she touched them in the right way, each would result in something happening—the right weapon, a tracking spell, or something useful for hunting.

She'd made a similar belt for me, though not as complex. Mine had room for weapons, potions, and some odds and ends. I saw Elena took care of Nix, making sure she had one too.

My younger sister was pretty amazing for a lower-level Apprentice. She's a monster hunter and a Meta, a shapeshifter. I only discovered her a few years ago. I thawed her from a prison of solid ice, but that is another story.

"Elias has got himself involved with a girl none of us know who wants to come on the mission." Elena huffed. Her eyes glared at the Shadow-Elsh, then back at me.

The blue woman spoke. "I can help." Her words sounded like the wind that howls through caverns, deep and echoey. I turned to see her standing right behind me. Her face was narrow and angular, and her irises were dark blue with an oily sheen to them. I thought she smelled of dark caves and the underground—and of something else that tickled my mind—something from long ago that I—then I remembered. I shut it out of my mind.

"I want to help," her voice came to me again, winding its way around me. "My name is Jessamine."

"I wanted you to stay out of it! "Elias hissed." I didn't tell you about the prophecy so that you would join us. Quite the opposite, actually." Elias stalked up to her and spun her to face him. "You need to leave."

"I don't have to do every little thing you want, darling. I've been around prophecies before. You'll need me; they're tricky little things to navigate. I should know."

As they bickered, I studied her again. Quick movements, good at hiding in the shadows—the skills of a Shadow-Elsh—and much older than she appeared. More than that, she was familiar to me. I remembered seeing a picture of her in classified files during an Arcane Alliance meeting, back when I'd still been an Apprentice, back when she was famous for a failed prophecy.

"Jessamine Caverns," I said aloud, and everyone stopped talking. "Everyone thought you died." Around us, the stars shone bright, and all was very still, almost as if the Celestials were listening.

Jessamine's dark blue lips, full and luscious in contrast to her thin face, quirked up when she faced me. "Yes, as planned and as necessary. But I'm back. I'm in love with our dear Elias, and I want to show the Guilds that I can succeed. I made a deal with the Grand Guildmaster Maganti." She showed me her wrist. A band of pulsing black and blue circled it. "An Oath Band. You know I cannot remove it or even try. It requires me to answer to the Guilds until the deed is done."

I didn't know what had happened when she'd taken up her prophecy quest. All I knew was that it had gone completely wrong. Nearly everyone on her mission had died, and the Arcane Alliance had held her responsible.

I stared at Jessamine's band. It was authentic. I guessed that instead of banishing Jessamine to Lethenthril, the Grand Guildmaster before Seraphina—High Priestess Maganti of Hecade Guild—must have gone easy on her.

Elias's mouth fell open. I almost laughed. The others simply watched in quiet confusion while Jessamine nodded. "I want to support this prophecy and prove that I was exiled for no reason. What went wrong . . . it was *not* my fault."

Without hesitation, the words came from my lips. "I'll allow it."

Somewhere, hunting cries and howls of Crayites sounded in the mountains. I pictured them running in packs, their five tails snapping viciously. The stars still twinkled above, cold and hard, bright. Were the Celestials pleased or not? I didn't know. But I had work to do. My eyes shifted to Nix, tracing the lines of her face, her neck, the pulse of her vein. And I had a woman to protect.

"What?" Elias whipped his head to look at me. "No! It isn't safe."

Jessamine crossed her arms, about to respond, but I was done with this. I didn't want to be a part of this fight anymore. My challenge was to get everyone to the Omnipatos, to the main portal, so we could go to Zeleel since I couldn't transport them all.

We struck out across campus. The ground started to shake. Elena glimpsed around.

"Um, Daris, what time is it?"

"Shit, Elena, just after eleven. You ready? Want to handle this one?" I glanced at Nix. She seemed like she was recovering, and she was going to need the practice. "Give me your pack, Nix."

"What?" Nix looked dazed.

"It's after eleven, girlfriend," Elena broke in as I took Nix's pack and grabbed Elena's from her. "Time to see what happens when you stay out late and play. INCITER!" She bellowed the last word like a battle cry as she took a fighting stance.

I motioned Elias and Jessamine forward toward the Omnipatos to stand a safe distance. We'd be nearby, just in case.

The ground rumbled again, and then, in front of Elena, the earth shot up and formed into a giant dirt snake. It reared back and struck at Elena, sending her rolling across the ground. Then, it reared back, ready to pound Nix. Nix stood there dumbfounded as the earth snake hurtled toward her.

Elena pushed a button on her belt, and a massive shower of water formed above the snake and pounded down on the creature, turning it into a huge wasteland of mud.

Elena smacked her hands together, wading through the wet muck. "See? Easy shmeasy." She and Nix made their way toward us when the mud began to form, and we watched as, instead of dirt, the snake was now a ropey mud serpent, slicker, and more nimble. And now had three heads.

"Cosmic.   Hydra.   I   should   have   remembered that one," Elena said dryly. Her gaze flicked to Nix. "You got this one, girl."

"ME?" Nix cried out, wide-eyed. "What am I supposed to do?"

"Well, it's MUD. What do you think?" Elena flashed a look at Nix's hands.

Nix shook her head, and Elena nodded as the mud serpent bared down on her. Nix positioned herself into a fighting stance—put a hand over her head and one out in front of her. The move looked very graceful and practiced. Her wrist tattoos glowed red and blue.

Ah—her true Ignitor magic is about to come to life.

Swirls of blue and orange fire streamed from her palms. Amused, I watched as she scrunched up her face, closed her eyes, and aimed at the serpent, blasting it. When she opened her eyes, we all took a moment to admire the nicely fired statue of the serpent mid-strike in front of Nix. Nix stood and bowed to it. Elena didn't miss a beat.

"Splendid job!" She passed by Nix and patted her on the back. "Next time, keep your eyes open. Let's go."

Nix glanced down at her hands in wonder. The way she could release that much power with so little training . . . I can't lie; it turned me on. I looked forward to seeing what we could do together on the road. At the same time, I had to push away thoughts of caressing her body, of kissing her lips, of running my hands along her curves and sinking my fangs into her sweet neck, drinking down . . .

"You coming, Daris?" Elena grabbed her pack from me. I caught a knowing little smirk at the corner of her lips. Damn. This was going to be a wonderful, terrible long journey.

"Actually, can you take my pack for a moment, sister? Keep walking. I won't be a minute." A group of raucous young Apprentices were out late, and they were admiring Nix's handiwork.

Her eyes whipped toward the sound of the laughter. There were five strapping lads in all. They could each spare a pint, and I'd be quick about it.

"Try not to get too drunk, okay?" To her credit, she left me to it and kept Nix moving forward even though my new Apprentice wanted to wait for me. It didn't take me long.

The portal at the Omnipatos was a central thoroughfare. It had several gates all linked together so several visitors could arrive or depart as needed from different Realms. Lupine sentries were almost always the primary security forces due to their supreme sense of smell and speed, followed by Grasha Warriors.

Grasha were a species that occupied several Realms. They were muscular, their strong jaws accented by short lower tusks. Their warrior-like nature and raw strength made them naturals for Bellator Guild, and they were practically born with weapons in their hands. It was nearly unheard of for a Grasha to choose any other Guild than Bellator. They were amazing fighters and had solid magic capabilities. Most only had one Elemental gift.

Four large Grasha and two Lupines were on guard as we approached the Omnipatos portal. Variant stood waiting, dressed in his predictable black leggings, boots, and jacket. He gave Jessamine a chin lift in acknowledgment as if they knew each other. She did the same. They were both Oscuro Guild. I suppose they did somehow.

I was a little unsteady on my feet. My 'meal to go' must have had an Ulnarthi Bomb, or ten of them, floating in there somewhere. Shuttling everyone in past security, I prepared to recite the words to get us to the Zeleel Realm. Shouting blasted through the air. Lupines howled. Grasha started to shut down the gates to the Omnipatos portal.

One Grasha was a friend of mine. "Beethi! We have to leave on Alliance business." I showed her an official seal Seraphina had given me that I wore around my neck.

Beethi nodded her head once.

"What happened?" I tilted my head toward the outside. Beethi's jaw clenched in anger. "A Magisar is dead. Burned like the last one. Discovered at the Parabellum."

"Who? Do you know?"

Beethi shook her head and pulled out her Celcom for an update. Shook her head again. My heart pounded. "Best get going," she said. "I have to shut the portal down."

The group around me was quiet. Everyone looked at Nix. I sighed and began the words.

They were complex, bringing back very old memories. My tongue tasted the blood of the thousands that died here, some under my fangs, as the mists appeared. Rather than remorse, I only felt—hunger.

Thank Chaos that I'd fed before coming here. However, Ulnarthi Bombs did tend to make me crave more of what I loved and decreased my ability to hold back from getting it. And I wanted Nix so bad. I was pretty sure no one knew, not even Nix, that I had a little sip of her during transport.

A gold and silver mist swirled around us till I could see nothing, and then it spread out in front of me. Through it, the faint outlines of enormous evergreen trees lined one side of the sky, while in front of us, the rest of the open air was carpeted with more Celestial presence than I'd ever remembered seeing in my lifetime.

I stepped out under the heavens and dropped to one knee, gazing up in wonder.

"Great Chaos," I breathed.

NIX

BLOOD

My entire world was like a worn sock some-one had turned inside out, except on the other side, there was no sock. There was only something else beyond what my sock should be.

As the gold and green mist covered us, I still stared at my hands, thinking. I'd turned that huge mud Inciter into a giant clay statue. Basically, I'd Raku fired it with my own hands. And then, I'd snuffed the flames off much easier than I ever had before. I just thought, "off."

The news of the new murder haunted me. This time it was Magisar. Someone experienced and powerful. Burned the same as the last murder, the guard said. Would everyone start blaming that one on me too? It wouldn't help that I was gone. I decided to try not to worry about it. I couldn't do anything anyway.

Following Daris out onto what they called the Zeleel Realm—I was starstruck. Were there ever so many stars visible in our Mortal Realm? I didn't think so.

I did hope the area was safe. It was difficult to see across the field ahead. The clearing of grass I stood in came up to my shoulders, making me feel like a bug. The trees to the left were so tall that I couldn't see the tops of them, much less even think about climbing them.

"Wow." I felt like an idiot. All of this beauty and nothing more profound managed to come from my lips than 'Wow.' When I tilted my head back, I noted that there were two purple moons in the sky close together, and both were full. I couldn't wait to see this place during the day.

Jessamine sidled up to me, looking up to the sky as well. "They remind me of Tarot cards. The two of Pentacles. I don't know if you know of them. They represent balance and harmony even in the wake of turmoil. Even reversed, they can signify standing up for oneself and gaining control. Taking one's rightful place." She moved away from me, and I didn't have a chance to respond.

Daris was scrolling through his Celcom, the light reflecting on his face. Then he paused, his hand shaking. "NO!" he bellowed. A flock of strange birds screamed from the trees, and other night creatures scattered. Daris collapsed on the ground, his head in his hands.

The others were scrolling through their Celcoms, too.

"Don't bother, all of you," Daris said. "You'll need to maintain your device power."

Elena gasped. Elias nearly dropped his. Variant turned his off and put it away. I heard him swallow. I wanted to run to Daris, to hold him. Whatever had happened, this had to be bad.

"What?" I asked. No one was saying anything. "What happened?"

Elena spoke up, tears rolling down her face. Daris's face was so pale, and his expression was devoid of all cheer. It was as if a whirlwind of sorrow and darkness had found its way to his face and settled in there. He seemed numb, as if he couldn't believe what he'd read.

"The Magisar who was murdered," she said. "The one the guard said they found burned in the Parabellum. It was Daris's friend, Hemere."

Daris did everything he could to try to get back to Arnexis to help with the investigation, but the Arnexis portals were closed. Completely shut down for now. He texted Seraphina and told her who was next in line to run Skia Guild while he was gone. He begged her to let him come back, but she said the investigation was in good hands and that he needed to focus on completing his task.

"I'll kill the person when they catch him or her," Daris growled. "If they haven't caught the killer by the time I'm back, I will make it my personal mission to hunt them down. And I will bleed them dry, over and over again until they beg to die." I watched as his fangs protruded a little over his lips. He was roiling with anger.

For the first I'd seen, Variant dropped his knife.

My body shivered, hearing Daris talk like that. His voice was cold and calculating. His tone was merciless. I wondered for the first time, could I be with someone like him?

My eyes traced his face. My gaze fell to his mouth, where I saw those teeth that could drain a body—that could rip and tear flesh. And I felt no fear. I couldn't explain why. Yes. I could be with him. My palm itched. I stared at my bond.

I could be bound with him till the end of time. Somehow, I knew it.

Daris seemed to switch gears as if promptly deciding that getting this quest over was the single most important thing to focus on at the moment. Maybe he thought that by finding the items in the prophecy, he'd get us back to Arnexis, and then he could find Hemere's killer.

"There should be a native settlement that way." Daris pointed toward the giant trees. Our trek in the direction that Daris indicated was a silent one. What had seemed like a glorious and stunning landscape seemed sinister and spoiled now.

Elena conjured light orbs for us. Soft enough to avoid disturbing wildlife or attracting attention, yet bright enough to allow us to see. The moons overhead helped us see as well.

I trained my eyes on Daris's back as Jessamine walked beside him quietly. Soon, she indicated a path marked by glow-stones. That made the traveling easier, though I guessed we needed to be aware of coming across other travelers.

I was grateful when Jessamine rested a hand on Daris's shoulder. "Maybe we should stop and rest. Your troops look weary." My legs were throbbing. Elena was rubbing her eyes, and I thought I saw a red glow in them. Elias yawned every so often, and the strange noise that accompanied it sounded feral. Variant was stoic. The only indication I had that he suffered any fatigue was that his feet seemed to fall on the path a little heavier than before.

His maroon eyes swept over us, and assessing our state, he nodded. "I agree."

I tried not to let my relief show. Jessamine smiled, her blue lips curling at the corners, and I thought maybe she was trying to develop some camaraderie with us. She got some points from me.

I found a wide, inviting space between some gnarled roots at the base of a towering tree, its branches stretching up towards the starlit sky. The space seemed protected enough, a natural shelter from the elements and any prying eyes. I started to gather moss, my hands working to create a soft, comfortable bed to sleep on. The moss was cool and damp beneath my fingers, each handful a vibrant green that stood out against the rich, dark earth.

As I worked, Elena approached me, her footsteps soft and quiet on the forest floor. She gave me a gentle half-hug, her arm wrapping around my shoulders in a comforting embrace. With a wave of her hand, she conjured a tent, its canvas walls shimmering in the moonlight. Inside, I glimpsed something that looked like a sleeping bag, its soft, plush material beckoning me to rest.

I couldn't help but think how much I could have used something like this back in my Scouting days, when I had spent countless nights huddled beneath the stars, my body aching from the hard, unforgiving ground.

My mind wandered, and I found myself wondering what else might be available on Zeleel. Were there fish to catch in the nearby streams, their scales glinting silver in the moonlight? Could we build a campfire, its flickering flames casting dancing shadows on the trees around us? Would there be Smores to roast, their sweet, gooey marshmallows and rich, dark chocolate a perfect end to a long day? And what about morning coffee, its rich, bold aroma wafting through the crisp, cool air? Or the simple pleasure of cleaning dishes in a bubbling brook, the water cool and clear against my skin?

But then, with a mental smack, I reminded myself that I was on Zeleel, not Earth. It was best if I kept my brain focused on the here and now, on the challenges and dangers that lay ahead.

Elias and Elena offered to take the first two shifts as look-outs, their eyes sharp and alert. They shapeshifted into birds, their feathers gleaming in the moonlight as they flew up to the branches above, their keen eyes scanning the surrounding forest for any signs of trouble. Daris told them to wake him next, his voice low and serious.

Jessamine curled up on her own, her eyes focused on something far away, something that only she could see. Elias was still upset at her for coming, their interactions brief and tense, their words sharp and angry. Variant, too, found his own section of the camp, his back resting against a gnarled root as he closed his eyes, his face etched with worry and concern. I think everyone was still disturbed by the news about Magisar Hemere, the weight of it hanging heavy in the air.

As I settled into my tent, I was acutely aware of Daris's presence near me, his body close enough to touch. My mind wandered to his need for blood, and I found myself wondering how long it had been since he had last fed. Would he ever want to drink from me? And if I offered myself to him, would our protection bond allow it? The thought sent a shiver down my spine, a mixture of fear and excitement that I couldn't quite explain.

I shook my head, trying to banish the thoughts from my mind. I was being ridiculous, wasting time with these idle fantasies when Daris probably didn't even think of me in that way. With a sigh, I closed my eyes and tried to sleep, but my mind wouldn't rest.

The night stretched on, the sounds of the forest a constant backdrop to my racing thoughts. I tossed and turned, my body restless and uneasy. Sleep seemed to elude me, dancing just out of reach as the hours ticked by. And through it all, the thought of Daris lingered, a constant presence that I couldn't shake.

I couldn't sleep.

It should have been easy. I was exhausted and the sleeping bag Elena conjured was extremely comfortable. But it was like I could feel Daris right next to me. Outside, I heard Daris's voice.

"I've been to the Mortal Realm, you know. I've even been to Drade. It was beautiful."

My breath caught in my throat. *How? Well of course he knew I was awake. He could hear my movements, my heartbeat. He heard everything.*

I laughed. "Beautiful? I don't think I've ever heard that word anywhere near my hometown's name."

"It has a rough look to it. I loved the way the fog crawled over the mountains in the mornings and how the sun pierced through it as it started to rise. The waterfalls had crystal-fresh water and sweet caves to hide in. When I was there, I was looking for Elena, actually."

"Why was she in Drade?" I poked my head out of the tent to look at Daris. He was on his side, on top of a sleeping bag, under the stars. He turned to regard me with an amused smile.

"That's a long story. She got involved with some black-market groups and went missing. I tracked her down and found her in Drade. I remember the surprise I felt when I found her, and she told me she didn't want to leave yet."

That made me laugh. Elena confided to me she loved every little bit of the Realms; I'd seen it in the way she gazed out the window during the classes we had together or how she went silent to observe the world around her. And for her to go silent—that was a big deal.

"Your sister makes for the best roommate I could have asked for."

"She's the bubbly one. I've got the dreary, depressing genes."

"Don't talk about yourself like that." I threw a handful of moss at him, and he batted it away. "I think you're amazing, too," I said.

He stared at me then like he'd been waiting his entire life to hear words like that. I wanted to stay in that puppy gaze of his for the rest of my life. My heart broke a bit when he tore his gaze away and changed the conversation. "Aren't you tired?"

I shook my head and kept picking at the moss. "No, strangely. I feel restless. And I can't wait to learn more about my new magic. And my fire—usually, it's tucked away deeper in my chest, but right now, it feels like it's lying in wait just under my skin."

"Like today, right? That's your Ignitor magic. You've had your Blaze ceremony now. Your Elemental magic will come faster. It will be at your command much easier now.

"Maybe that's it," I conceded.

My eyes kept seeking out the darker part of the sky, the direction we'd keep going when it got light outside. Something in that direction was calling for me. Maybe it was the Magus Seraphina had sent us to find. Maybe it was something else.

Sometimes, the reality of this situation came crashing down on me. I was in a Realm I'd never been to, on a quest that seemed impossible, with people I didn't know well enough to trust. Of course, there was Daris and Elena, and even Elias, but Variant and Jessamine seemed like wildcards to me. What was I doing?

Daris moved swiftly to my side, his warm hand resting gently on my wrist. I peered down and realized that sparks were flaring from my skin, betraying my inner turmoil. Meeting his gaze, I felt a wave of misery wash over me. "See? Something's wrong. My flames are quicker, and I don't know why."

He guided me through breathing exercises, but like before we'd entered this Realm, it felt like an impossible task, especially when his hands glided tenderly over my skin, cupping each of my cheeks with a touch that ignited my senses.

"This isn't a good idea," I whispered, even as I leaned into his touch, unable to pull away. "I'm dangerous."

"I don't care if I burn, Nix. You've already set my soul ablaze." His words were a promise as he leaned in, and we tumbled into the tent together.

Laughter filled the air for a moment as he gently brushed a strand of hair from my face before capturing my lips in a passionate kiss. It was a kiss filled with wild hunger, desire, and an unspoken need that threatened to consume us both.

My body melted against his, returning the kiss with equal fervor. I'd yearned for this moment for so long, wondering if I'd ever be sated by his touch.

We curled into the tent, our limbs intertwined. Breaking the kiss, he took a moment to caress my hair, his eyes darkened with raw hunger and an aching need that mirrored my own. At that moment, I knew I could give him what he craved, what we both desperately desired.

Gathering my courage, I decided to take the plunge. There wouldn't be a better time than now. He was leaning in to kiss me again when I found my voice.

"Daris?"

He paused, his eyes lingering on mine, waiting for me to continue.

"I want to ask you something. I'm—I'm—okay." The words stumbled from my lips, my nerves getting the better of me. Taking a deep breath, I tried again, his intense stare making it even harder to form coherent thoughts.

"I'm just going to say it. You need blood on this trip. And—and it's such a personal turn-on, having you kiss my neck. I'm attracted to you. I know you feel the same. We're bonded. If I give you permission, can you drink from me—can we be safe? I'm asking you—will it be okay?"

Daris stared at me, his lips parting slightly. The barest hint of his fangs pressed against his lower lip, a tantalizing sight that sent shivers down my spine.

Abruptly, he left the tent, leaving me stunned and aching. My insides felt like a submarine crumpling under the immense pressure at the bottom of the Mariana Trench. What had I done wrong?

In the span of a hummingbird's heartbeat, Daris returned, his arms encircling me, his lips claiming mine with a hunger that stole my breath. He brought his palm to his face, revealing the blue glow of his stone.

His voice was measured, each word carefully chosen. "I don't want to be selfish, Nix. But this act, if I agree—it will be selfish. And yet, not completely. You will feed me, and I already crave you more than you can imagine. But know this: having a blood source helps me stay strong, helps me protect you, and keeps my magic at full strength. So—not entirely selfish. Do you understand?"

"Yes," I breathed, my voice steady with unwavering conviction.

"Are you sure?" he asked, his eyes searching mine. "You offer this freely?"

I held his gaze, grasping our bonded hands and holding his over mine. Though I had no magical words or Celestial stone, I made the promise anyway. "Daris Ravencroft, I, Phoenix 'Nix' Emberwind, do solemnly swear to be your primary energy source throughout this quest and beyond until our lives end or until you release me." A tingling sensation coursed through my hand, as if the universe itself bore witness to my vow. Daris seemed to glow with an ethereal light, his eyes filled with a primal hunger that both thrilled and terrified me.

"Do you want to feel anything?" His question hung in the air, a dagger poised before a willing sacrifice.

Did I? Uncertainty gripped me. "What will it feel like?" My breaths quickened, shallow and hitching, anticipation warring with the unknown.

Daris's sensual Sangor voice hummed like a beehive underwater, hypnotic and alluring. His hands pinned mine down, his fingers tightening around my wrists as his body moved over me, anchoring me to the ground. I shivered when his lips brushed my ear, his words a whispered promise.

"It will feel like agony. Ecstasy. Insanity. No regret." I couldn't tell if he was describing the sensation for me or for himself. Perhaps it was both.

Hell, I thought. *I'd imagined this moment, dreamed of it ever since I'd discovered he was a Sangor.*

Focusing my eyes on his, I sank my very soul into the depths of his gaze. Gritting my teeth, my next words escaped as a mixed gasp and hiss.

"Do it."

If I had believed I'd known true pleasure before, I was sorely mistaken. I hadn't even scratched the surface until the moment Daris's fangs pierced the soft tissue of my neck, his mind merging with mine in an instant. His heartbeat deepened, guiding mine to match its rhythm. With every contraction of my heart, the essence of my life flowed into his body. I felt him drink, savoring each swallow of my blood.

Slow. His voice echoed in my mind. *Slow.*

Coherent thought eluded me as pure sensation overtook my being.

His lips pressed like fire and ice against my neck. I sensed his joy as he tasted me, and I reveled in his savage lust for my blood. As if suddenly aware of my own internal celebration, his excitement grew, and his hands gripped me hard with inhuman strength. I was trapped beneath him, latched in his arms, the perfect offering for his survival.

A sudden, intense pain wracked my body within my innermost core, and immediately, my brain broke free. I understood that he was a predator. Of course. His body would flood me with a chemical. A venom? Paralytic?

Part of my brain wanted to work it out, and the other told me to file it away and let go. Get lost in the pain, and prepare for the best to come.

Or was it Daris telling me that in my head? Did it matter? I'd already offered myself. I listened. I rode the pain and let go.

In seconds, chills traveled through my muscles and over my skin, wiping away the pain. I felt my nipples harden, and sudden heat warmed between my thighs. My body quaked, and I heard my own breath quicken—faster and faster.

Internally, I shuddered, my inner world twisting with an intensity of pleasurable sensations I'd never known before—feelings and emotions that were impossible to describe. They touched my mind and tantalized the furthest reaches of my very soul, bringing everything together as if I were suddenly THE Goddess of all living beings across space and time.

Darkness surrounded me, but soft like a satin blindfold. I thought I would break with this feeling—as if I were standing on the edge of a cliff, with this ultimate warmth, this knowledge of life, lust, and love pulsing within me, around my breasts, between my thighs—

And then, I stood on the pinnacle of the highest mountain in dark space, my arms opened wide—glowing—my fire running in yellow, orange, and blue waves up and down my body, I grew brighter and brighter until the greatest explosive and pulsing release of light I'd ever known burst from me. Stars flew from my fingertips. Universes were born from my glow as

I showered space and time with a pulsing release of pure light over and over again.

The room spun around me, and our hearts fluttered. I sensed the internal struggle Daris suffered as he battled with himself, working to pull himself away from me.

Nix. Dazi.

I   sensed   Daris's   mind   wanted   to   say more—but then—he was gone.

He slowed our heartbeats once more, and then his fangs retracted. His tongue lazily lapped around my wounds, and I felt them heal. He nuzzled his face against me and I could have sworn I felt a hot tear on his cheek. But Sangors didn't cry. Did they? I shivered. Part with cold and part with residual ecstasy.

My mouth was dry, but I managed to swallow. "Wow. You weren't lying."

I caught a flash of a wicked grin, and then the air was ice cold as he left me and returned.

"Drink," he commanded.

I smiled. Good old Aphrodite Gold juice and a Hecate Shake—this time chocolate. Back in the Mortal Realm, when we donated blood, they gave us orange juice. This was better. And donating the blood—that—I never wanted to stop donating blood if it was like this.

I drank the bottles down fast and felt energy return to me. "Thank you. I dreamed about that, you know. I wanted . . ."

Daris placed a finger to my lips. His head snapped around.

"What's wrong?" I breathed.

His   ears   twitched. I hadn't known they could do that. As fast as lightning, he whisked me out of the tent just as a group of beasts with tusks descended on it and started tearing it apart.

Daris yelled out loud to the others in warning, "Warsharms! Warsharm attack! Everyone, get up!"

I had no idea what a Warsharm was, but I learned soon enough. These guys were huge. I thought they looked like enormous wild boars, but with scales of armor instead of fur and four giant tusks, two on each side of their snouts. They had two eyes on each side of their face as well, and a long whip tail in the back. Their feet were razor sharp.

Daris dashed with me toward a pile of rocks far away, dumped me there, and then rushed back for the others. That pissed me off. I had other magic now. I didn't know how to use it, but I could at least try. I had Cielo—Air Elemental magic.

"I can help," I yelled. But everyone ignored me. Elena and Elias shifted into Warsharms, mimicking the animals as best as they could, but they were smaller and less proportionate. They didn't look as if they could do more than delay the other beasts. They moved awkwardly in their new shapes, careening against them, attempting to gouge them with their tusks only to suffer being gouged themselves.

I ran forward, trying to use air to help me—focusing my mind on it. Wind, I thought, and brought my hands up, imagining flying to help my friends. I was partly successful. I ended up throwing myself into a tree and crunching my face into it. I almost knocked myself out. Blood streamed down my torn cheeks.

I guess Daris had Cielo too. That's how he healed wounds. He caught sight of me and used air to shove me back. "No, Nix! Stay back!"

But I wasn't going to be a coward. I ignored him. I at least had my Ignitor magic. I was better at using fire. I planted myself in a backstance and raised my arms, almost as if prepared to do a throw. One of the Warsharms caught Elena in its giant maw. It started to chomp down, digging its teeth into her. I let my fire loose and blasted. The beast let her go.

Variant and Elias battled two of the other beasts. I aimed my flames at them and let them fly—the beasts roared, and both Variant and Elias were able to take them down. Daris had two Warsharms down, and Elena was helping him with a third. The Warsharm I'd blasted off Elena was charging toward me now.

I tried to aim at it, but to my dismay, my fire wouldn't flare now—it only fizzled and sparked. I'd used up my power or burned myself out. I still didn't know how this all worked.

"Shit!" I had a fire when I didn't need it, and I didn't have a fire when I did. What great power did everyone call to here? "Sweet Chaos—" I muttered. And that was exactly what was happening as far as I was concerned. Chaos.

The Warsharm bore down on me, and I ran, dodging it. I picked up a large branch and tried to fight it off. The animal snapped at the branch, opened its giant maw, and suddenly had me in its teeth.

"Shit, oh holy HELL!" I screamed, and the excruciating pain of the Warsharm's jaw crunched down on me.

It grunted. I heard it roar, then wince. My body fell, tumbling in the air until I smacked the ground, and the dark black of space and time opened up and swallowed me.

"You're gonna be alright."

My eyes fluttered open to see tears streaming down Elena's face. I tucked my chin to get a view of myself. My abdomen was crushed, and blood oozed from my ribs. A gash on my right shoulder and down my arm gushed blood as well. My entire body shook, but I couldn't feel much now. My legs were numb.

Elias was kneeling down, pressing his hands hard over my injuries, trying to stop the blood. He had a wound on his head, and something had pierced his leg. Variant stood behind him.

Daris was on his knees next to my face, across from Elena. I gaped frantically between her and Daris, but Daris appeared strangely calm.

"Nix, my *dazi*, I need you to drink." He brought his wrist to his mouth and pierced his own skin. Everyone else moved back, even Elena and Elias.

"What are you doing?"

"My blood can heal you. You need this." He pressed his wrist to my lips. I shook my head, but Daris didn't move. "You have to, Nix. Or you'll die."

"No." My word was muffled around his arm.

Elena returned next to me and stroked my hair. I didn't like the thought of drinking Daris's blood. I didn't know what that meant. What would it do to me? But we didn't have any medical supplies or anything in this Realm to heal me properly.

Daris lifted my head. "Your wounds are beyond my healing skills. This is the best way I can help you, Nix."

I looked from him to Elena before closing my eyes. I opened my mouth and swallowed, trying not to think of the irony. I wondered how to tell when I'd had enough. I wasn't hungry. I was injured. Did I wait till I wasn't injured anymore?

When Daris pulled his away, I stared in fascination as my wounds knitted together, and soon, all of them were closed. A sick part of me couldn't help but smile a little and think that some of the blood I drank was mine anyway. My breaths grew stronger. Steadier.

I laughed, and Daris sat back, looking me over. It only took a few minutes for me to appear as though I'd never been in a fight.

"That's amazing," Elias said.

"It's forbidden." I glanced behind me to see Jessamine taking large strides toward us. She had two nets of fresh fruits and a couple of birds with her.

"Where have *you* been?" Elias stormed over to her, Elena following in his wake. Daris stood by me and helped me up. His eyes narrowed. We were all angry and suspicious. Jessamine hadn't been at camp to help with the fight.

"I was out scouting ahead, checking to see what we might come across. I disarmed a couple of traps along the way. Brought these back for the rest of you for fresh food." She surveyed the area. "By the time I realized there was trouble, the fight was over. And I wasn't the one on watch. I believe the BIRDS were."

Elias and Elenas cast their eyes down guiltily and turned red. "We didn't see the beasts until it was too late," Elena said. "The tall grass made it hard to see them."

"Never mind. We need to get going. Camp somewhere safe next time." Daris turned to address everyone. A look of concern crossed his face when he met Variant's eyes. I wondered what it was about. "Cook the birds. Have the fruit—Jessamine, you brought it, you test it first."

The dawn had already streaked the sky with ribbons of crimson, violet, and magenta, and colorful birds took to the air as we started on the path. Our surroundings appeared different by day, less menacing, though as we hiked along the tree line, I wondered if Warsharms were a regular thing in the area or if there were worse things to worry about in Zeleel. I tried not to think about it right now.

Daris and Jessamine led the way, discussing what Jessamine had discovered as she'd scouted ahead. I felt a hand on my arm. Elena jutted her chin toward some thick growth. I understood she needed to tell me something but couldn't do it here. We stepped off the path, but Daris paused and glanced back, an eyebrow raised.

"Just a relief break," Elena assured him with a smile. She shooed him forward with her hand. "We'll catch up."

"We can stop," he offered, looking at me. I shook my head. He turned back to the path but walked slower. Variant was behind him, still flipping his knives. Elias still sent lingering glances back for us as if he wished he was with us.

When we were out of earshot of people other than Sangors because I was pretty sure Daris had supper-hearing, Elena took my hands. "Listen to me, Nix. When we fought the Warsharms, Variant used a move to kill one that I'd never seen before. He gouged out its chest." She stared at me expectantly.

"So?" I didn't know where she was going with this.

"It was the same kind of wound described in the murdered Hecade Apprentice. Daris said her chest had been gouged open, and then her body was set on fire later, along with the inside of her chest cavity. I need to ask Daris more about it—see what he thinks, but I don't trust Variant."

I knew Variant was Oscuro Guild and, of course, was training as an assassin, but the full realization of what that meant hit me heavily. Variant was training to kill people for a living, and the idea that he might have murdered someone innocent, that he might have some other purpose . . .

"It couldn't have been a different assassin?" I thought about how angry Daris had been. If he thought for a second that Variant had anything to do with it, and we were wrong, it could be bad.

Elena shook her head. "They do most of their training alone and in secret. I know a part of it is to come up with a unique, signature death blow that others are unlikely to have. I could be wrong, but I *could* be right."

I sighed. "I hope you aren't."

DARIS

CHALLENGE

Thoughts of Nix consumed my mind. Now that she had offered herself to me as my Prime and her magic had sealed our bond, our connection was becoming more intertwined. The act of sharing my blood with her to heal her wounds had only deepened the intensity of our relationship. My mind reeled from the magnitude of what was happening between us, and I couldn't fathom what Chaos and the Celestials had planned.

For a millennium, my life had been one of solitude, with few close friendships and even fewer loves. Those I had known had met horrific ends, and my closest relationships had been with family, which came with their own challenges. Now, there was Nix—this impossible woman who called to every fiber of my being, tempting me to break every vow I had ever made just to be with her.

As we trekked towards the mountain range, I was acutely aware of her presence behind me, her scent drifting my way with every gust of wind. During a break for lunch, Nix approached me. "Elena and I need to speak with you."

I swallowed nervously, wondering if she had confided in my sister about the depth of our relationship. I followed her upstream without question, where Elena perched in the form of a crane. With a swift motion, she darted her head into the water, plucking out a large, silver fish and swallowing it whole. I never had to worry about Elena; she was self-sufficient and unafraid of the harsh realities of survival.

When Elena shifted back to her human form, her demeanor didn't suggest that she had just discovered her best friend's intimate involvement with her brother. Instead, she checked to ensure we were alone before divulging what she had witnessed—the fatal blow Variant had dealt to the Warsharm. It was information I already knew, having seen it myself. A sense of dread settled in my gut as I realized the danger they had put themselves in by revealing this knowledge. They were risking not only their own lives but the success of my carefully laid plans.

"Stop," I commanded, putting a finger to my lips. I made sure Variant was nowhere near. Fortunately, he was preoccupied with Jessamine, engaged in a knife-throwing contest. "I know. You must behave as though you are unaware, as if you trust him. I will handle the surveillance."

Nix's voice was high-pitched with fear. "We can't do that. What if he kills one of us? We're in danger, Daris." The sound of my name on her tongue sent a shiver down my spine.

"Listen to me," I urged. "If Variant is here for sinister purposes, it means Seraphina assigned them to him. This goes far beyond Variant. Besides, I don't believe Seraphina orchestrates murders. That's not her style."

Elena's eyes blazed with determination. "If Variant killed that girl, then maybe it is."

I understood their concerns, but my mission remained unchanged. I had to keep everyone safe and complete our objective. "Between the three of us, we have transformative skills, ancient Sangor magic, and fire." My gaze lingered on Nix, whose eyes were fixed straight ahead. "And maybe more. We will keep an eye on Variant and intervene if he threatens one of our own, but that's it."

They nodded reluctantly. I shared their unease, but I knew that Seraphina's plans unfolded slowly. It seemed unlikely that Variant had come to kill us; that wouldn't align with her methods. It was more probable that she was using him to gather information, though the specifics eluded me.

"Let's keep going," I said, rounding up the group to resume our journey. As we hiked, the hours crawled by, and part of me yearned to use my Sangor speed to race ahead. The sluggish pace was tedious and having Nix behind me—sometimes beside me—engaged in conversation was a sweet, slow torture.

As early evening approached, we reached the village nestled at the foot of the mountain. Its buildings resembled dense undergrowth, with green leaves and brown strips of bark woven together in wide, circular shapes.

Long before the others, I heard the crackling of flames and caught the scent of something savory, like smoky meat. My mouth watered at the prospect of a hearty meal, even if it wasn't the blood I craved. If the villagers welcomed us, sharing a meal could be an opportunity to build trust and possibly find some answers.

The forest thinned at the base of the mountain, giving way to long grasses. In the distance, I spotted figures dancing around a fire to the beat of drums and the melody of flutes. As we proceeded along the path, one of their lookouts spotted us, and a series of birdcalls rang out—not as an alarm, but as an announcement.

Some villagers broke away from their dancing, and a group of children ran up to us, their eyes gleaming with excitement and their smiles wide. A girl held out a small, roasted creature to me, its aroma matching the enticing scent I had detected earlier.

"No!" a couple of adults called out, rushing after the children and beckoning them away. From behind them, an older man wearing feathers in his hair and wide pads of colorful feathers on his shoulders approached, flanked by two guards.

I noticed that the villagers were all much taller than us, with lean, muscular bodies. Their long hair was adorned with feathers, vines, and other natural decorations. They had sun-kissed skin and wide, dark eyes. Some possessed animalistic features, like pointed ears and sharp, nimble fingers with claw-like nails, but they still appeared very human and seemed to understand our language.

The older man stopped before me, carrying an intricately carved staff topped with a large crystal orb that sparkled and glowed with a blue light. The guard on his right was a woman a head taller than him and at least two heads taller than me, with horns that resembled twisted branches protruding from her scalp. On his left stood a man who must have had Giant genes, given his immense stature. A thick vine around his waist carried an array of weapons. All three of them focused on me expectantly.

Unsure of the proper protocol, I decided to bow, hoping my team would follow my lead. I sensed their movements behind me as I spoke. "Greetings, and May Chaos Reign! I hope we have not disturbed your evening." I paused to clear my throat, the tips of my ears heating up. Were my words too formal? Would they understand? I noticed a mist swirling up from the crystal in the center man's staff. "I am Daris, the leader of our group. I am a Guildmaster. We are from the Guilds of Chaos in the Arnexis Realm. We seek safe passage and a place to stay for the evening. We believe there is a Magus among your people who can assist us."

"May Chaos Reign," the man returned my bow, as did the others with him, and I took note that his eyes glowed the same shade of blue as the crystal on his staff. "I am Orion, the Elder of the Hatuni tribe. I know why you have come." The mist from his staff brightened. "I am aware of your mission. I even recognize one of you. You are welcome here, friends. It has been too long since our Realms have connected. Come with me. I have had a meal prepared for all of you."

"Thank you." I bowed my head to him before leading my group after his. I quickly explained to them that the Hatuni were a tribe of Wood Orcs who lived in harmony with the forest and possessed strong magic.

Orion ushered us into one of the larger buildings ahead, much taller than the others and circular in shape. He invited us inside to sit at a round stone table laden with smoked meats and steamed vegetables. It was not the blood meal I craved, but my mouth still watered as I took a seat. Nix sat beside me, and as her arm brushed mine, a ravenous hunger stirred within me, knowing that the food before me would not satisfy my deepest desire.

Variant eyed the food warily, and I studied him closely. An assassin would be the least trusting of strangers. While he excelled at stealth, he lacked training in protocol. He should have understood that a Sangor's keen sense of smell could easily detect poisons. As Variant reached out to pick up a piece of meat and sniff it, Jessamine, who had seated herself between him and Elias, slapped his hand away.

"Wait!" she hissed. She glanced around to see if anyone noticed Variant's disrespect. Elias let a laugh escape his lips, and Variant threw daggers with his eyes.

Thankfully, Orion had offered them to enter the room first and then stopped outside to talk with the others. The man entered with the others after Variant had almost started sniffing the food and sat in the largest chair. We all introduced ourselves.

"Wonderful! It is a pleasure to meet each of you. Now, before we begin," Orion smiled, "a test of trust." He stared at me. "Daris, is there any one of your group here suspected of murder?"

I was floored. Bound to Nix with my Celestial stone and now linked with her curse—I had no choice but to tell the truth or turn bright red in front of everyone. And I immediately realized I hadn't told Nix about this. She had no idea.

I could either offer up that she was suspected of murder in Arnexis or that we suspected Variant of the crime. I had to hope she would understand.

"Yes," I admitted.

"Who?"

"My Apprentice, who you just met. The one called Nix—Phoenix." My gaze remained steady with his, and I prayed to the Celestials he would ask me no more questions. He did not. Instead, he went to Nix.

"Nix, have you killed anyone?"

My heart raced. Nix only just discovered she'd killed her parents in a fire she'd accidentally started right before the Blaze Ceremony. I watched her face, which remained placid, but inside I sensed her inner turmoil.

After a long moment, she lifted her eyes to Orion and said, "Yes."

"Who?" he asked, leveling an intense stare at her.

"My p-parents. And—and my brother. In the Mortal Realm. It was an accident. I killed them when I burned down—"

"That is enough," Orion interrupted. Now, tell me a lie, Nix—something that isn't true."

The confusion rolled over Nix's face like an ocean wave. Her eyebrows knit together as her eyes widened. "What?"

"I want you to tell me something that is false," he insisted. His tone was very serious, but his eyes—I thought they glittered with amusement.

Nix's eyes swept over the table laden with fruits, meats, vegetables, and other delicacies. "I am not hungry, and this table looks like garbage," she declared.

Orion burst into a huge fit of laughter. His chitter was not at all what I imagined his laugh would sound like. It was high-pitched, musical, and infectious.

"Scarlet skin!" he cried out. "By Chaos. I really wanted to see that in person. Forgive me, child. I just could not pass that up." Orion grinned and winked at Nix. He gestured to the food. "Please begin. I will tell you about myself while we eat. I'm sure you know little about the Zeleel Realm."

I stared, wondering how he knew about Nix, and then wondered if he knew about me. If he did, then that was awkward and —and what? Unplanned. But it didn't change anything. We still had a mission. I didn't have to do anything differently.

Elena sat on my right, eyes huge as she watched the Elder—Orion— speak. Nix sat on my left. I had to resist the urge to rest a hand on her thigh. We were seated so closely together that her leg brushed mine, but she didn't look at me. The room was lit with fire—but the fire was magic. It emitted no heat from the torches placed around it. Along the walls inside, vines grew—and flowers bloomed of different varieties I hadn't seen before. Various oranges, yellows, and reds.

Orion told us of the history between our Realms.

"Once, the Zeleel Realm had close connections with the Guilds of Chaos. But there was a Grand Guildmaster who sought to take over the Zeleel Realm—to make it the seat of the Guilds of Chaos because of Zeleel's origin. Zeleel has deep magic—arcane and raw. It is a dangerous place for any who haven't been born here to wield it."

"Wasn't the Zeleel Realm the first place the Celestials lived? And they created the intelligent species?" Nix asked. I was impressed she'd remembered.

"Our ancient books say that, yes. All beings created by Chaos and the Celestials are *Caeli* or 'of the heavens', and those who are beings we consider—not necessarily more intelligent but within our gene structure and within our nature to understand well—we call *Mentis* or 'of memory, understanding and mind' as we know it. Species such as Elsh, Orc, Mortal, Arnexin, Sangor, Garsha, and so on—these are Mentis, while the Warsharms you battled are Caeli."

Orion had Osculus magic. It was the only way he could know these things. And he had to be strong with it too. I noted the Magus colors decorating the room, as well as the red and gold feathers he wore. Was he the Magus we sought?

He paused to gather some of the vegetables in his hand like a cup and loaded the meat into it. I imitated him, relishing the sharp flavors. Elena and Jessamine both drank down a bowl of steaming soup with flowers in it. Elias sat between them, still not sure what to eat.

Orion then placed some strings of meat and chunks of a slimy neon green salad on Elias's plate, along with some vines of fruit, smiled, and continued, "When the Maestro of the Guilds tried to overtake us, we fought. You remember that battle."

I did remember. All too well. It didn't last long. Once the large portal was destroyed, large numbers of troops from Arnexis could not be transported. It was poor battle strategy to try to transport troops through a known entrance anyway—the *only* known entrance at the time—in a war. Guildmaster Straxer was insane. He claimed Zeleel had historical significance, and therefore he should own it. Guild troops needed to already be in place in Zeleel to win. He was sending them in for slaughter with his strategy, expecting to portal them in when needed, but he wouldn't listen. In the end—

He *knew.* He knew I was the reason his people were cut off from all the Realms for so long, with the exception of traveling places one by one and only by skill level. It had taken years for them to build a large portal again. I had acted alone, destroying the portal. But no one knew. Each side blamed the other instead.

"I was protecting everyone." I pushed away my plate. "Protecting our Realm from your powers and your Realm from our . . ."

Orion held up a hand, cutting me off. "You did what you thought was right. Just as I will."

I didn't know what he meant by that, but I was sure I wasn't going to like it.

Orion shifted his attention to Elena, who was seated by Variant. He leaned forward in his chair, his chin on his hand.

"Elena, when you fought the Warsharms, a member of your party killed one in a way that concerned you. Why did it concern you?"

Elena had just put a mouthful of food into her mouth. She took her time chewing it. A long time. And she kept chewing, picked at a fingernail, grinned politely at Orion as if to apologize for still chewing, but cut her eyes toward him with a confidence that said, 'You know what it's like to have to finish chewing,' and she pointed to a pitcher as she chewed, motioning for an empty glass as she kept chewing, and chewing some more—then—finally—she swallowed—holding up a 'wait-a-minute' finger while she poured water, and drank it down, then poured another water and drank, then poured another water . . .

"Answer his question, Elena," I growled.

Elena took a bit of time clearing her throat, then said, "The creature's chest was ripped out."

Orion leaned back. "I see. And why did that concern you?"

Elena narrowed her eyes at me. *Oh shit. She's not even going to try.*

"Because the description of the bodies at the Guilds of Chaos is exactly the same."

At the same time she uttered the words, a tiny dart punctured my neck. I felt a drug release into my bloodstream, and then everything around me began to move in slow motion.

Variant lunged at Elena, and I rose to confront him, pressing a button on my belt to summon my chosen sword, Dragnot. Variant's daggers sliced through the air, tearing my shirt and grazing my skin. Despite my sluggish movements, I managed to stab his right arm, forcing him out of the building and back to the village. Elena followed, her steps behind me unsteady.

"What have you done?" I roared at him.

Variant ignored my question, his lips twisting into a smirk as his daggers cut at me. I dodged, but my efforts were futile, my mind racing. Had Elena been drugged or poisoned? If Nix were in danger, the stone in my palm would be red, but it glowed blue.

Variant slammed me hard against a nearby hut as the harsh red sky darkened to a deep purple, the last remnants of sunset fading. Disoriented, I spun around, the drug still hindering my movements. A vision consumed my sight.

"Looks like you have to choose." When I turned back to Variant, he once again held Elena against him, a dagger pressed to her arched throat. Why had she followed me outside? "Save the village and lose your sister or attack me and lose her anyway." His grin was positively triumphant as if he had won a match at the Parabellum.

It doesn't sound like much of a choice, really. I thought Oscuro Guild Apprentices were supposed to be intelligent.

I stepped toward him, fists clenched, but Elena whimpered, and blood trickled down her neck as Variant pressed the dagger harder against her throat.

"Let me go." Elena's eyes blinked slowly as if she couldn't comprehend what was happening. The more I studied her, the more convinced I became that Variant had done something to her.

The acrid scent of smoke rose in the air.

Nix.

That had to be because of Nix. Orion was nowhere in sight, either.

"I'll find you," I assured Elena. It seemed that was all Variant needed to hear. He dragged Elena a few feet away, and then they vanished. I considered tracking them once more and launching a surprise attack on Variant, but the glint in his eyes told me he would make good on his threat and kill Elena the moment he noticed my presence.

I raced back to the village, where a blazing trail cut through its heart. Elias and Jessamine were battling the fires. Elias used Teragos magic to raise earth and smother any flames on the ground, while Jessamine harnessed Aquane power to conjure small rain clouds over the burning rooftops. No one was hurt, but Nix was nowhere to be found.

"Where did she go?" I grabbed Elias by the shoulders when he shifted back into his Arnexin form. His eyes were wider than I had ever seen them, brimming with panic.

"Variant took Elena."

"I know that! We will get her back, Elias. First, I need to know where Nix went."

Elias shook his head in a daze, his gaze fixated over my shoulder. He then shoved me aside, attempting to storm up the mountain after Variant. Orion emerged in front of him, blocking his path.

I turned, gripping my hair in frustration. Not only had my sister gone missing, but no one knew where Nix was, either. Now, I would have to face the consequences with the man in charge of the village my people had nearly destroyed.

"Orion, my apologies—"

He chuckled, his wizened face showing no sign of displeasure, let alone anger. "I was curious about what she could do. I only wish I could have seen your sister's abilities, as well. As for you . . ."

It took me a moment to speak, his words seeming to carry a deeper meaning than what they conveyed on the surface.

"I don't understand." I was in charge of this team, and I was failing. Failing to keep them together, to keep them safe, and to complete our objective. I had it all worked out until things fell apart. A group of children ran by, playing a game in the dark. I realized I still held my sword, Dragnot, in my hand, and pressed the button on my belt to sheathe it.

Orion tilted his head, a look of sympathy on his face.

He focused on his staff as he spoke next, gesturing to it. A breeze kicked up, ruffling his feathers on his shoulders. Elias and Jessamine closed in to listen. "This is all that remains of our connection with the Celestial Realm and its power. What I failed to mention earlier was that we are involved in every prophecy. It is written in the ancient texts binding all of us together.

I know of Tooth, Claw, and Staff. I know them to be three of your own people. However, I do know not all the threats you face. One seems to have shown himself tonight. But I do know some."

"What else do you know?" My voice came out as a growl. The more time we wasted, the further away Variant took Elena, and I didn't know where Nix could have gone. Air that tasted like smoke still hung heavily around me.

Orion bowed his head as though he regretted the words he'd said. "Variant will be back. Nix has disappeared into the tunnels of the mountain. He will take her next if he can. If not, he will take someone else."

"Would have been nice to know this all a lot sooner." Elias lunged for Orion, who stepped back and shook his head.

I pressed a hard hand against Elias' chest while Jessamine took hold of his arm. She stared angrily at him, her hot gaze boring into him. I tried to calm my own unsteady fury. "Are you saying Elena is a part of the prophecy?"

"Yes, as it seems, you and Nix also are. There's a reason she went to the mountain."

"Don't tell me you sent her there." The thought of her alone, trekking into the twisting caverns and tunnels that crawled through the mountain, terrified me. Still, my stone remained blue. I shook with anger when Orion nodded. This time, Jessamine held me back. "I'm going after her. Let me go," I commanded.

"What about Elena?" Elias grabbed my head, trying to force me to calm down, but there was no way in the Realms I was capable of that right then. The choice was unbelievable: go after my sister or the girl I loved more than anything.

Even as logic ran frantic laps between the two, unable to pick, my heart settled. "Seraphina won't . . . Variant won't kill her. They won't." My thoughts tumbled from my tongue. "If they took her, it's for information. They wouldn't do that.

Listen to me, Elias, as a Skia Guild Apprentice, you are my responsibility. I can't risk your life sending you on a rescue mission without me. You and Jessamine return to the Skia Guild and learn whatever you can about where Variant took Elena but stay safe. Keep to the trees at night. Avoid dangerous wildlife until you get to the portal. I'm going after Nix."

"Daris, think. We have more chance of success together." Jessamine stood at Elias' side, some of her blue hair billowing loose around her face. A deep sadness settled in her eyes, reflected in Elias's gaze as well. I didn't have the mind to comprehend it.

"Swear that you'll do as I said."

Elias knew he couldn't change my mind. His jaw clenched. I hated ordering him not to go after Elena, but I needed to be responsible. I had to order the right thing. But I'd also be lying if I said I didn't have a spark in my chest that hoped he and Jessamine would ignore my order. If anyone could save her, it was him.

He nodded. I watched as they slung their packs on their backs after receiving some travel food from some of the people, and they disappeared into the wilderness. Suddenly, splitting up didn't seem like the right call.

With them out of sight, though, my entire being returned to focusing on Nix. Orion nodded and gestured to a dark-shadowed creature behind him. It was immense. Not as large as an Agon, but with a strange golden fur. Larger than a Griffin, but with feathers like razor-sharp metal. It seemed to shift between soft feathers and fur and shiny hard armor as it eyed me.

Orion held out a hand to Nemar in greeting. "Ho, Nemar." He bowed. Motioning me to come forward, Orion made us acquainted. "Nemar, this is Daris of the Arnexis Realm."

I repeated Orion's greeting and bowed. Nemar pawed the ground, taking a softer form.

"Nemar is a Grigon," Orion walked over to nuzzle the beast. "As I've explained, we have very deep and dark magic here. Many strong Myrocans have come—some independents, some from Guilds or various trades—seeking to—create things. Grigons were one such creation. A blending of Agons and Griffins. They can transform their soft fur and feathers into battle scales and impenetrable wings sharp as the sharpest blade, and each one has a particular 'breath' gift. Nemar exhales electricity, like lightning, in battle. He's extremely intelligent and very loyal.

Orion took a moment to turn away and spoke quietly with Nemar. I found it curious that though they were close to me, I couldn't hear a single word Orion said. Did he have a mental link? But I thought his lips were moving. It was some kind of silencing spell, then. I didn't fault him. I used them as well. But usually, there was not a silencing spell that managed to keep my keen hearing out.

Turning back to me, Orion said, "Nemar has protected this village for a very long time. He has trained a young Grigon who will do well on her own." Orion rubbed Nemar's great head against his hand. "He uses emotion for energy. Finds his own food as well. Small game, vegetation. As an omnivore and emovore, he's versatile. I offer him to you as your guardian and travel companion. Nemar is a very special creature, as are all Grigons—because there are so few. He can transport you wherever you'd like to go with great speed, nearly equal to an Agon. When you bond with him, you will have a mental link with him. When you need him, you need only call on him by focusing your full mind and intention on his name and his form. He will come to you."

I didn't have any more time to waste. It was very late, and my only hope was that Nix had stopped to sleep for the night and I could track her while she slumbered.

I thanked Orion with deep gratitude. This creature could make all the difference in finding Nix. I could tell he was precious to the man.

Nemar came to my side and sniffed my chest. His Grigon eyes widened briefly, a startlingly human expression, before he offered his back for me to mount. I grabbed my pack, made sure my belt was in place, and we took off toward the mountain at a speed that would make the wind jealous. As we did, the stone in my palm started to glow red.

NIX

DESTINY

Though the mountain paths were wide, I didn't trust them. I half expected to find Daris next to me any moment, berating me for taking off. But Orion convinced me. As Daris fought Variant, Orion had come to me, and in that circular room, he'd grasped my hand—the one with my protection bond, and he'd showed me his visions.

He showed me how I was meant to walk this path—and what would happen if I did not. He showed me Elena's death at Variant's hand. Daris wandering in Lethenthril. Me caught in some dark oblivion. Apprentices suffering horrors at the Guilds.

I'm sure he could have shown me more, but I ripped my hand away before he was done. It was too much.

I didn't need much convincing after that. Deep down, even though I didn't know how to use my Osculus gifts, I knew he was telling the truth. And I knew I was going to do whatever it took to make things right—to save Elena, clear my name, be with Daris, and help him finish this mission. I decided I wanted to learn to be stronger, to control my power more. I was tired of feeling weak and out of control.

It wasn't hard to gather my jacket and my belt to strike out for the journey. I wasn't sure what all was in my belt, but if I really needed something, I was sure I'd find it. Elena had helped to pack it after all.

The tunnels ahead welcomed me into the dark. I didn't trust them, even though the pathway was marked sparsely with glow stones. Every step made me feel like the walls were closing in on me, and the few glow stones didn't guarantee my footing. My heart beat wildly beneath my ribs, longing for light.

Be brave. Be strong. Save Elena. Be with Daris. Help him finish the mission.

The words became a mantra in my head, cheering me on. I wondered if, maybe, I could conjure a ball of fire in the palm of my hand to help me see—kind of like a torch, but without the stick. I figured the worst thing was I'd burn some rock—maybe my pants.

I stopped and imagined a ball of light in my left hand. My sparks started around my wrist. They started spinning in circles rapidly. I focused.

Now, form a round ball on the palm of my hand.

I visualized it—what I wanted it to look like, the shape, the color, and even the smell. And wonder of wonders, a ball of fire grew in my hand. I had some decent light to walk with rather than relying on a few glow stones.

I thought of Orion's words before I left.

'The Magus you seek is not part of the prophecy in the way you think. He lives at the top of the mountain. You must find him.'

I hadn't questioned him about it. I'd only nodded, too frantic because of my flames to do anything else except do what he told me. He'd sent me off into the tunnels, searching hopelessly for a Magus that I was beginning to think I would never really meet.

Something flapped over my head. The sound of wings. Fairly large ones. We had bats in Drade, but if these were bats, they were humongous. I pushed myself to keep walking.

Thoughts of Drade put me into a funk. I'd never go back. I missed my family, but I missed my father most. And my family's deaths were on my hands. Home was a tomb to me now—not home anymore.

Focus, Nix. Be brave. Be strong. Save Elena. Be with Daris. Help him finish the mission.

Thoughts like those kept me moving, as did the mountain itself. They were my thoughts, weren't they? I felt the mountain as if it were a live presence within my own veins. It was steady and strong like I so desperately wanted it to be.

As I hiked further in, I learned that, in certain directions, that feeling grew stronger. My flames became more and more restless under my skin if I followed one path versus the other. Soon the paths led upward, and I fought to catch my breath.

"Yep," I told myself out loud, "Got to get back to the cardio."

I stopped cold in my tracks. The mountain opened up into a giant cavern—as if it had been a volcano at one time and cut in half at the top. In the center of the cavern—a huge hole opened up, a wide gap that revealed the purple moons and stars above, allowing the heavens to illuminate a pool of shallow water at the bottom. I smelled rich mineral deposits here, fertile earth, and a scent so intense and achingly sweet—but I could not describe it. Maybe I'd smelled something like it before.

In the center of the pool sat a skinny man with gray robes. He was bald, and his thin white mustache and beard hanging straight into the water like a taproot. His small eyes were closed, and he had thin lips pressed together. His hands were palm to palm in some sort of prayer.

As I stepped forward, shadows shaped like massive fish rippled over the surface of the water. The man opened his eyes but did not turn his head. "Welcome, Your Royal Majesty. I am Drishti. You have come to claim yourself."

I knit my eyebrows together and approached him. As I did, he skimmed the water with his fingers in an invitation to sit. I settled across from him, surprised to find that my clothes—my body- everything submerged in the water remained dry. Amazed at this wondrous place and this mystery man, I searched his face.

He spoke. "I have long awaited your arrival. Just as you have."

Every word out of his mouth only further confused me. I got to the point. "Orion told me you would help me control my flames."

"Only you can do that, but I will set you on the right path." Suddenly, he flung his hand up, a trail of water droplets following the dramatic gesture, but they did not return to the pool. They hovered in the air like tiny, glistening stars, and as I watched, they became something else entirely.

Pictures flashed before me as the man spoke. They first showed a group of three people: a woman with a tilted crown and crazed blue eyes, a man holding a gilded staff similar to Orion's, and a man with his hand outstretched toward the woman's free one as though they'd just made some sort of agreement. The woman with the tilted crown glared furiously at the two. "Your prophecy has shown itself in different forms throughout the years." Drishti narrated the tale for me as I studied the image.

"This was the most recent one. The Queen, you see, was a powerful monster hunter who went mad from misuse of her magical gifts. She practiced the art of killing monsters with all her skills— her touch, her words, and her mind. She became the ultimate killer—killing everything she desired. Eventually, she tired of the sport of hunting monsters and chose to hunt Mentis —all species related to our kind. Mortals, Elsh, Orc, Grasha, and others. She hung the heads of the strongest, most difficult kills on her walls."

The picture changed to show the Mad Queen as a ferocious killer hunting a wild-eyed woman through the forest as she rode a snake-like beast. My stomach lurched. The enjoyment on her face was sickening. When she wounded the woman and came in for the kill, she got off her beast and tortured her first—and blood drenched the ground.

Drishti didn't show me that one for long. The vision switched back to the other two visions I'd seen earlier. At second glance, I noticed the shadow of a man on the grass near them, stabbed through with a sword. The shape of a crown had fallen near his side while the two other figures gaped at him in horror.

"The woman you see standing there was an heir and an extraordinary Magus, and the man a Sangor, as well as the Queen's best friend. They could find no peaceful solution to the Mad Queen's reign, except to end her life and ensure her power never drove anyone in her bloodline mad again."

The next image showed the woman, holding a child, surrounded by gilded halls, cupping something bright gold in her hands. It moved like water, though no force acted behind the ripples. When I scrutinized her face, I felt she looked familiar. Then I realized—her nose and cheeks resembled mine.

"You come from the same bloodline as the Mad Queen," Drishti told me. His eyes were closed once more. I leaned forward to observe the picture closely.

"What is she holding?"

"The second soul of the young heir to the Mad Queen's throne. This is how your bloodline has stayed sane: by taking a part of you and locking it away until you are capable and willing to wield the second half of your true self."

Was this why I'd felt so drawn to the mountain? No. It was ludicrous to believe my blood contained royal properties or that my powers could be so strong. I could barely create a fireball with intention. I could blast devastating fire in battle, but so far—that was the extent of any control I'd felt.

As though he'd read my mind, Drishti spoke. "The part of yourself that you're missing is the key to controlling your powers. I know it seems cruel to be without it for so long." For the first time, he focused on me, really gazed at me, as though he remembered my soul. "Sometimes, not having control is the best remedy for a heart in a storm."

And now was when I desperately needed Elena—because those words did not make any sense to me.

"How do I . . . find this other part of myself?" The words sounded strange. I wasn't quite used to knowing half of me was missing, but the knowledge almost comforted me. I hadn't yet become my true self; I could learn the balance, learn how to wield my flames without hurting anyone I didn't want to.

"You must go deep into the depths of the mountain now. Your half of your soul will guide you. I believe you're ready—but be on your guard. This is not a safe place." He stood and bowed his head. I returned the gesture.

"Thank you." So many unasked questions were settled in my mind, but my chest started glowing a faint blue, and a trail stretched before me, illuminating the first of my paths. I gazed once more at Drishti. But he'd returned to his meditative state.

"There is one more thing I must say." I jumped, startled. I hadn't expected him to speak again. "Your genetic code has not been unlocked. It remained dormant in the Mortal Realm. If you desire to unlock your full potential, to become the one you were designed to be, you must walk through The Eye of Chaos."

With that, he returned to his perfect silence. I was on my own now. I conjured my fireball and continued along my path.

Designed to be? I thought. Visions of clothing designers came to mind, with Veronica Beard, Georgio Armani, and Dolce & Gabbana hitting my brain, and I shook my head. I had to FOCUS.

Got it. Eye of Chaos. Full potential. Crazy stuff about who I need to be. Later. Meanwhile, in the mountain—half of my soul is playing Marco Polo with the other . . . Marco?

I wished Daris was with me. I rubbed the protection bond on my palm. It helped to know that if I were in danger, the stone in his hand would alert him. He'd have to find me, but how would he find me?

I realized there was no use in worrying about that. I'd just have to have faith. With a deep, steadying breath, I followed the trail before me and kept to my mantra.

Be Brave. Be Strong. Save Elena. Be with Daris. Help him finish the mission.

I couldn't remember which paths I'd taken and which I hadn't. At first, I worried I would never find my way out, but a familiarity deeper than what I knew from traversing a few tunnels warmed my bones. Somehow, I knew everything would be okay.

Then, a light stream of blue light beamed from my chest and bent along tunnels as if showing me the way forward. I followed the blue magic as quickly as I could. My body moved without urgency. I began to feel like I wasn't fully present within myself.

Was the missing part of me calling me to myself? I thought how stupid I sounded believing that—asking myself that question—but the blue light was undeniable. Overhead, I heard more flapping wings.

I entered another smaller cavern, where yellow balls of light hung on the walls, illuminating the round room. Blue incandescent eyes stared at me, and her ears flattened against her head. Sharp silver teeth shone from her snarling lips, and her nose was like a beak as if it could rend and tear. Her forked blue tongue flicked out as if tasting the air as she pawed over to me, her claws clicking on the floor. Each step rose like the pulse of a heartbeat.

My heartbeat, I realized, was the one in my human chest.

I knew this creature before me. Somehow, I was her. I could feel the faster rhythm in her chest, the uncertainty sending her cobalt fur and multicolored blue feathers standing on end. Through her wide eyes, I saw the human part of me.

Through her eyes, I was a frazzled figure, unkempt and terrified. My frame was small, and my bones were too large for my skin. I moved unsteadily on my feet, in shock that this frailty before me was mine.

How strange the split perspectives were. How different everything seemed. One half of me controlled herself, flaring only when she wanted to, steadying the rhythm of her heart, and forcing her fur and feathers to lay flat. The other half of me shook uncontrollably, terrified to take what belonged to me from this beautiful creature.

Tears fell from my human eyes while my blazing blue ones narrowed. My great beast self gently butted a great head against my Mortal self as though to say it didn't have to be like this.

An ache spread between us, the two of us. We—I—wanted to go home.

I wrapped my arms around myself, both chests glowing. I pressed a hand to my furred chest while panic threatened to seize the other. Two gentle blue lights merged, and with a gasp, I became whole again.

The creature that was my soul's vessel remained gentle. She breathed deeply, too. Both of us felt relief: her because the weight of my soul was lifted from her chest, and me because now I knew what it felt like to be whole. I never wanted to feel anything else again.

The flames she'd just possessed disintegrated like ash into her dark blue fur. Her eyes turned bright blue, and her tail fluffed out like a dark blue shadow. She remained hovering near me. I offered a hand and stroked her soft back. She arched into it, a sound between a growl and a purr rumbling its way from her throat. I smiled.

I opened my palm and thought simply: *fire.* I wanted flames. They appeared, following the stitched patterns of my skin along my tattoos of my forearms to my hands, and a sharp laugh emerged from my lips. I could control the direction they went in, making them brighter or dimmer. With little more than a thought, I extinguished the flames. All was silent and dark for a moment as I reveled in my perfect control.

I examined the beast, whose eyes had been tracking my flames like a game. Now, she met my gaze. "Would you like to accompany me on my quest?"

The beast seemed to understand me well. I named her Cobalt. She let me climb to her back, and I was thrilled to have her show me out of the cave . . . until we were attacked.

Giant wings smacked into me, nearly knocking me off of Cobalt. I heard her screech, crouch low to the ground, and dash faster along the passageway. I conjured fire in my hands easily now and didn't hesitate as I aimed a blast behind me. I figured something would probably be there chasing us. I was right. A high-pitched cry that could have shattered glass reverberated through the tunnel. I thought I heard part of the cave crumble.

There was no time to look around, though, as I hung on tight to Cobalt, praying I wouldn't fall. She banked a corner and slipped through a narrow arch. I thought for sure, as big as those things seemed to be, we'd be done, but no, in moments, I felt a claw at my back, trying to lift me off of Cobalt. I blasted the thing as it lifted me into the air, catching a momentary glimpse of it. Batlike in a way. The wings were moist and leathery. It had rows of long yellow teeth shaped like piercing needles. It looked desperately hungry.

My body tumbled toward the ground, only to have another one of the ugly creatures grab me. I heard a roar and then saw a blast of blue fire. My heart catapulted when Cobalt launched into the air and let loose flames that incinerated the creature that held me. She dove and managed to catch me before I hit the ground.

There was no time to be afraid, though I should have been terrified. Still, it was not like I expected. Something was different. Did the other half of my soul make a difference? Did this change how I felt about heights? I climbed back on her, none the worse for wear with some gashes I knew I'd have to heal when I returned—when I felt Daris's arms around me, holding me tight.

Then, Cobalt nearly threw me off, grinding too a halt. She reared and growled. I raised a fireball in my hand, ready to hurl, and—smiled.

"It's all right, girl. Cobalt, this is Daris. Daris, Cobalt."

Daris was on Cobalt with me in less than a second. He pressed his lips against mine, holding me tight, and he kissed me like I'd been gone for a million years. When he pulled away, it was too dark for me to see his face, but I heard the emotion in his voice.

"Don't you ever, ever leave like that again." He held me close for a few more moments, and I wished we could be close forever —forever without the interruptions of the world.

Introducing Nemar to Cobalt was a strange affair. He backed away at first as if surprised—and Cobalt advanced, tilting her head. Then, they both touched foreheads and a strange silver glow formed around their heads as a sound I couldn't accurately describe—like a high-pitched buzz of a mosquito, only pleasant like a meditation tone—hit the air. And then, they moved away.

We made our way out of the mountain quickly, and the words Drishti said to me rose in my mind. I needed to tell Daris. It had to be part of his plan. He needed to know.

"Wait," I halted Cobalt, and Nemar dug his claws into the road, stopping too. Daris turned. "When I was inside, in the upper cavern, the old man I spoke with—a Magus named Drishti—told me about The Eye of Chaos. He said if I wanted to know my full potential, to become who I was meant to be, I needed to walk through it."

Daris glanced away, and I sensed his deliberation in responding.

"You know where it is, right?" My question was direct.

"Is it so important now, Nix? Elena is missing. We need to find her."

I hesitated. Daris was right. Elena was more important. I wasn't significant. I was just some girl from the Mortal Realm who had killed her family with out-of-control powers.

Except that, I *knew* that walking through The Eye would transform me. It would help me understand my full potential. Orion sent me into the mountain, certain I'd find the other half of my soul and knowing I'd meet Drishti. And Drishti told me I had to go through The Eye. He showed me the visions. There was a purpose to this that had to do with the prophecy—and we wouldn't succeed without it.

I felt that after everything that had happened so far, this was something that had to happen next—before anything else. It wasn't selfish; it was practical. When I examined my mind, I was terrified of doing it. I was more terrified of not doing it.

What if I went mad? Or became a hideous monster? But Orion had Osculus magic, boosted with his staff. I had to believe he wouldn't encourage me if he didn't see some good coming of it. Drishti showed me death and destruction if I avoided it.

"Yes, it's that important now, Daris. It can help me reach my full potential, which I believe—no, I know—can help us defeat Variant, Seraphina, and anyone else we need to. I have so much to tell you, Daris, but first, I need to walk through The Eye of Chaos."

DARIS

LET IT GO

The Eye of Chaos.

It was a detour I didn't want to take. We could run into Seraphina. Nix's transformation could be anything. I had no idea—she had no idea—what it would be. She explained a little about royal blood. Great. And the mad Queen. Lovely. But that was one side of the family. What was the other side? What were the recessive genes? What were the possibilities? What were her moon signs in the Realm where she'd been born? There were so many factors.

But here we were: Elias and Jessamine stood guard near the portal just in case. Nemar and Cobalt wandered near the fountain, observing the koi. I really hoped they didn't try to eat them. That would be a disaster.

Getting the Grigons here had been interesting. We had to go in small groups. Unfortunately, at the Cor, it was the one place a person couldn't just portal in and portal out. The central portal had to be used. So, only three or four people could come and go at a time. And if you were caught here by accident, when you weren't invited, you were stuck. Only The Eye of Chaos could help you then.

We walked along the polished floor toward the far room. "Okay, Nix. You understand, right? There's no going back. Once you walk through, that's it. You could become a Meta and shapeshift like Elena, or an Orc, or . . . "

"Yes, you told me." She didn't snap, but her lips were tight, and I felt her tension. I got the sense that she was getting irritated with me trying to talk her out of doing this.

I was the one that was scared, after all. I needed to let her go. Let her be her. I was the one with the problem of change.

I grasped her hand and walked her past the round table we'd all sat at a few days ago. Beyond it was a curtain of white mist.

"I can't go any further." I cupped her face in my hands. "The room is only for one person at a time. This is your time. This is for you. When you go in, you'll see a large archway with a large stone eye on top. You will not see anything on the other side. The Eye of Chaos will tell you what to do. Good luck."

I kissed her gently on the lips. She smiled, grateful, and vanished into the mist.

NIX

THE EYE STARES BACK

*C*ome.

That same deep, reassuring voice. I was sure it was the same one I'd heard when I was here before—when I was a dumb klutz and made a mess of things.

Part of me felt like I was in a Wizard of Oz movie, and that I should be looking around for the man behind the curtain. But I knew better. This was way different.

I placed one foot steadily in front of the other as I moved toward the archway, then stopped before it. Did I just step inside? Yeah, I'll ask.

"Do I just step inside—go through?" I waited.

Yes.

So, I did just that.

It was like standing in the middle of a blank artist's canvas if I were the size of a speck of dust or in the middle of a blank white computer screen if I were the smallest pixel imaginable. I was lost in white space—undefined, blank, and nothing.

Then—my entire surroundings shifted. Colors, universes, electrons, cells, storms, insects, beasts of all kinds, species throughout all Realms—they all flew around me—inside me—my mind reeling from the sheer knowledge of it all.

And then, as fast as a hummingbird heartbeat, I was standing in front of the archway of The Eye of Chaos once more.

I felt like I should ask some questions, get some answers to what it's all about—understand the meaning of life, but—The Eye of Chaos had just told me everything. My brain just didn't know how to handle it. I didn't even know what questions to ask. I took a breath and exhaled. I should at least be polite.

"Is that all? Am I —done?"

Yes.

Thank you.

You are welcome, Nix. Live well. Learn well. Guide others better than you did the day before.

I turned and walked out, not feeling like anything had changed but knowing that everything—everything in *my* world— was different now.

DARIS

THORNS

Nix still looked like Nix when she came out of the room after entering The Eye of Chaos. My skin would have turned scarlet if I'd said I wasn't relieved.

And she looked utterly amazing, even with her torn shirt and ripped pants. I wasn't sure what her transformation was, but there was something to her that had, if possible, enhanced her physical attraction. Increased her muscle definition—made her seem more athletic—like she'd just returned from super-hero camp.

I wanted to examine her more, but we needed to leave. Elena was next on our stop. We needed to find her quickly. And I knew a seer—a very good one, who might be able to help us.

I provided part of my plan to the team: "We all need to portal to the Omnipatos with Nemar and Cobalt. Once we are there, we'll make sure Nemar and Cobalt have Access Arums placed upon them so they can fly out—come and go across GOC wards as they please. We will rendezvous at Hecade Guild and meet at Guildmaster Myst River's office. She owes me a favor.

Like arriving at the Cor, there wasn't enough room for us all to travel together from the Cor's portal. Jessamine and Elias portaled first, then Daris and I managed with Nemar and Cobalt. It was a tight fit.

Before we transported, I ran my hand along Nix's chin and gave her a kiss. "I need you to know, I care about you Nix. You are everything to me." I gazed into her eyes. Then I froze. Why hadn't I seen it before?

She noticed my concern. "What's wrong?"

Two things happened.

I said, "Nothing," and immediately turned scarlet. The portal promptly transported us to the Omnipatos.

My day was *not* going as planned. All because I noticed Nix's eyes were no longer hazel. They were a deep shade of maroon.

Like mine.

We prepared to step out of the portal, and I was ready to explain to Nix about my lying link to her when we were immediately slapped with the hard metal of magic restraining handcuffs.

"Grand Guildmaster Moonshade requests your presence," a Lupine guard grinned as he started dragging me forward. Looking ahead, it was clear she'd asked for the presence of Jessamine and Elias as well. "Get out of here!" I yelled to Nemar, "Go! I'll call for you! Go to the mountains! Take Cobalt with you!"

Nix joined me in shouting at the Grigons to leave. They screeched and roared and tried to attack the Lupines to save us, but when the Lupines threatened to kill us, Nemar and Cobalt backed away.

Go, Nemar, I thought to my Grigon. *Now is not the time. We will call you soon.*

I hoped they understood they would be more useful alive—that we'd need them in the future. After our desperate shouts, and when a Lupine drew blood from my neck with a blade, they flew off. My mind eased. At least it was daylight. They'd have a chance to get the lay of the land before dark.

As we were marched to Seraphina's office, we were silent until Nix finally glared at me. "Just when were you going to tell me that you can't lie?"

"Nix—I didn't have time. Really, I—"

"Shut it," said the Lupine guard holding me, and they threw us to the floor in front of Seraphina. Her office was an opulent mixture of golden satin and red velvet everywhere. A red velvet sofa with gold trim and stylish accent pillows was placed against one wall opposite two matching velvet chairs, and sheer golden drapes covered the windows in a delicate fashion. Her desk was intricately carved mahogany with accents of pure gold in places that made it stunning.

The carpet's golden color shimmered. On the walls were works of art by Pyrosh, a fire artist known for using live magic fire, which transformed her work into three-dimensional views of controversial themes.

Seraphina stared down at us with a wicked smile.

"Daris, oh Daris, you had a single mission. How hard was that? Did you fulfill it? Did you answer the questions about the prophecy and find me the people included in it?"

Great. Nix and I are in a room being questioned by a woman we don't want to tell the truth to, and neither one of us can lie. Well, that sucks.

Nix had the most experience with this, and I admired her as she tried a diversion tactic. She stood up tall, and I regained my footing beside her. "His sister, Elena, was abducted by Variant. I believe you wanted him to come with us? Well, now, she's gone," she retorted. "You can hardly expect him to complete a mission with his sister missing."

Seraphina didn't hesitate. She waved a hand and air-slapped Nix to the floor. Rage flared inside me, and the protection stone burned in my palm. I struggled against the cuffs. They might restrain my magic, but they didn't stop my species . . .

"Don't even try, Daris. Don't even try to use your Sangor wiles on me, or Nix will pay. Got it? Now—the prophesy. Let me explain it to you so you understand. I needed to find these people to STOP it. I have a lot invested in what I'm doing. I've worked hard. I plan to succeed. And you both are going to help me. Variant said Elena may be one piece of the puzzle. Is this true, Nix?"

Oh, Chaos. She's put her on the spot. She'll have to say it.

Nix stared at Seraphina with hatred. "Yes. But we don't . . ."

"That is all. Now, Variant went back to the village after you left. He questioned the old man. Unfortunately, Variant is inventive in the way he questions people, and he has to use some rather distasteful methods—" Seraphina reached behind her desk and brought forth Orion's staff. The blue crystal orb on top of it no longer glowed.

Nix's eyes widened, and my heart wrenched as a scream tore from her throat—"No!!"

"Oh—yes," Seraphina   smiled.   Her voice was smug—taunting, "but in the end, Orion let Variant know, Nix, that you are tied to this, and—"

"I'm not!" Nix yelled, "and her skin stayed its normal color. You all think I'm something I'm not. I am not part of this prophecy—whatever it is. I'm just a girl from the Mortal Realm who can't control her powers. All I'm trying to do is learn how not to hurt people—and I can't even do that!" Tears streamed down Nix's face, dripping onto the carpet.

Seraphina paused and stared at Nix thoughtfully. "Given your curse for having to tell the truth—or 'truth will out' with your scarlet color—I can see you truly believe that. Shame. But whether you believe it or not, Nix, I happen to know differently.

Seraphina swiveled her frosty gaze toward me. "And you, Daris. You are a prime part of this as well. So, you see, you have no more secrets to tell me. I have every bit of information I need from you."

As she turned, I noticed two things. The scaly shimmer of her skin that darkened gray for just a second and the momentary change in the shape of her pupils, which had turned to horizontal slits. With a jolt, I realized Seraphina wasn't just a cruel, unimaginative serpent's ass. She was, without a doubt, a Demomancer.

Somehow, she'd managed to disguise herself and cover her scent. Quite well, I might add. I was usually excellent at sniffing the vile things out. But it explained why I found her scent unsettling in the past.

Had she been a Demomancer all this time, or had one replaced her? Were there more than one? I suspected she wasn't alone. A sense of deep dread crept over me. Demomancers in the GOC. How had we let this happen?

The Lupine Guardians came in as if summoned. Again, I was surprised the Lupines hadn't sniffed out the Demomancer—recognized her for who she was. Did I dare let her know that I knew her secret now? Or keep that knowledge for later?

I looked at the guards. They wouldn't believe me if I told them. Best to keep it quiet for now.

Seraphine pointed at us. "Take them to the Magus Guild. Be discreet," she ordered, wiggling her long ring-covered fingers. "Devereux knows what to do with them."

My one consolation was that Seraphina hadn't seemed to notice the change in the color of Nix's eyes.

NIX

TORN

Orion was dead. Seraphina had his staff. Jessamine and Elias were prisoners somewhere. Daris and I were powerless under the magic restraining cuffs, and Cobalt and Nemar were likely somewhere in the mountains.

The Magus Guild loomed ahead in its golden glory, shining like a happy place full of wealth and promise. A brilliant fiery yellow and orange ball of light hovered above the guild—and bright red sparks streaked from it now and then like fancy streamers.

And I was starving. Hunger and a thirst pulsed through me—something far greater than I'd ever known before. My body was changing every second—I felt it. Each step across campus toward the Magus Guild was sheer agony. Pain tore at my abdomen as if it were being ripped in two. I dropped to my knees.

The Lupine beside me prodded me with the tip of a spear to get up. It had some kind of electrical charge that zapped me as if I needed the extra painful incentive to stand.

When I tried to rise and crumpled on the cobblestone, he groaned, picked me up, and threw me over his shoulder. Then, I heard his heartbeat—so strong! I felt like I could almost hear the blood coursing through his veins. His scent was not the best, but I felt my mouth widen, and with speed I did not know I possessed, I curled around him and felt my teeth elongate. They latched onto his neck.

His hair was a minor inconvenience—but sweet heaven—the warmth of the succulent liquid that came from him once my fangs sliced into him was beyond description. It was like I'd been in the driest desert baking under a hot sun for days, and someone had handed me the best ice-cold smoothie in the world. I drank deeply, filling myself—satisfying my need—wanting more—

A blast of magic knocked me away, though too late. I'd drained the Lupine dry, and still, hunger overwhelmed me. The other Lupine next to Daris aimed a razor-edged spear at me, his thick, shaggy hair drooping down between his furrowed brows. He wore the leather armor of Magus Guild gold and red colors on it.

"Down!" he ordered me with a terrible growl. The dude's dog breath was revolting—like he'd eaten a garbage can of shit for breakfast, but underneath that horrible stink was a scent that I knew would satisfy my hunger. I'd smelled better by now, but this would do.

I wiped my hand across my mouth, noting the tremble in the guard's gloved fingers. His heart rate was elevated, galloping like a hundred horses. My eyes flicked to Daris. He stood there calm—unsurprised. His black T-shirt was torn, as were his black jeans. He hadn't been able to snag his jacket, but he still had his all purpose belt. His red eyes leveled at me, unblinking, filled with serious comprehension but also love and understanding. He *knew* what was happening to me.

I launched myself at the other Lupine, heedless of the deadly spear tip aimed at me. I was too fast for the beast to counter my move. Magic cuffs didn't suppress my species' gifts, and having walked through The Eye of Chaos, I had new gifts now.

In moments, the Lupine fell to the ground, its form shriveling back to that of some male creature I'd never seen before. Daris stood in front of me, unlocking my cuffs. He'd fished the key from the Lupine guard's pocket and removed his own cuffs first.

Daris grabbed my head with both of his hands, pressing it between his palms. His eyes fixed on mine.

"Nix—it's very important you listen to me now. You walked through the Eye. You *changed*. You are *Sangor*, now, like me. Understand?"

I didn't really understand—and I didn't feel like what he said was quite right—but I nodded anyway.

Daris pressed his lips together and stared into my eyes with an intensity that made me feel like I was falling. "In the beginning stages of your transformation, you are going to feel an insatiable hunger. You *must* control it, Nix. You must not kill unless absolutely necessary. You can drink from others, then stop and move on. You are what we call a *nacen*—a new Sangor." He let go of my head and tucked a piece of hair behind my ear while maintaining his gaze. "An uncontrolled *nacen* can decimate towns—wipe out all of the people there if left unchecked. You do not want to destroy your friends."

Those words shook me. I swallowed, then dropped to my knees again, my red hair sparking around my face. With nothing to restrain my magic, I'd have to control my fire in addition to my thirst. I was just getting better at the fire control. And now?

"We need to hide the Lupine bodies," Daris, hefting a corpse onto his shoulder. He nodded to the other as if he expected me to do the same, but these were huge and heavy creatures—even when they weren't in Lupine form. He half-smiled at me. "I think you'll find, as a Sangor, you can manage it."

A flash of anger filled me. We'd just traveled back from a different Realm after being attacked by Variant, gone to The Eye of Chaos, where I'd been forever changed into a Sangor, captured at the Guilds of Chaos, and now my body was undergoing this crazy transformation—and he treats what I'm going through like it's yesterday's news! Like, 'Oh yeah, you're a Sangor now—so you've got super speed and can pick up Lupines—or heavy dead bodies, so go get to it . . '

Yeah, danger or no danger, love or no love, I wasn't putting up with that. Sudden pain jolted through me again, but not quite as bad as before, and I worked not to show it. I straightened and then turned toward the Magus Guild. Elena, Jessamine, and Elias needed us. Daris could damn well hide the bodies on his own and join me when he was good and ready. I was not going to put up with being ordered around like that. Not now.

I expected to feel a twinge of guilt at the thought. I didn't.

A vision of the note Elena had found in my burned, tattered clothing the night Daris and others had found me—the note I had no idea where it came from—rose in my mind.

You will See
When You Pass Through the Eye
And Turn for Blood
Eternal Love
Ascend As You
Were Meant to Be

Well, I'd certainly passed through the Eye and "Turn for Blood"—that seemed obvious. And Eternal Love? My mind immediately flew to Daris. His word for me: "*Dazi.*" I thought of our protection bond together. His lips on my neck—I'd never feel that again, would I?

Now, I was a Sangor. In the Mortal Realm, Vampires didn't drink from other Vampires—they were dead or living dead.

Sangors were different,   I   guessed.   I was different. What that entire difference was, I couldn't explain. I realized my body and my spirit were transitioning, phasing to exist on two different planes of reality. I saw wisps of spirits as they swept past me on the cobble path as I sped toward the Magus Guild.

Ascend as You were Meant to Be. The words from the note made no sense. Orion had said I was descended from the Mad Queen. Did it mean something related to that? I knew nothing about Arnexis. Was there even a King and Queen of Arnexis anymore?

It seemed to me like the Guilds of Chaos ran everything. I might have changed dramatically in just a few days, but I realized I still knew next to nothing.

It took only a few moments for Daris to catch up with me as I veered from the Magus Guild path to perch on a crop of rocks nested under some lilac trees near the building. It was, indeed, an impressive Guild. There was an obvious way in through the front gates, and Apprentices entered and exited through the gilded archways studded with jewels and decorated with protective symbols, then there were side entrances I noted—used less frequently. Daris would know this place better than me.

He held up something to my face, and the screen swirled with a misty multicolor. The metallic scent of it was strange. "It's a Celcom. It belonged to one of the Lupines. They won't be needing them. It's imprinting on you. Say your name."

It seemed he wasn't going to be bothered by my ignoring his order to help him. That made me even more irritated. I bet he was chalking it up to female Sangor PMS or a *na-*

cen tantrum (if there were such a thing) instead of his poor manners. But I really wanted the Celcom.

I shrugged. "Nix Emberwind." A gentle flame appeared both inside and just outside the screen. *Cool.*

"Okay," Daris nodded, seeming satisfied. "It's programmed and set to your biometrics. It should be on vibrate. If we separate, to call me just say my name, and we'll connect."

Wouldn't it be magnificent if it were that easy in the Mortal Realm? I thought. I pocketed it and then caught the scent of more people—more blood passing by. My body trembled. I felt my incisors enlarge. I had absolutely no control over it. It was an automatic response.

Daris gripped my arm. "Not here, Nix. Now now. It's a group of Apprentices. *You can't.* You'll kill all of them. Hey. Look at me!"

He forcefully turned my head toward him, but the scent of the Apprentices was nearly unbearable. I felt Daris wrench my hand. "Come, Nix, this way. I'll feed you. Show you how."

If he hadn't been so fast, I would have decimated that group in one fell swoop. He raced toward two Apprentices standing in a wooded area practicing Teragos magic and showed me the proper technique to paralyze them. "Remember when I asked you if you wanted to feel anything? Paralysis stops all pain. It blocks all thoughts. Otherwise, you send your thoughts when you drink—you become one with your prey."

Oh, I remembered. I hungered for that sensation again, but for now, I just wanted to feed.

"Now," Daris said. "Practice a quick sip and release. The release will be hard. You will want to stay—but do not."

I bent over the female Apprentice and swept her long blonde hair away from her neck. Just a sip, I told myself, as I sank my fangs into her and drank, and oh, dear god, she was so—"

"Enough!" Daris barely had the strength to rip me away. I almost took the woman's neck with me. I bared my fangs at him, then stopped, realizing what I was doing—the extent of my reaction. Daris cleared his throat. "That was a poor first effort." He demonstrated how he healed her neck wounds and then put the blonde woman to the side. "Let's try again, shall we?"

We shifted to the male Apprentice. He was larger. I felt encouraged. If I messed this up, at least he had more blood to spare. It was like Daris read my mind. "A sip. A quick drink only, Nix. Practice."

The logical part of me understood, but the wild, new part of me just wanted to break free with abandon and feed like no tomorrow. Then, I remembered Elena. And Elias, Jessamine—and Cobalt and Nemar. Orion was dead, and Variant had killed him. If there was anyone's blood I wanted most, it was his. I realized I wanted control over myself, my capabilities, my life—and I was tired of feeling like I didn't have it.

My whole life had been about feeling out of control—feeling like my fire would explode at any second. Feeling like I was a threat to my family. At the trial, I'd discovered I'd killed my own family. I'd been whisked away on a prophesy quest because of Seraphina. Discovered a part of my soul was missing and then reunited with it, though I had no idea what I was doing.

When I'd gone through The Eye of Chaos, that had been my choice. Becoming a Sangor was not—still I knew there were no guarantees what I would become. It helped to know that no one really knew what they'd become when they stepped through The Eye of Chaos.

I thought of the vision I'd seen on the mountain of the Mad Queen and her closest Sangor friend. I realized he likely wasn't just her friend and that Sangor genes ran through me too—they were part of my makeup. I wondered if that was part of what attracted me so much to Daris and him to me.

"I got this," I growled, and I sank my teeth into the warm neck of the Apprentice. Again, as his blood flowed into my mouth and my body—the flavor of it so much better than Lupine—sweeter. I found it a monumental feat to yank myself away, but just as I felt Daris's hand on my shoulder, I did it.

"Better," he said. "But you need to be faster. Now try the healing." As he talked me through it, he explained that blood made our magic stronger. "Good." He seemed satisfied with my healing result. It needed to be faster too, but he said that came with time and practice. "Now, we make them forget what happened."

"How do we do that?"

"With your Sangor seduction voice. It takes practice as well. Just listen as I use it on these Apprentices." His voice was smooth, low-toned, and silky—hypnotic—as he told the Apprentices that they were practicing Teragos magic and accidentally knocked each other out. "Now, back to Magus Guild, and let's find our way in before Seraphina realizes we never made it there."

We returned to the rocks and the group of trees where we had been. The sun was starting to dip toward the horizon, and night would soon cover the campus. A sudden thought occurred to me: "Daris, did you ever use your Sangor voice on me?"

DARIS

TAKE OUT

Rather than risk turning scarlet in front of my *na-cen dazi,* I elected the element of distraction instead. "We don't really need a way to get inside, Nix. We already have one." Of course now that we didn't have the magic restraining cuffs on, I had Guildmaster privileges. I could simply portal us inside the Magus Guild. I took Nix's hand.

Nix raised an eyebrow as I motioned with my fingers. The mists swirled around us, and—nothing. I tried once more. Again, the mists swirled—, but that was it. The mists fizzled and died around us.

"And what was supposed to happen?" Nix tilted her head at me quizzically in a manner I might have found cute, except that I didn't at this very moment. My fangs snapped out as I growled in irritation, and I had to pull them back in quickly. Nix pressed her lips together.

I'd never had my Guildmaster portal spell fail before. But if Seraphina was on some kind of wild takeover, she could have placed a ward over the Guild—something that allowed only certain spells to get through or something that kept certain spells out. I stared at Nix thoughtfully and remembered her Blaze Ceremony.

"Nix, when you portaled here, and when you left the Blaze Ceremony, you used a spell," I held onto her hands. "Do you know if you can carry a passenger or not?"

She shook her head. "All I got from my dad was the note about the Guilds of Chaos, the Skia Guild, and the spell, which I memorized. And I can't guarantee where it will take me if I haven't been there before. I think I was lucky the first time. I've never been inside the Magus Guild. I could put us in a closet or Deveraeux's office—I have no clue."

Damn. Not that, then.

Trying to use Nix was too risky. We'd have to rely on our speed then and hope there weren't any Sangors I didn't know about on the Magus side. I wondered how deep this conspiracy ran.

The two Sangors I knew who were recent Magus Apprentices had graduated last year and gone to work in governing positions. Others I knew were in various positions in the Queen's Guard, Oscuro Guild's Secret Operations (which was humorous to say because all of their operations were secret), or Bellator Guild as top warriors. Most of us knew each other—or learned to know each other. For many reasons, we were a rare species. My bet was there'd be none inside. I tried to think of who else would be inside.

"Okay, Nix. Here's what we are going to do. The upper levels of the Magus Guild building housed the Apprentices, and the ground levels were where the common areas and classrooms were, generally, for beginners—like our Skia Guild—right? Younger Apprentices would be none-the-wiser about what was going on."

Nix nodded, but with all of her new Sangor senses, I could tell she was getting distracted. I grabbed her chin and forced her to look at me.

"Stay with me, Nix. Now—Elena, Elias, and Jessamine will be in the Magus Guild caverns below ground. The Guilds of Chaos has a deep underground network of tunnels and chambers under each Guild, with passageways connecting them in secret ways. Usually, only Guildmasters, Magisars, and higher-level Apprentices know how to get through these passageways—"

"We can't use those to get in?" Nix jittered her heel impatiently. A breeze kicked up, and a pair of Apprentices passed by, chattering about a magical metallurgy and its ethical practices in different Realms. Nix's eyes followed them. Saliva dripped from her mouth.

I shook my head, bringing her face back to look at mine gently with my hand. "They'll have the same wards on them, like what's keeping me from portaling into the Guild. Seraphina and Devereux would have thought of that already. The back entrance is open right now, and Apprentices are still coming and going, but—like every Guild—the Magus Guild requires each visiting Apprentice to have Guild amulets for the late evening hours, or the gargoyles will sound the alarm."

I was starting to see that *nacen* wild look in Nix's eyes. I needed to find her some blood to snack on before she outright killed herself. And it was dark now. We couldn't wait any longer. We had to get inside.

I pointed to the back of the Magus Guild. "Follow me." On the way, I carefully grabbed up a mound of Gargoyle shit.

Hoping desperately we wouldn't run out of time, I motioned Nix to the Pegasus stables. This was part of a plan I desperately hoped would work. The intricately carved and quite large stables would help to hide us, and Nix could snack on a Pegasus. Of course, Pegasus blood had psychoactive properties, but if we could manage not to upset a mare and not get caught by a Meta (someone who could change into a Pegasus), then it would help Nix for the moment.

I did not bother explaining how the Pegasus's blood would make her feel. There was no time, really. I brought her to a gentle mare I was sure wasn't a Meta (they smell very different)—and asked the mare for permission. She eyed Nix dubiously and flicked her long purple and pink mane in the air. I said I'd heal her—no worries. That Nix was new. The mare tilted her head, swished her purple and pink tail, and nodded. She seemed used to Apprentices. Maybe she'd even fed the Sangors who recently left, though I'd never seen this one before. She bared her neck.

Upon the assent, Nix suddenly launched forward and clamped onto the beautiful creature's neck with crazy fury. She looked like a wild beast attacking the poor creature.

"Nix! No!" But there was no stopping her.

Thankfully, the creature was paralyzed, standing upright, but I had to bite her too, on the other side, to inject some extra paralysis venom and to merge my mind with Nix.

"STOP, Nix. Stop now. You are killing her."

"She's so good—so good, Daris. Amazing!"

"You MUST stop, Nix. She'll die. Elena will die. Elias will die. Everyone we are trying to save will die." I felt her fight herself. I felt her reluctance. Finally, just when I was afraid I'd have. to rip her away, I felt her withdraw. I healed the wounds, which were quite extensive.

Wrapping her arms around the mare's head, she nuzzled against the girl. "Thank you. That was wonderful. You are wonderful. Thank you, Thank you Jimson-Bee!"

"What did you just call her?" My stomach lurched, and I had a very sick feeling overcome me. I could not have heard what I'd just heard. "Why   did   you   call her that?" Chaos crickets started singing, their voices filling the air.

"When I was feeding on her. We talked. She told me she didn't mind talking. She told me her name was Jimson-Bee and that she belonged to—"

"—the Queen," I finished. The Queen was here. Every particle in my body, in this plane and the other, told me this was not good. The Queen was very old. She never went anywhere but stayed in the palace for safety. Nix had no idea. She was busy loving on Jimson-Bee and giving her kisses.

It is very difficult to make a Pegasus forget a Sangor feeding. This is generally because the Sangor, having just fed on the Pegasus, is under such an elevated, ecstatic state that they can't do it properly. I wouldn't have been able to do it if I'd had more than a few sips of the mare's blood, and oh, dear Celestials, how I wanted more.

In this case, I still asked Jimson-Bee for her permission. The majestic creature deserved a choice since she'd bonded a bit to the *nacen* Sangor. Surprisingly, she would not allow it and preferred to keep the memory.

The Pegasus stable was near a field, which let us call the Grigons, Nemar and Cobalt. I wasn't sure they'd hear us, not knowing how far a mental call traveled, but they must have been nearby because in moments, they swooped down and landed—Cobalt following Nemar's lead, since Nix wasn't thinking straight. I pictured in my head what I wanted Nemar and Cobalt to do and showed him the gargoyle droppings.

I wasn't sure any of this would work. Orion had only explained how to call Nemar. He hadn't explained the depth of the bond. But I sensed, somehow, that this would work. To what extent, I didn't know.

It's very explosive if you can manage to send a fireball or electric jolt after it—I sent my thoughts to him. *Be careful, but gather as much as you can and drop it there.*

I pointed out where we needed it to hit on Magus Guild. Nemar and Cobalt both grunted and flew off into the night sky. I had to hope they could see in the dark and didn't get blown up.

The next was imperative, and I only hoped it would work. I pressed a button on my belt, retrieving pen and paper. I penned a note to Interim Skia Guildmaster since I had no idea who had stepped up now that Hemere was dead, and Seraphina never answered me when I made my recommendation.

I advised them of the Demomancer presence and made a call for help in the Magus Guild Underground. I ensured that only a Skia Guildmaster properly assigned, or their second, could read it. Then, I folded the paper into the shape of a bird, blew a life-direction spell into it, and sent it on its mission.

As I watched the paper bird fly away into the dark, I realized it was a desperate attempt. Nix and I might very well be on our own on this venture, which meant we'd likely fail. But we had to try. My sister, Elias, and Jessamine were in there, and this all had to do with something big that Seraphina was planning—something that included Arnexis, the Queen, and the prophecy.

Now that Nix had practiced on Terra Guild Apprentices, it was time to practice with Magus Guild Apprentices. She wasn't as hungry, but she wasn't exactly stable either. I was going to try to explain it anyway. I sat her down on a crate next to some fresh pears the beautiful creatures were munching on.

"Nix, listen. I know you're feeling stellar, right? But now, we have to get into the Magus Guild to save our friends. Remember Elena? Elias and Jessamine? Variant and Devereux are probably there—they could be hurting them right now."

Nix seemed to sober and focus for a second. "Oh—right. We can't have THAT." Then, she giggled and snorted.

Holy Celestials. Her hands sparked with fire, the little flares arching like flaming rainbows to the ground. We couldn't have *that* either.

"This is serious, Nix." I really wished sobering spells worked on those of us who drank Pegasus and Unicorn blood, but they did not. "If we both can manage to 'sip' blood from Magus Apprentices and gather some strands of their hair to wear as we make our way to the lower levels, then technically, we'll pass for Magus Guild members after hours. We'll have to remember to do it every fifteen minutes or so." I'd tried it on several occasions before I became a Guildmaster. What I didn't know was exactly how long it would work. "And you're going to have to keep your hands under control."

She looked down at them. Her index finger was burning, and her sparks were getting awfully close to the straw and the Jimson-Bee started to look anxious. I prayed the creature was smart enough not to flap her wings, or we would definitely have a fire. Instead, she pawed the ground and whinnied nervously, looking toward the Magus Guild. She was right. Giddy Nix or not, we had to go. I suddenly had an idea. It wasn't perfect, but it would do. I pictured the items in my head, my eyes roving over Nix's hands, and I spoke the summoning words.

Praise Chaos, I think I did a fair job.

"What are those?" Nix's eyes widened as she looked at what was in my hands. The muddled lump was quite an unattractive brown-orange color and had a very unappealing smell. The wind was picking up, and there was no more time to waste.

"Gloves," I said. "They're used to gather explosive items, things that are hot or fiery as well." I shoved them on her hands and used a shrink spell. "I hope this works," I muttered.

"Wait. You just put gargoyle shit-gathering gloves on my hands? Is that what those are?" Nix wrinkled her nose.

I grabbed her face. I shouldn't have. Despite the gloves, with her new Sangor smell, something about her—she smelled more enticing than ever. I wanted so desperately to kiss those lips, to . . . I stopped myself and focused. "Nix—remember Elena. Elias. Jessamine. We need to go. Now."

Thankfully, she sobered. For the moment, the sparks seemed contained.

The back entrance to the Magus Guild was well-lit. Not some shadowy affair like you'd expect a back entrance to be, no—the Magus Guild made a production out of everything. Its double doors blazed with golden lights outside, and jewels studded the archways along with the intricate symbols similar to what decorated the front. The only benefit of this entrance was that it was used less frequently because it was inconvenient, and fewer Apprentices tended to travel through it at night. There were a lot more Incitors positioned here after eleven.

Nix and I dashed to a fairy willow. Its leaves, each a different pastel color, were shaped like fairy wings, hanging from long, fine tendrils that waved in the wind.

"When the doors open again, we are going to sprint in and bank to the left," I said to Nix. "You'll see a set of stairs that go down. Take those to the next floor, then go left, and you'll find a place under the stairs—a small alcove. We'll meet there."

Nix was quiet, which worried me, but the doors started to open as a group of Apprentices entered. "Oh, by the love of Chaos—" I took a deep breath and I sprinted. I chanced a look back. Nix was gone. I didn't see her in front of me either.

I prayed to all the Celestials as I sped through the doors past the Apprentices, grabbing a sip from one of them, as well as a tendril of hair, as I went through and banked to the left. From there, I catapulted to the small alcove and stared in shock. Nix was pocketing some hair she'd just taken off two young Apprentices, their bodies sitting neatly back-to-back. The gloves I'd painstakingly summoned for her lay discarded on the ground, and I watched as she wiped the blood from her face.

"I really did   try   the   sip   thing," she moaned, "but there were two of them, and they struggled. I don't think I did it right, but they were tasty." She smiled apologetically. "I did try to stop in time . . . "

NIX

SKY FALL

What the hell was the matter with me? It was like I was watching one side of myself I couldn't control have a party while the other side was powerless to do anything about it. I felt like I was in the passenger seat with a drunk driver swerving on the road going a hundred miles an hour, trying to tell the driver to pull over, but the driver wouldn't listen.

And there was Daris, looking at me like I'd lost my mind. And I had. But man, that Pegasus blood—that stuff was no joke. Their necks should come with a warning label.

Anger flared inside me because Daris had to know this would happen. I guess he thought this was better than me going on a full Sangor rampage inside the Magus Guild, but I wasn't so sure. Still, the effects seemed to be wearing off. If I could just get the muddle out of my brain and think more clearly.

What was he saying now? I gazed down at the two Apprentices I'd only meant to 'sip' or 'snack' on so I'd have some Magus Guild Apprentice blood in me.

" . . . pulses are weak, but they'll live. They won't die. It wasn't a cosmic solo venture, but it was not bad, especially given the circumstances. And you did a good healing job. Now, let's get going."

What? Praise from the Magisar? Guildmaster Ravencroft provides approval? *Yay,* I thought.

I shook my brain. Again, I had to remind myself: Elena, Elias, and Jessamine. This is what we were here for. But Daris—he looked so good, even with his messy hair and haggard face . . .

Daris grabbed my arm. "Nix, listen. We have two more levels to descend before we get to the Magus Guild Underground—the part of the GOC Underground. From there, we'll have to use our keen senses to find out where they have Elena and our friends. Do you understand?"

I nodded, remembering he'd called Nemar and I'd called Cobalt. I was betting we'd need them soon, and I said so.

He nodded. "Once we reach the Underground gate."

I was slowly beginning to realize that we were actually inside the Magus Guild. I glanced around. Damn, this place was bright. Downright opulent.

The gold and red Guild colors abounded. Red velvet seats with gold trim, crystal glasses—it was a building dedicated to opulence. I zipped behind Daris as we descended the next two flights of stairs, and thankfully the alcove under the stairs there was vacant.

Daris peered down, and we both realized he still had his belt. So did I. They'd forgotten to confiscate them when they took us to Seraphina. Maybe they didn't even realize what they were—but Daris and I had our belts.

Unfortunately,   I had no   idea   what was in mine. Only Elena did. If I pressed a button, I got a surprise. I told Daris as much, and he grimaced.

"Well, I've got weapons. That's something. And we have magic and a few more things that might help. So, let's find that door and call for a little distraction."

Finding the door ended up not being pleasant. When we got close, Daris gave the signal to stop.

The door was made of thick black iron, and many intricate latches and locks that held it closed. Guarding it were several Lupines, well known for their keen sense of smell.

"You still got those gloves?" Daris asked.

"Unfortunately, yes," I answered and handed them over.

He took one glove, rubbed it all over himself, and motioned for me to do the same.

"You gotta be kidding me." I wanted to hurl. With my heightened Sangor sense of smell, I could barely take it.

He shook his head. "Trust me," he said. "It could be worse. Cover yourself good. Even your face and hair."

I nearly gagged and held my breath. I'm not a girly girl, but gargoyle shit gloves all over my face—I really tried not to think about it much less breathe while I did it. We rubbed each other's backs, then sent thoughts to Nemar and Cobalt to literally let shit fly.

I hoped the explosions would work—that the doors would open, and someone would come through so we could zip in. Otherwise we wouldn't have a fireball's chance in a snowstorm of getting through that gate.

We waited.

A Lupine Guardian with a snaggle tooth sniffed. "Something stinks, dudes. Ugh. Who didn't take a bath!" He pushed another one next to him who was unkempt, and probably needed two baths.

"No, man, I think it's Goyle shit. But stuff shouldn't be down here. Maybe I should check it out—"

"You heard the Great Grandmaster. She said not to leave the gate unless we smelled intruders. That's Goyle shit, or it's your breath. We stay here."

The messy Lupine tried to straighten his red and gold leather uniform and push back his hair, but it only fell back into his eyes. "But—"

<<BOOM!!>> The Magus Guild walls shook.

Both of the Lupine's eyes went wide, and they gaped at each other. More Lupines rushed to their spot.

"What's going on?" One of them cried out.

<<BOOM>>!! The Guild walls shook again.

The hinges of the black gate creaked loudly, and latches and locks clacked as they started to open.

<<BOOM!!>> <<BOOM!!>>

Wow, I thought, *Cobalt and Nemar are not going half-assed.* I didn't know if it would do any good, but I mentally sent Cobalt a message to stop after two more, then they needed to disappear so they could be safe. The gates were opening.

The doors started to swing open. Daris and I positioned ourselves like sprinters. I was finally feeling like my old self, except that Lupine blood was starting to smell good.

Control, Nix, I told myself. *Control.*

When the doors fully opened, over twenty Lupines poured out along with other species in Magus Guild guard uniforms. One was Grasha, but I wasn't familiar with them all.

Daris looked at them sideways, and I had the feeling he wasn't telling me something. I also noticed my sense of smell was changing. Some of the species smelled different from the others. Some caused the hairs to rise on the back of my neck, similar to how they did when I was with Seraphina. I wondered why.

"Get ready," Daris whispered, and his fingers ran along the back of my hand. I felt a warm thrill go through me and thought, second to blood, there was one thing I'd really like right now, and that was to be alone with this amazing man. That thought was sadly dashed to pieces with his next word—

"Go!"

DARIS

Uninvited

Nemar and Cobalt had come through, and somehow, we'd made it to the Underground of the Magus Guild. Nix's Pegasus blood trip seemed to have worn off, and so far, she wasn't blazing with fires of fury from her hands (or anything else), and we were through the complex Black Gate!

Now, all we had to do was find Elena, Elias, and Jessamine, escape without being caught, expose Seraphina for the evil Demomancer that she was, and save the Guilds of Chaos and the Arnexis Realm. Then, the mugs of blood were on me at the Oneg Run blood bar.

Thinking of the place made my thoughts drift to Hemere and how Variant had killed him. Rage filled me, a burning desire for vengeance consuming my mind. I wanted that bastard. I wanted to make him pay for all he'd done. For the killing, but especially for killing my friend Hemere, for killing Orion, and for hurting my sister.

And she better be alive, Variant or your death will not be as quick as those you dealt out. This I swear.

I was not a malicious man, but I believed in justice. And justice meant a person received the punishment they deserved. One that fits the crime—or series of crimes. Did I have the right to make that call? Damn right, I did.

I felt Nix with me. Now that the Pegasus blood effect had worn off and her transition seemed more or less complete, it felt as if we resonated together. We were Sangor together, like a Vamsat, a sacred Sangor family. I felt in touch with her almost as closely as if I were sinking into her neck, drinking her. I pushed the thought away, feeling myself getting aroused, and this was not the time for that.

I sniffed the air and caught her doing the same. Good. She was tapping into that sense, too. We zipped behind some stone walls, the low levels of magic light casting a soft glow around the room.

This entranceway was expansive, and several species of guards were still arriving from different corridors. There were three main directions: straight ahead, left, and right. I caught Elena's scent from a guard who came from a corridor on the left. Nix nodded that way as well.

As soon as the guards were running off and there seemed to be a break in the numbers exiting, we dashed around the corner, hoping to find the next place for concealment. But the corridor was long, its length stretching out before us like an endless tunnel. I realized this corridor may actually travel toward the mountains. I couldn't imagine it going that far, but I'd never been down here before. We sped ahead, passing by four guards who didn't see us. I stopped to sip. Nix didn't chance it.

We passed by two Grashas. I didn't see any other guards. I stopped her and made her feed. I took a moment for a lesson.

"Look," I showed her, "you won't smell it at first because somehow they've managed to cover their scent, but see the gray shimmer?" I turned their heads while they were para-lyzed. "See their pupils?"

"What are they?" she whispered; her voice barely audible.

"Demomancers," I said, pressing my lips togeth-er. "And one of the worst meals you'll ever have to survive on if you have to. Now, drink. You might as well find out now what you're in for." I watched her face, and to her credit, she didn't spit or vomit.

For the first three days, a *nacen* will pretty much drink anything anyway—their hunger is that para-mount. But Nix's body shuddered in obvious revulsion. I shared in the drink, so she understood this wasn't a hazing but a true lesson in survival.

Before we began sprinting again, I gripped her arm and stared hard at her, my eyes locked with hers. "Nix, Seraphina is a Demomancer. They are a species that wants to destroy the Guilds of Chaos and allow all dark magic to take over the Realms. They want everyone to believe they desire ultimate liberation in magic but make no mistake—what they want is ultimate control over all living beings."

Her eyes widened at this news. I heard her heartbeat race faster as we launched ourselves along the corridor in search of Elena. There was so much I wished I had time to prepare her for, but she'd have to learn it as we engaged. It wasn't fair. But that was the nature of Chaos.

After a few more moments, the corridor opened up into a large domed room. I thought it had to be under part of the nearest east hills, perhaps just before the mountains. Several corridors broke off here.

One turn to the left was larger, and I sensed that this was the direction we needed to go. The passage descended downward, the stone walls transitioning into a silver, glittering substance I was not familiar with. Glowing orbs of bright blue lit the way, very different than the Magus Guild colors of gold and red.

The path was no longer stone but white, smooth, and polished, though not slick.

We stopped short of a large archway, an entrance into another room. Nix and I peered inside. A vast domed room lined with glistening ice appeared before us. Along the walls were several magic-infused iron cells, frosty cold.

Iron was particularly good at holding magic spells, and I detected the aura of magic around them. This had to be Seraphina's doing. She was the mistress of subzero temperatures.

I scanned the vast room, and my eyes were drawn to one cell on the second level in particular. I heard a moan. Elena! It had to be her.

Nix gripped my arm, the heat of her hand grabbing my attention as I noted a few sparks dripping from it. I looked into her deep, reddening irises. She jutted her chin forward.

Demomancers. In their natural state. They looked very close to Arnexin but for the gray shimmer of their skin and their eyes.

I inhaled. And there it was. That characteristic Demomancer scent. So, they'd found a way to mask it, but temporarily. I wondered how and for how long.

I counted four Demomancers on the ground floor and spied two more on the next level. I pressed a button on my belt, silently drawing my sword, Dragnot. Nix was unarmed, and she had no official weapons training that I knew of, but she had her fire. And I'd seen her take a fighting stance with that Incitor. I hadn't had a chance to ask her, but I was willing to bet she'd had some form of battle training. She'd taken down those two Magus Guild Apprentices in the alcove without a problem.

"Now or never," I hissed. "Let's be fast and take them out. Demomancers have different powers, Nix. Be careful. Be fast. Now is the time to use your flames."

We both took in a deep breath and raced in. I quickly dispatched two Demomancers with Sangor speed, slicing through their necks and ensuring their deaths.

Nix sped in and ripped out the neck of one with her teeth, and the vile taste of Demomancer's blood was enough to make her pull back. She blasted it with fire, but she was attacked by the other as it paralyzed her with a magic spell and moved in for the kill. This allowed me enough time to move behind it and slice its neck as well.

The two Demomancers above hurled magic bolts at us: one of thick black lightning and another of a dark, foggy goo that I suspected would be bad for our health if we were struck.

"Dive!" I instructed Nix, and we both dodged the magic missiles just in time. Nix's reflexes were beautiful because no sooner had we come to our knees than she aimed at them and blasted a fireball so powerful from her palms it looked like a comet.

Her fire obliterated one Demomancer, turning it to ash. The other was severely burned on one side. It crumpled near Elena's cell but rose up to cast another magic bolt with one hand.

"Break!" I directed Nix, pointing to a set of stone stairs. I ran for the other set on the far side. The Demomancer's magic bolt missed us, although flying rocks struck me as I dashed up the opposing stairs on the other side. I closed in on the creature, but Nix was already there, advancing on it.

Damn, how had she become so fast? The Demomancer was on its knees, its burns clearly causing it difficulty breathing, and it was probably in a great deal of pain. I saw no remorse, no surrender, no request for mercy in its eyes. Its horizontal pupils flicked from Nix to me.

"Your sister is as good as dead, and so are you!" it spat. "You'll never get your sister out of that cell without Demomancer magic. The prophecy will not be fulfilled. Long live the Infinite!" With that, the Demomancer uttered words beyond my understanding, and as I prepared to move in to slice its throat, it pressed its hand to its chest. A sick green glow grew brighter and brighter . . .

"Get back!" I   screamed   at   Nix.   Not   trusting that she heard me, I hurtled myself toward her, catching only thin air. She was already gone as a loud explosion rocked the cavern.

The walkway crumbled, and I tumbled with the stones and mortar to the ground. Nix was there in a flash, tossing stone off me and pulling me up. My left arm was broken. To heal properly, I needed blood. Nix was my Prime, but now she was a Sangor. I'd just have to make do.

There was a loud clang above us, and then a figure dropped down, dangling from an iron chain hanging over the crumbled walkway, where the magic-infused iron cell door now stood open. Elena!

"So, is this what you're looking for?" The taunting voice above us was chillingly familiar. "She's quite dull. Unremarkable, too talkative about unimportant things, and not talkative enough about what I need to know. But none of that matters now that you're here."

NIX

EVOLUTION

My friend Elena was suspended in iron chains, a cluster of icicles around her chained neck. Her arms were yoked across her back. Her legs were tied together, and every inch of her skin was bruised as if she'd been beaten all over and hard.

Her face was the worst of all.

One of her eyes was swollen shut. Her other was barely open; I didn't know if she could even see us, but I could tell she was conscious from the breaths puffing like ghosts from her bloodied lips. One of her cheeks dripped red, too, and her throat was inked the same color, like she'd been stressing against the chain collar.

Variant stood in front of her, twirling his blades. He cocked his head, and a sharp smile cut across his face. "Nothing to say?"

I would have blasted him, except that he stood right above Elena, and I didn't want to hurt her. I stared at her chains. Magic-infused iron.

I didn't know anything about it. The Demomancer said only Demomancer magic could neutralize it. So, how could I even help Elena? Certainly Variant had to have a way. He did not seem to be a Demomancer. Only a traitor.

I watched Daris's eyes flash with fury. In seconds, he'd rushed up to meet Variant, his sword drawn. I cringed, suspecting his left arm was damaged by the way it hung. He probably had broken bones.

As a Sangor, he healed quickly, but he'd heal faster with blood, and he wouldn't have any unless he could score with Variant. I readied to try to save Elena at least, but felt the sharp tip of something at my back.

"I wouldn't move if I were you," came the goaty voice of Devereux. "I am very fast with my blade, and this tip is poisoned. One wrong move, and you'll be dead."

I smelled two Lupine Guardians with him, heard their heavy breathing, and berated myself for not hearing them as they came in. I'd let myself get distracted. I did know one thing. If Devereux wanted me dead, I'd be dead already, so he wanted me alive. He wasn't going to kill me.

I tried to think very quickly about how to get out of this. The last thing I needed was another set of magic restraining cuffs. If those got slapped on me again, Daris and I—Elena, Elias, and Jessamine—wherever they were—we'd all be doomed.

Apparlusio, a voice whispered to me. I tried not to turn my head. The voice was inside my head, I realized a second later.

But yes, I had Apparlusio power. I had the ability to conjure illusion. I just hadn't used it since the Blaze Ceremony. How could I use it now?

Devereux did not want me to move. Could I create something that quickly? I concentrated. I imagined an image of myself outside of myself—just like myself—and gave it form.

Devereux gasped and stepped back for just an instant, and then two Lupine Guardians reached for my wrists but grabbed my apparition instead as I dashed away. I sprinted to the right, whirled, hooked one Lupine by the neck, and quickly drained most of him, gaining energy. The other I blasted with a ball of fire. My eyes widened as I glanced around. Devereux was gone.

I didn't waste time searching for him as Daris continued to battle Variant. Variant wasn't so lucky now that Daris wasn't under the influence of any drug, and though Daris was injured, he was fast. As I dashed up the side, I glanced into a cell and caught sight of two figures. Elias and Jessamine! They were pretty beat up, but they weren't in the iron chains that Elena wore. Only inhibited by the magic-infused iron cell itself.

Daris seemed to be holding his own against Variant. He had speed, but Variant was a chameleon and could easily disappear, making himself hard to see.

If I could free these two—we'd have extra hands. But I couldn't break through the iron. Still, the stone around the iron was not infused with magic. Could my fires burn hot enough?

"Elias! Jessamine!" I called out. They were both at the iron cell door but unable to grip it. Even touching it elicited pain.

"Sparks! Don't touch the door," Elias warned.

"Hey, Golden Boy," I said with a wink. He returned a weak smile. His blond hair lacked the golden luster I'd seen before, and he, like we all, needed a good cleansing. "Stand back, you two. I can't do much for the iron, but I'm going to give it a go on the stone."

Elias and Jessamine both cocked their heads, pressed their lips together, raised their eyebrows and backed away to a far corner of the cell. I pushed my palms against the stones beside the magic-infused iron door and let my fire go. Yellow. Orange. Blue. Then darkest blue.

The rock heated until it glowed, and I felt it melt beneath my hands. I pressed harder until I had a hole in the cell big enough for them both to fit through. It took seconds.

With an opening to the outside, Elias and Jessamine were able to make their way through the hole very carefully. Though they weren't in magic-infused iron cuffs, they still wore magic inhibitor cuffs. Lucky for me, I'd snatched a key off one of the Lupines. I unlocked and freed them.

Elias immediately gave me a quick embrace. "Where's Elena?"

I pointed to where she hung. "We've got to free here. But only Demomancer magic can do it. Daris is fighting Variant—" I caught Daris's eye for just a second. I heard him yell out.

"Nix! The gloves! Gargoyle droppings might neutralize the effects and let you touch a key! The Demomancer bodies!"

I didn't know what he meant for a second, but then it made sense. I grabbed Elias's arm. "Elias, there are two dead Demomancer bodies down there. Take these gloves," I pulled out the disgusting gargoyle shit-gathering gloves Daris was having me wear—the ones we used to cover our scent—and handed them to him. "They're used for . . ."

Elias nodded vigorously. "I got it! If I can find a key to Elena's locks, I can touch it with these, and unlock her chains!"

I didn't have time to say anything more. The golden-haired boy was off and running. I turned to find Jessamine. She was pale and gaunt, her skin a darker blue than I'd ever seen it. Jessamine took time to give me a big hug. "Glad to see you, Fireball," she said and winked at me.

Elias returned, brandishing a long iron key that glowed and shimmered. "Got a key. Hope it's the right one." He placed it down near the cell and gripped the chain holding Elena. I tried to think of what I could do to help him. I couldn't touch the metal.

Cielo, a voice whispered in my head. Yes, I could try my air power. I'd tried that before in Zeleel, but I'd overdone it.

I didn't want to hurt anyone, but time was of the essence here—I felt it. I raced down the stairs and positioned myself below Elena as Elias strained to pull her up.

I pictured clouds—white, puffy clouds—soft, full. I turned them into a rectangular elevator platform and positioned them beneath Elena's feet, making them denser and imagining them pushing up. Doubt crept into my mind.

What if this was stupid? Had no one taught this to me? I hadn't learned how to use my Cielo powers yet. Then my eyes traveled to my friend's broken face, her body bruised and beaten. Anger flared inside me.

Air. Wind. I pressed into my mind. I didn't want fire now. I reformed the platform beneath Elena's feet, solidified it, and pushed with air, with wind, and my own breath caught as she moved. She paused. Because my concentration broke.

I focused again. *Air. Wind.* This time, I doubled down.

As Elena's body rose, Elias pulled, and in moments, we had her on the part of the walkway that had not been blasted away. Elias grabbed the key. It fit into the locks of her shackles, and she was free.

Elias took her into his arms and held her close. I was surprised at how closely he held her. We lifted her away and put her gently to the side, each of us performing what healing magic we knew and were able to help her for the moment. It was enough that she could move—then she could stand.

I hugged her gently. "I missed you, El," I whispered into her ear.

She drew back and gazed at me with pained yet curious eyes. She raised her eyebrows. "It seems I have some catching up to do."

"Time enough for that later," I called out to every-one, "Now, let's help Daris and get out of here!"

"Oh, I don't think anyone is going anywhere." The room shook as the booming voice echoed around, and the temperature started to plummet. My breath frosted in front of me, and I started to shiver.

We looked down. Seraphina—the Grand Guildmaster—stood there glittering and covered with a sheen of ice, with Devereux by her side and a mass of Lupine and other guards. She seemed to be right.

"Well, crap," growled, Jessamine. "Someone forgot to scrub the guest list."

I couldn't fully comprehend what happened next, but Jessamine was beside me, and I grasped her arm, words tumbling from my mouth without conscious thought. "*Don't despair. Battle on and engage. Aid comes to you in your greatest need, for your written wings were read and answered. Fight! Fight! Fight!*" I bellowed the last words like a battle cry awakening within me, my hand raising as I hurled a violent fireball toward Seraphina, unleashing my power.

Seraphina's team scattered, and the temperature drop faltered. I glanced over to find Elias transforming into a monstrous green lizard—large, with long teeth protruding from his jaws. He leapt towards Daris and Variant. Then, Variant was running—escaping Daris, disappearing somehow. Daris bore several wounds, and both he and Elias wore snarling faces.

Seraphina's guards headed for the stairs, and I hurled more fire. "Daris! Help is on the way!" I yelled, unsure if he heard me amid the chaos as he and Elias fought off the oncoming guards.

My primary concern was Elena. She was still weak, a perfect target for Seraphina. How would I protect her? Jessamine touched my shoulder.

"It's my turn to join the battle, Fireball. I'm a Shadow-Elsh, but also a Meta. My transformations can be quite—large. You might want to move away."

I stepped back into the magic iron-infused cell, bringing Elena with me as Jessamine transformed, and I marveled at her enormity. She became a massive beast of snow and ice, her diamond crystal skin impenetrably hard. She had massive tusks and horns protruding from her head, nearly touching the ceiling, And her hooves seemed razor-sharp. Jessamine bellowed, and the rest of the team backed off.

All except Devereux. I exited the cell and prepared to fight, glancing back to check on Elena. But she had vanished. My heart raced until I noticed a small mouse skittering down the stairs. I stared in horror as it positioned itself beside the colossal Jessamine beast and then grew into an identical diamond crystal-skinned monster form. Elena's enormous tusks swooshed in the air—and she rubbed up against Jessamine as if to say, "I will not let you do this alone."

Devereux was dressed in his finery—the same slithery snake suit he'd worn to my trial. The day I'd gone through my Blaze Ceremony—the day I discovered I'd killed my parents. The snakes on his shirt seemed particularly active; even from this distance, I could see them move.

"You seem to have forced my hand, my beauties," he sighed, remaining just out of Jessamine and Elena's reach. "Your great forms throw such a lovely, BIG shadow on the floor, don't you think?" Then Devereux changed ever so slightly, his horns receding, his fur turning to scales, his eyes morphing into vertical slits like those of a serpent. Fangs protruded from his mouth. "I must admit, it has been such a long time since I've had a satisfactory meal. The ones that Variant has given me have been far and few between."

Daris yelled out in rage, and just then, a small dart hit him in the neck. I heard it first, then spied it on his skin. It had to be from Variant, hidden somewhere. He'd taken advantage of Daris once more.

Elias quickly shifted into a stocky bronze creature with a snout and armored plates for skin. Daris dropped to the ground, not dead, but limp. I was in shock. How was aid coming? Where was it?

Elias ran to his side of the stairs and battled the guards pounding up them. I ran to my side, blasting my attackers with whips of fire, trying to keep them at bay while watching the scene unfold in horror, fearing I could not stop what was happening to Jessamine and Elena. I didn't know what Devereux was about to do, but something deep within me knew that something terrible was imminent.

Jessamine and Elena bellowed and roared, striking out toward Devereux with their hooves and horns but missing him as he slid back into an area too narrow for them to reach. Devereux held out his arms—stretching his fingers forward, but it was not his hands that acted. It was the shadows beneath them. The shadows of his hands and fingers lengthened and grew, widening until they became serpentine things themselves. Jessamine and Elena stomped at the shadows, but the tips of the shadow fingers split and became fangs, each set curling and biting where they stamped. Their beast forms howled in pain—they were supposed to be impenetrable, but these shadows slipped right through their armor.

Devereux's shadow hands wound around the necks of the giant Jessamine and Elena, and the fingertips split into fangs again—rearing back and striking, wriggling into their skin. They seemed to suck the life and soul essence from them greedily. Elena and Jessamine's beast forms shrank before my eyes as they screamed horrific sounds. I spared every moment I could between the assaults on me to sling fireballs at Devereux, but Seraphina simply blocked them with blasts of ice and laughed as her guards continued their assault. Daris and Elias fared no better on the other side as more and more guards flooded in with spears, swords, axes, and magic assaults.

I wished desperately for peace, tranquility, and fresh air with my entire being. I remembered Elena's sweet face when I first came to Skia guild, her talkative nature, and suddenly I smelled—Leander. That tall, willowy Immaru with the huge pale blue eyes who'd healed me when I first arrived.

How strange to think of him at a time like this. So many times, he'd been on my mind. It reminded me of my link with Cobalt, and I wondered if maybe, somehow, there was something there—something I didn't realize.

I stretched out with my thoughts, *having no clue what I was doing: Leander, if ever I needed you, I need you now. In the depths of the Magus Guild Underground, we are in a prison chamber where Demomancers abound, and are about to be destroyed. Me, Daris, Elena, Elias and Jessamine. We need your help. Seraphina is a Demomancer. We need the true Alliance.*

With all my might, I threw another fireball, taking time to pull a Lupine into me so I could latch onto his hairy neck and drain him dry.

Ugh. I spat out the hair. *Still. Waste not, want not.* I needed energy, after all, despite having to deal with the fur on my tongue. I was desperate—still wracking my brain—trying to figure out what else I could do to get through this battle and save us.

Elias was fighting his monster butt off, tooth and claw—hurling some fire when he could. Daris was down. Variant could be coming after me next, and Devereux was somehow leeching the very essence out of Jessamine with his shadows.

Jessamine's form was shrinking, nearly half the size it was before.

Then, the room shook. My eyes cut to Seraphina, but she was also glancing around, and it dawned on me that this was not part of her plan. In the center of the room and in different spots all around, Guildmasters and Magisars appeared with their Seconds.

Behind Seraphina's guards, I heard a great thundering yell, "Bellator!" and what sounded like hundreds of stampeding feet. Hoots and war cries followed.

Seraphina blasted ice, snow, and freezing cold in every direction, and her voice shook the entire cavern. "What is the meaning of this!"

A tall man with white hair stepped forward, blasting Seraphina back. With a simple flick of his fingers, he had her in magic restraining cuffs. He stared at her and then at Devereux, then at Seraphina. I'd never seen him before, nor the white-haired woman beside him. They both wore crests on their chests that were different from any Guild symbols I'd seen.

"Seraphina Moonshade, by the declaration of an emergency meeting of the Guilds of Chaos, you have been declared a criminal within the Guilds, having violated its sacred trust. You are a Demomancer who has posed as the Arnexin, Seraphina Moonshade. You are also charged with her death and stealing her powers. You are under arrest."

Seraphina stared coldly around the room. "You can take me to the Truth Teller. I did not kill her. That privilege went to Guildmaster Devereux. He is, after all, a Sevvir. He killed the original Devereux not long after I took Seraphina's place."

The room went silent. Then there were whispers. I didn't know what a "Sevvir" was, but it didn't sound good. And not good at all for Jessamine or Elena.

Devereux backed away, the snakes on his suit swirling wickedly. "Don't let his shadows touch you!" I called out in warning.

Seraphina yelled out to everyone. "You think this prophecy will save you? You think she—" Seraphina pointed at me, "will save you? Oh no, dear friends. This is just the beginning of a long plan for my people. This little prophecy will not stop what's to come. Do you hear? Do you hear!" Seraphina raged. Devereux turned to run, but I thought I heard him scream. I guess he had a weakness after all.

I felt a hand on my shoulder. I turned. Leander. His smell. Somehow, though I was dirty and tired—I felt better. I pointed to Daris. "Can you help him?" I asked Leander. And Leander was flowing to Daris before the words left my lips. At the same time, the Guildmasters were taking Seraphina and others into custody.

I surveyed the enormous room where the ice hung in various places, and the Demomancer magic-infused iron cells lined the walls. Help had come just when things seemed like all was lost. Then why did I feel like something was still wrong?

I thought back to our visit to Zeleel, to my talk with Orion and the old man. I remembered Orion's staff. It was devoid of life in Seraphina's office. Was it still there? And the Queen. Where was she? Jimson-Bee—her Pegasus, had been in the stables. I gasped for a second, realizing I'd actually fed on the Queen's prized Pegasus—oh dear, god, I'd fed on a Pegasus! But seriously, I'd yet to see who I thought might be the Queen. Was she even here? Where was Variant?

My gaze went to where Elena and Jessamine were on the floor. Elena had returned to her normal Arnexin form, but Jessamine—somehow, in all of the commotion—she was gone.

A very large yellow creature bearing a double-bladed ax the size of a cow burst in and fixed its gaze on the two figures with white hair. "My Lord, my Lady—the creature posing as Devereux—he managed to slip away! He's on the loose!"

With so many warriors responding, how could he have slipped away? I realized I knew very little about Devereux. I imagined the creature he was had a number of survival skills. I dashed down the stairs to Elena, who had a number of people around her, but I pushed my way through.

"Elena, we're getting you help. Leander is here!"

Elena's complexion was so gray. Her green eyes, normally so full of life, rolled up at me as if barely able to see. She seemed as if she were trying to speak.

"No, don't try to speak. You're hurt—"

"Nix—the Queen—the staff," Elena stopped and coughed, blood ejecting from her lips. I tried to stop her, but she pressed on. "The Queen is secured in Seraphina's office. Magic space. Use Orion's staff to show you . . . " She coughed and coughed again, and then the Immarus were there, bearing her up, taking her to Leander. I kissed her hand, though I knew she wouldn't feel it.

"I love you, dear Elena, and if I can make Devereux pay for what he's done, by God, the Celestials and Chaos—by all the stars—I'll do it!" I prepared to follow them so I could meet Daris, but a hand gently touched me.

A small man with chestnut hair stood before me in blue, red, and gold robes, and behind him were the two white-haired figures who'd spoken earlier and had Seraphina arrested. He wore the same golden crest as they did, and now that they were closer, I could see that the crest was a crown with a sunburst in the middle, and there were other designs stitched in it, but I couldn't take time to look closely. They also wore clothing with blue, red and golden colors.

"If I may, Ms.—er—Apprentice Emberwind—may I introduce you to Lord Apollo Inferno and Lady Corona Inferno. Family to the Queen Essembra Inferno, who is currently missing." The man regarded me expectantly, as did the Lord and Lady. And here I was, torn, dirty clothing—smelling like a sewage rat—and looking like one as well—and having no clue about proper protocol. I defaulted to what I'd seen in movies and went down on a knee and bowed my head. Whatever would get me out of her faster—that was my best play.

"My Lord, my Lady. How may I be of service?"

Lady Corona smiled. "Isn't she so sweet, Apollo?"

Apollo grimaced and got to the point. "First, no need to take a knee at an affair like this. Next, our Queen Mother is missing. We need her back. She's quite old and unwell. If you can help, we'd much appreciate it. And lastly, out of curiosity, you say you come from the Mortal Realm I hear? How old are you in Mortal years—Earth years, to be exact, if I might ask?"

"I'm eighteen," I responded, without so much as a 'my Lord' following the words, which I think caused some displeasure.

The Lord and Lady glanced at each other. Lady Corona said, "I've heard you display quite a force of Ignitor power. That's something that runs very strong in our family."

Lord Apollo spoke once more, "Before I send you on your way, I'd like you to meet someone. He will be the new Guildmaster for the Magus Guild. Guildmaster Lux Amber." A golden-haired gentleman glided forward, and before I knew it, he'd taken my hand.

"It is a pleasure to meet you, Apprentice Nix. I look forward to seeing what you can do with those Ingnitor powers in the future, along with the others. Take care of yourself and your team."

Before I could respond that they weren't *my* team, they'd all turned, and in a flash, they'd portaled away. Just like that.

I whipped my head toward Daris. We had a Queen we needed to find and save, and we needed to find Jessamine before Variant or Devereux did. I needed him with me.

DARIS

RESPONSIBILITY

T he Celestials had smiled upon me, and I was grateful that Variant hadn't loaded a poisoned dart designed to kill me, although it wouldn't be easy to kill a Sangor that way. Still, I believed it proved that Seraphina wanted Nix, Elena, and me alive—that she truly believed we were part of this prophecy, whatever it was.

Leander's antidote counteracted the drug's effects, and I felt better almost instantly. However, my body went cold when I saw my dear sister Elena lying helpless on the icy floor, her dark auburn hair limply covering her face, her freckled body thinner than I'd ever seen it. I couldn't believe what I'd heard while drugged, unable to see clearly what was happening. I grabbed Leander's arm.

"Leander, thank you for your help, truly. I must ask one more thing of you, please. I cannot believe it's true, but if I heard correctly, while I was drugged, Devereux seemed to be some kind of Sevvir serpent. But this can't be. These serpents have been extinct for thousands of years. Is this possible? Could some have survived and evolved over time?" My hand went to the pouch around my neck. It was still there.

Leander's eyes slowly swiveled to Elena, his gaze lingering over her. "I don't know how it can be, but it seems true. I sense she doesn't have much time left unless she receives an antidote. From what I know, only an antidote made from Sevvir venom itself can help her."

I yanked the pouch from my neck. "There's a vial in this pouch—I carried it with me to Zeleel just in case we needed it for other purposes. Make what antidote you can from this, please," I pleaded. "As fast as you can. Do you have someone who can take her to the Immaru Guild?"

He nodded, and immediately, two Immaru Apprentices floated toward Elena and bore her toward Leander. "I will see to her myself," he swore. "You need to heal, brother. This is a dark time. Let me embrace you before I go."

I felt Leander's mind touch mine ever so gently, offering his blood to give me energy quickly where no one would see or judge. He was a healer, after all. My heart swelled. Then he told me something even more curious.

"You should also know, Nix is not a pure Sangor. She can still be your Prime. What she is remains to be uncovered, but it is more than any have known or will see in an age. Now heal, and I will return your sister soon."

I reached out to tell him about Jessamine, realizing she was no longer there. I had no idea where she'd gone or why she left. Damn her—why did she do this?

Oddly, Nix was talking with Lord and Lady Inferno near where Elena had fallen. I never could have predicted that. Perhaps they had something to say about the Queen. Her Pegasus was here, after all, and we'd seen no sign of the Queen.

Then, Nix was at my side, along with Elias, and Leander had already disappeared with Elena. I hadn't even been able to touch her or tell her I loved her despite her unconsciousness.

I took a deep breath, needing a moment to regain my strength before finding Jessamine and getting her to the Immaru Guild. She would die without the proper antidote to Devereaux's shadow bites. I stared at the face of the golden-haired boy whose unpredictable monster form terrified much of the GOC.

I guessed Elias had to be worried about Jessamine, though I never got the impression they were in love or together. I tried to speculate on Jessamine's real reason for coming along on our quest or understand why Elias had let her know about it in the first place, but I came up empty-handed.

"How are you?" Nix placed a hand on my back—much more familiar than an Apprentice would to a Magisar in front of people, and I straightened.

"I'm fine, thank you," I said formally. "We'll get going in just a moment. I saw you met Lord and Lady Inferno. Did they have any news to pass?" I would not be the reason she had to leave this place or why either of us ended up in Lethenthril.

Nix dropped her hand, understanding my meaning, but I thought I saw her red eyes gleam with anger. "N-no," she stammered for a second, then recovered. The Hammerfists from Bellator Guild pounded with their boots along the walkways, checking cells, freeing anyone else they found as prisoners. No one found the Queen.

"The Queen is still missing, Variant and Devereaux are gone, and so is Orion's staff. I did get some last words from Elena before she passed out," I told him. "She said we should look in Seraphina's office."

He tilted his head thoughtfully at this and said, "I'm sure someone's already been in there to check for her, and the staff is useless. I think it died when Orion did."

Nix didn't back down, and Elias pressed in with her—their insistence was almost infectious. "What if they didn't know where to look? Elena said something about a magic space. One of the first things that occurred to me was Seraphina's paintings. They seemed to be such a prominent part of her office and something she loved."

I had improved feeling in my limbs now, and my muscles engaged. My mind was working faster, and I thought Nix was onto something. But the staff . . .

"I know you're thinking about the staff—but maybe something just needs the right trigger. A blood offering, or placing the staff in front of the painting—something. We can't just give up—that's all I know, Daris. And, when we get there, maybe I can use . . ."

Here, she hesitated, and I suddenly thought I knew why. Our bond was stronger now, and I got a picture in my mind of her Blaze Ceremony and Master Coes. Damn, she shouldn't have remembered that, but she did.

And now, she's thinking about trying to tap into her Umbrani magic and speak with the shadows or the dead to find the Queen or the secrets of the staff.

I placed a mentor-style hand on her back. "We'll get to that if we need it, Nix. You're thinking about your Umbrani magic but you have no training in it yet. Let's see what we're dealing with first, okay? We could be walking right into a hornet's nest."

I glanced around at the three of us. Technically, Seraphina was under arrest. The new Grand Guildmaster had not been named yet and would not be until the Guildmaster vote. That put Lord and Lady Inferno in the lead with the task of finding the Queen, and me in the lead of finding Jessamine under my care and the criminals Variant and Devereaux.

Straightening myself as best I could; I caught Gauge's attention as he finished overseeing his Hammerfists collecting prisoners, setting them free from inside the giant amphitheater of cells here, subduing the Lupine Guardians who'd been working for Seraphina—and disguised Demomancers—and sending them to prison. "Can you take over all primary security decisions per our protocols since Seraphina is officially declared unfit for service, an Enemy of Arnexis and the GOC?"

"Only if you arrange a time for a proper ass-whopping in front of our friends when things settle down. I need some public festivities, Daris!" bellowed and pummeled his chest. I liked him as Guildmaster for Bellator. In all my years, he'd been one of the most—fun.

Though I didn't feel like it, I puffed up and stuck out my chin. "Count on it, brother!" We both shot our fists into the air in a brother salute and turned to take care of our corners. Duty called.

"Now," I said, as I returned to Elias and Nix, "I will take Elias with my Guildmaster portal spell. Nix, it's practice time for you. With Demomancers in our backyard, our world just got a lot more complicated. As my Apprentice, you need to level up in your Apprenticeship ability, catch up with your class, and go beyond it. With your Apparlusio magic ability and the spell you used to come to Arnexis, I know you have your own portal capability. You've been to Seraphina's office. You need to portal there. I'll meet you with Elias. Let's see how you do."

I grabbed Elias's arm and quickly transported just as I heard Nix say, "Daris! How the hell . . ."

Yeah. She'd figure it out. She had to. I loved this woman, but I was her Magisar, too. She was my Apprentice. That meant I had to care enough to make sure she had the best training. I had to love her hard enough to train her hard.

And I meant it when I said this world just got a lot more dangerous. Demomancers were infiltrating our ranks, using our magic against us, killing us, and doing anything to interfere with our prophecies to ensure that they did not come true.

I was going to love her so hard that she just might hate me for it.

THOUSAND WORDS

Yes, I'd been to Seraphina's office exactly once. *Thank you, Daris.* This wasn't funny.

Okay. I'd made it to my room on my Blaze Ceremony day. Here goes. I closed my eyes and pictured the place—Seraphina's office—that velvet sofa. I started the words when I was sure I had it. But then, her face intruded. Master Coeus. I felt my body whirl and twist, and I tumbled quite unceremoniously onto the Arena in the Omnipatos courtroom.

No, no, no! I mean, at least at this moment, as I fervently glanced around—the huge room was empty. But this was not Seraphina's office. I'd started thinking about the trial and my Blaze Ceremony and I'd lost focus. That had to be why I was here.

I darted for the protection of one of the larger Guild statues. What was likely a Mernai Guild statue—the figure draped with water fountains splashing around it and a small pool of fish swimming at the bottom—loomed above me. I'm sure I would have found it lovely and awe-inspiring if I'd had time to appreciate it, except there were three figures stepping into the room. One was Variant, practically dragging Jessamine along, who could barely walk. The other was Devereux.

I shrank into the shadows, wondering if Daris's Celestial stone in his palm was alerting him to anything right now, or if I had to actually be undergoing an attack. The vast darkness of the inside of the round courtroom was lit only by some soft orb lights at various entrances and exits.

"Surely, with all of that time on the mountain in Zeleel, you learned where it is, Jessamine. Tell me now, and there is still time left to save your life. Just a little of my blood with the right ingredients, and you'll be right as rain," Devereux crooned. "We only want Seraphina returned to us. She's no good to us as an empty sack on Lethenthril. She has information we need."

"I swear to you, I don't know. I learned nothing. I tried. I did. I followed the girl. Nothing came of it that we could use."

She followed me? What does she mean she followed me? But then I remembered I'd seen Jessamine transform into a giant beast like Elena. What else could she transform into? Was she versatile like Elena? A versatile Meta?

It seemed some Meta were aligned with a certain species while others could shapeshift into anything. I wondered why. Jessamine had to be lying though—she'd gone with Elias when I was in the mountain. Still, it had no bearing on my problem now, which was how to get out of here undetected and warn Daris.

Just then, my Celcom buzzed. I froze. It was supposed to be on silent!

Of all the times I didn't need it to vibrate—to do anything—this was the time. In this great hall, even though it was on vibrate, in the large silence, it might as well have been a trumpet.

Damn. And I'd wanted a Celcom, too. I'd been excited about it. Was looking forward to using it.

Fire burned in my belly. If things were gonna go sideways, then I might as well get it over with. That was, I could start dealing with the problem now rather than waiting on it. I whisked the phone out of my pocket at lightning speed. "Daris, I'm in the court—"

That was all I got out before Devereux plucked the phone out of my fingers with one hand and gripped my neck with the other. I didn't realize he could move so fast or that his grip was so strong. He put the phone to his ear. "I have Nix, Daris. Your little secret co-Sangor—not so secret anymore. I saw her move—her speed—when you were trying to save your sister. Too bad she won't make it—but maybe it won't be too late for her or Jessamine here. Given that we have some common goals, I think you need to tell me where you are."

I didn't mess around. I saw how this was going to go. "Seraphina's office," I croaked out. "We have to save the Queen."

"Ah," Devereux blinked. His eyes raked me up and down with disdain. "And you think you can get her? Well, she's a much better bargaining tool to get Seraphina back, so let's go to her office, shall we?"

I watched as Devereux cast a glamour over the three of us, making us appear as if we were average GOC workers, and he guided us around to Seraphina's office. A Bellator Magisar appeared to be guarding the arched gilded door. He was a Grasha species with thick and well-defined muscles. He held a heavy battle-axe at the ready. He was probably supposed to ensure no one entered Seraphina's office after her arrest.

We walked up to him, and his amber eyes just stared straight ahead. I'm sure Daris hated having to cast whatever spell he did to freeze him in place. We all stepped inside, and before Variant closed the door, I glanced over my shoulder at the green-skinned

Magisar, who was likely quite very proud of his battle skill. *Epic fail.*

It was a good thing Seraphina's red and gold office was spacious with lots of seating, not that we would use much of it. We'd use the space though. The room had a rich smell of amber, sweet patchouli, and some smokey incense I wasn't familiar with.

It helped cover up any trace of that nasty Demomancer scent, I thought. Daris and Elias were standing by one of the paintings, staring at it.

"Now," said Devereux, "what is your plan to get the Queen back?"

"Can you help Jessamine first?" I pleaded. "We need her. She'll die soon without the antidote. Please, Guildmaster." I practically begged and hated doing it, but I had to try.

He tossed a calculating eye my way and said, without an ounce of pity, "No. Queen first. Then maybe I can spare some blood for the antidote if they release Seraphina to me."

Out of necessity and because my brain and body sometimes just performed when under pressure—not always when I wanted it to, but usually when I had to—I went into action mode. I thought about martial arts classes, Scouting, and some of the things we'd done since we'd been here.

"Okay, let's do it then," I said as I clenched my teeth. I felt like everything in my head was moving at Sangor speed. A picture of Seraphina holding Orion's dead staff flashed in my mind. "Where's Orion's staff?"

Daris picked it up—it was by Seraphina's desk, discarded like a dead thing. He tossed it to me, and I caught it mid-air. We all stepped back, myself included when the staff's crystal orb flashed a bright blue light. I nearly dropped it—fumbled— but managed to hang on.

The moment I grasped it, I saw Orion's face in my mind—wise and serene. He showed me a vision of myself holding the staff in the cave on Zeleel. Apparently, I'd return. He showed me the Queen, older, tall, beautiful but frail—her calm spirit divided from her body and stored inside another dimension.

I didn't understand it all, but she seemed encased in a protected bubble of fire underwater. He pointed to the staff and to me. I gathered that the staff was the key to getting her spirit out.

The light in the staff died down, all except for the tiniest little spark in the center of the orb. I held on to the staff, using it to keep me upright.

"Sparks . . ." Elias breathed. Daris and Jessamine stared at me wide-eyed and Devereux and Variant both wore angry expressions, though I sensed for different reasons.

"Shut up," Devereux snapped at Elias. His anger dissipated, and he eyed me with what I thought was, for the first time, a hint of fear. "It's clear the staff reacts to you a little. Now, go on."

I noted that his fingers trembled. The light above and on the walls cast shadows across the floor. I was acutely aware that doing anything life-threatening right now, like trying escape, wouldn't be smart, even if I thought I had an advantage. Devereux would call his shadows, and I'd feel those fangs. Or worse, Daris would.

I stared over at Daris, and as I met his eyes, he shrugged and jutted his chin toward the paintings.

Okay, so he's telling me to go with my gut. My earlier intuition.

Stepping up to one of the larger paintings, I spoke my thoughts out loud so others could help after I was done. After all, six heads were better than one.

"Each of these paintings represents a fire scene—all by the same artist. Seraphina came from the Magus Guild, a fire-element Guild, right? So Ignitor magic is the primary magic element for this Guild." No one said anything, but it seemed as if they expected me to continue.

"Orion also wore Magus colors. Now, the crystal light in his staff is not red or gold, but instead, the light in it is—"

"Blue," Daris said, adding to my thoughts. "And the hottest fire that burns is blue."

"Right," I confirmed. I held the staff in front of me, walked toward each of the paintings, and stood facing them.

One painting was a raging fire overtaking a range of mountains. Below, black shadows in a valley danced wildly in a circle as the fires ate everything in sight around them. When looking at this painting, it seemed as if the fires were trying to reach out and grab the viewer and draw them in.

Flames whipped out from the mountains and lassoed my hands as if to bring me closer. There was intense heat in them, but they didn't burn. I turned away, and the vision disappeared. We all shuffled to the next painting.

I continued to reflect, "Blue is also a primary color for other elements—water—and for air."

In this painting, a thriving metropolis burned. Fire burst through windows, and glass exploded into the air while bodies burned, plummeting to their deaths. The sky was partially blue, but smoke billowed up to obscure most of it.

This canvas glittered with the exploding glass splintering in different directions as the conflagration took over the entire city in a furious tornado of flame. No matter which position the viewer stood in, it seemed as if lethal shards of glass were exploding right toward the viewer.

I felt little prickles standing in front of this one—not harmful, just a built-in physical sensation that the artist included. *Curious.*

I moved to another painting—this one smaller than the rest—though it was still the size of a four-place tabletop. In this one, fire raged all around the borders, and steam rose softly from a central pool of tranquil and clear water. Figures around the pool either danced in celebration or pulled on their hair in anguish, but the placid pool only lightly steamed while gentle ripples traveled from the center outward in concentric waves. Glancing around the room, I noted it was the only painting in the room with water.

"This better be it, or I got nothin'," I said.

I placed myself in front of the painting and held the staff out toward it. The crystal orb glowed a soft blue—then the light pulsed in an intermittent pattern, like a heartbeat. I felt searing heat outside of me and cool water washing within me, and suddenly, I couldn't breathe. I quickly stepped away, the heat abated, and my breath returned.

I heard Jessamine inhale sharply. Daris, Elias, and Devereux leaned forward to examine the painting. Variant did not. He kept a watchful eye on me and Jessamine.

"So?" Devereux knit his eyebrows together, and Daris cocked his head. I told them all what happened—what I felt. I went from feeling smart and useful to being garbage again.

I sighed. "I admit, I can't tell you what this means. I don't know the GOC that well. I'm still new here. But if you've got a calm pool of water nearby and know where this place might be—the staff says this is important. Look at the painting. Something about it has got to tell you something."

Elias gripped Daris's arm and then glanced back at Jessamine and Variant. "I think she's in Oscuro's backyard, guys. Look at the name of the painting."

"Celestial Waters Inferno," I read. "What is that?"

"Only the best sacred waters for fortune-telling around all the Realms—and it just happens to sit right beside the Oscuro Guild," Elias murmured.

"That's dumbing it down," Jessamine remarked, barely able to get out a whisper.

"Shouldn't we leave Jessamine here to rest?" I pleaded with Devereux, gesturing to Jessamine. "Look at her. She's not going to go anywhere."

"Consider her your incentive to succeed, Apprentice Nix," Devereux wet his lips with a forked tongue. I watched him relax his eyes—his Sevvir viper pupils maintaining their vertical shape. "I have a feeling we're not done with you yet."

DARIS

PLUNGE

I kept searching for a way out of this—a way to escape with everyone or take Devereux and Variant out—but Devereux took no chances and hung on to Nix as we portaled to the Celestial Waters. I transported Elias. Apparently, Variant had some sort of hidden artifact that helped him transport himself and someone else, even though he was just an Apprentice.

The night sky blanketed us above, allowing the diamonds of the Celestials to twinkle brightly over us. I guessed it had to be around two or three in the morning. We were fortunate in one way. The Celestial Waters was one place where Incitors were not placed on campus. This was because the waters were strictly used for those who came to 'see' the past, present, or future of the lives of others. It was fairly close to what we considered 'hallowed ground.'

The other location where Incitors were not placed was the Observatree, where members of the GOC went to search for answers from Chaos, the Celestials, Ancestors, or other Spirits—or just to gaze at the Stars and find something they needed. Each place demanded a payment for the answers it gave. No magic, no answers were ever bestowed for free.

The moonless night worked to our advantage. Devereux had to rely on his magical capabilities alone and had no current access to his shadow magic. As a Sevvir—like a Demomancer—he had assumed the bodily form of the real Devereux and had stolen all of his power, knowledge, and magic, essentially becoming Devereux in all but the true mind.

The real Devereux was gone. The creature's true self and intention were still Sevvir, and its desire was to use magic for its own independent, selfish, and nefarious means.

We were herded to a secluded area of the Celestial Waters, where dream willows hung their silvery branches gently into the water. There was a grassy beach area here, where the green blades grew as dense as carpet, and the ground was soft and springy. The Stars reflected their diamond luster on the black surface of the water, and with the sky so clear, it was difficult to discern where sky and land divided except for where the trees broke the view.

Both Devereux and Variant conjured small balls of light, each the size of an orc's mug, to illuminate our surroundings. As a gentle breeze kicked up, carrying the sweet fragrance of freshly bloomed wisteria and jasmine, Devereux turned to face Nix and me. The familiar scents stirred memories of my mother, causing my heart to twist painfully, but I quickly pushed the thoughts aside, knowing that now was not the time to dwell on the past.

With a sweeping gesture toward the lake, Devereux proclaimed, "The Queen awaits," as if he expected Nix to simply reach into the water and pluck the Queen from its depths. However, knowing Seraphina as I did, I suspected that the task would not be so straightforward.

I watched intently as Nix approached the edge of the dark, mirror-like water, a frown etched upon her face. I was concerned. Both Devereux and I had borne witness to Nix's Blaze Ceremony. We were well aware that she had no affinity for water magic. I was certain that Nix herself knew this, assuming her memories were as intact as I believed them to be.

Ignitor and Cielo—these were the Elemental Powers that Nix commanded. Aquane and Teragos were not among her abilities.

With a determined expression, Nix raised Orion's staff high above her head. For a fleeting moment, nothing seemed to happen. Then, without warning, the blue spark nestled within the crystal orb atop the staff flared to life, its intensity growing rapidly. Brilliant light burst forth in all directions, fiercely illuminating the surroundings before gradually settling into a soft, steady glow.

Nix closed her eyes, and I watched in fascination as they darted back and forth beneath her closed lids as if she were absorbing and processing a wealth of information. Her eyebrows knitted together in concentration as though she were making a concerted effort to commit every detail to memory. In seconds, her eyes stilled, and she opened them once more.

I found myself utterly dumbfounded by what I saw. Nix's eyes, which had become the rich, maroon hue of a Sangor after walking through The Eye of Chaos, had undergone a startling transformation once more. In this moment, they glowed with the same mesmerizing, sparkling blue as the crystal perched atop Orion's staff, a sight that left me both captivated and perplexed.

Nix stepped away from the lake and turned to speak with everyone, her voice almost trancelike. I am sure we all listened, unable to tear our eyes away from her glowing features.

"The Queen is being held in the center of the lake—at the very bottom. She is cocooned inside the earth there, which cradles her body beside another cocoon of fire. Her spirit is contained within an air bubble inside that fire. Body and spirit in two different dimensions together. One cannot be liberated without the other, or she will not survive."

"I wish Seraphina had done this part with me," Devereux muttered under his breath, his crossed arms and down-turned mouth making his displeasure clear. The snakes adorning his suit slithered with a faint sheen in the light. His horns still gleamed, and I wondered at his desire to maintain his Arnexin appearance.

Curiosity got the better of me, and I asked him, "Are there many more like you?" I had to know. If they were allied with the Demo-mancers, this could devastate Arnexis and all of the Realms. "Are there many more Sevvir?"

His eyes narrowed at me, and then a grin slid across his face as if in pleasure at my curiosity. "Oh, dear Daris. There's so much you don't know, isn't there? The great Sangor lives for over a thousand years, and still . . . but I digress. You shall just have to find out. And you will, very soon."

Variant, having reached the peak of his impatience, inter-jected, "So how do we get the old woman out of there and be done? Sunrise isn't far off. I need to port."

Devereux hissed at Variant in response. Jessamine dropped to the ground, and though Variant prodded her with his knife to get up, she was unable to rise.

Elias's voice cut in. It was clear he was panicking and afraid that Jessamine would die very soon. He reached out to grab Nix. "Sparks, any ideas?"

Nix dropped her gaze to the ground, remaining silent for a moment. When she raised her head, her eyes had re-turned to their familiar Sangor maroon color. "As a matter of fact, I do. But they aren't going to like it." She nodded towards Devereux and Variant.

Devereux's voice challenged Nix as if he dared her to say something he knew was designed to help them escape or get him and Variant captured. "Why is that?"

As a wind whipped by, blowing Nix's red tresses in the air like a war banner, her gaze caught mine, and she inspired me. I stared directly at Devereux. I had to win his confidence. "You know how Nix can't lie, right?"

He nodded.

"Did you realize that when I bonded us with a Celestial protection stone, her inability to lie was also transferred to me?" I felt like revealing this weakness was one of the stupidest things I'd ever done.

"Really?" Devereux asked, his tongue slithered out to test the air almost as if he could determine the truth from it.

"No, I'm absolutely lying to you about that right now. I can lie any time I want and never turn a shade of red," I leaned near Variant's light so he could see my scarlet skin. The delight on his face was unmistakable.

"We can't use just one person to get the Queen. We need three. There are multiple layers to where the Queen is being held. To get to her we have to have a team. We are all Skia Guild. We have to have Elena with us. She can transform into the creature we need. Nix has the Ariparz powers to get the Queen out of two dimensions while we hold back the water, earth, and fire. Hopefully, Elena is healed and well by now."

Devereux carefully examined my skin— as if trying to discern the truth from it. "I see. And how do you propose we bring her here at three in the morning? I will not let you portal there and risk you alerting people to our whereabouts, and don't get hopeful about your Celcoms—those locators are neutralized.

I thought about that. Nemar and Cobalt. At least Nemar, though I'm sure Cobalt would follow. "If I can attach a message to Elena, on my Grigon, Nemar, then Elena will come. You can inspect the message. No tricks. Our goal right now is the same."

After careful deliberation and against Variant's protests, Devereux agreed.

In minutes, Nemar arrived, along with Cobalt, their wide, long wings blowing a whirlwind around us. They were wary and angry at our state, but we worked to calm them. I sent my thoughts to Nemar, along with a message I'd written on paper and pen, which I'd pulled from my belt. Devereux inspected it and approved it to go.

Placing the message in Nemar's beak, I watched as they launched off toward the Immaru Guild. I only hoped that Elena was healed, that she would receive the message and join us soon.

Jessamine started having a coughing fit, and Elias knelt at her side. I had a cup in my belt. I pushed a button. The Celestial Waters were safe to drink. Healing, even.

"Can I give her some water," I asked Devereux. He eyed me and waved his hand. Variant played with one of his knives, apparently taking pride in how he could hit the same spot on a willow in the dark.

When I went to the lake's edge to get the water, I stopped briefly to whisper to Nix in a voice only Sangor could hear.

"This is all about the prophecy," I said as I bent down to scoop the water. "*Tooth, Claw, and Staff will merge—Friends and Enemies the same.* This is it. I think this is all about saving the Queen. We were meant to save the Queen together!"

"Hey!" Variant yelled. "Get back over here with the water. No social parties."

Jessamine continued heaving, but together, we managed to get some water into her, and the liquid seemed to help. A few moments after that, we heard the sound of flapping wings. A very tired but much improved Elena slid off Nemar's back—and I sent them on their way, sending some additional thoughts with Nemar to watch carefully and listen since we may need them soon.

Relief washed over Nix's face when she saw Elena healed, though we both hated bringing her back into danger. Elias started to run to her, but Devereux yanked him back. "Everyone is fine, right where they are for now. Daris and Nix—tell me how this will work."

Devereux had Jessamine and Elias prisoner. He knew we wouldn't risk their lives, and we wanted to save Jessamine's life. I told him what I suspected, with Nix to back me up and correct me or adjust if I was wrong.

"Although I am a Sangor, I also have Teragos magic, Cielo, and Aquane. I will swim down to where the Queen is, figure out the spell holding her, move it, break it, or hold it back, letting Elena in. Elena is a Meta and has great transformation ability, and Aquane capabilities as well. I suspect that Seraphina has not placed the Queen down there unguarded. Though the Celestial Waters are supposed to be peaceful, no one goes to the central deep areas of the pool, usually, unless they are in Mernai Guild. She took a risk. Elena will serve as a guard and protector and fight anything that shows up. She is also a Grade Six Monster Hunter. Nix has Ignitor and Cielo powers as well as Umbrani, Osculus and Apparlusio. Combined with the power of Orion's staff, I believe she can bring back the Queen intact. If we die, then you've lost nothing except a way to get your Queen hostage since you were going to kill us anyway. And the sun is going rise in two hours."

While Devereux seemed to be pondering the process and Variant looked dubious, I glanced over at Nix. "Did I miss anything?"

Nix shook her head slightly but under her breath said, "Only that each of us can portal with one other person, but with the Queen, there'll be two extra people."

I realized she was right. That meant they had to leave—or kill—two of us, or all of us, to portal the Queen away as soon as we got her out of Seraphina's special holding cell. Unless Devereux believed he could use the main Portal Gate nearby. It was not far from the Celestial Waters.

I had to bargain that this creature was practical. If the Queen died, he'd still want bargaining chips. Me, Nix, Elias, and Elena would be valuable. Jessamine was expendable. He'd already shown us that.

Perhaps it would help if Devereux thought Jessamine was dead. I could get a little pick-me-up and poison myself in the process, likely making the love of my life furious with me. Without deliberating too long, I made a decision. Jessamine was part of my team, and I was responsible for her. I wouldn't abandon her, especially when Devereux could easily decide to kill her while we were in the water.

I hoped Nix would read my cue. I flicked my eyes to Jessamine and back and whispered what only Sangor ears could hear—*Fall.* Nix conjured sparks in her hand reminiscent of her uncontrolled fires, and her staff dropped to the ground. She tumbled with it.

Using my speed, I flew to Jessamine's side and sank my fangs into her neck, drawing enough of her blood into my mouth for some energy while releasing a paralytic. I stopped her heart and entire body process, putting her in stasis. Simultaneously, I sent calm and serene thoughts to her, letting her know what I was doing, though I was unsure if she understood in her weakened state. I had milliseconds to do this and heal her before returning to Nix's side, arching my eyebrows, and waiting for her answer as if I'd never left.

Nix even managed to apply an embarrassed expression to her face at her lack of control as she replied so everyone could hear, "I think you've covered it. I don't have good swimming skills, so I'll need help down to the bottom. And I might need help breathing if I can't get into the air sac in a reasonable amount of time. I don't know what extracting the Queen from two dimensions will be like." Nix glanced around as if surveying us for answers, though it was clear none of us had any.

I wasn't sure why she said that, but I wasn't going to correct her yet. As a Sangor, she didn't really need to breathe underwater. Her body systems could slow. She could just stop breathing for a while, and she'd be fine. But then I realized we'd never practiced that, and so she didn't know. Well, she was going to find out the hard way.

"Okay," I said. "Let's get going." I began removing my clothes, kicking off my boots, and tugging my shirt off over my head.

Nix stared at me in horror. "What are you doing?"

"Oh," I paused, realizing Nix hadn't come to the Celestial Waters with her Apprentice class yet. "Whenever you get into the Celestial Waters, it's an absolute must that you get in naked. Otherwise, they'll spit you out." I removed my pants and the rest of my attire, then waded in.

Despite our circumstances, Elena laughed at Nix's shocked expression as she shed her medical gown. "It's okay, dovie. You can bring things in your hands, like your staff, but the Waters won't allow clothing. No shirts, pants, shoes, undies, nothing . . ." She pulled off the last of her undergarments and waded in as well.

Nix stood there looking stricken, then swallowed and shook her head as if reprimanding herself. "Okay. For the Queen!" She placed Orion's staff on the ground, and the crystal went dark. She kicked off her boots and shimmied off her dirty pants, shirt, belt, and finally, her undergarments before picking up her staff. It glowed again, lighting up the soft curves of her body but showing the definition of the muscles she'd gained since coming here as well.

I tried very hard not to stare, extremely glad I was already in the water. When Nix's eyes met mine, I was relieved she was facing me and not *them*. It was bad enough that Devereux and Variant had a view of the backside of my *dazi*.

My eyes roved over the curves of Nix's breasts, waist, and hips. I was supremely grateful for Sangor night vision. Nix sucked in air through her teeth as she entered the lake, not prepared for the chill, and came close to me. I knew she didn't really mind so much. It was a Mortal reflex.

Elena cleared her throat. "Ready, guys?" Despite all she had been through, I heard fire in my sister's voice. She was ready to kick butt. Good for her.

Nix nodded. "Let's do this. Help me breathe down there, Daris. I'm not sure what I can do—how my body will react."

"I got you, but you're gonna do fine," I said, again, not having time to explain. "Ready, Elena!" I took Nix by the arm, and we dove down.

NIX

NOVDIM

How many people live life every day feeling like they have no idea what they are doing? It's a common feeling, I thought, as I kicked my feet next to Daris, attempting to swim alongside him. I certainly felt like I'd been caught in a whirlwind, still clueless as to why I was here.

Our Sangor sight enabled us to see clearly in the depths. It was as if our vision automatically switched to an infrared mode, allowing me to perceive the plants and other aquatic creatures, including small fish, swimming around us.

Turning my head, I moved closer to Daris. Elena had already transformed into a strange gray creature with gills, long webbed hands, and webbed flipper feet. She resembled a frog, but her skin seemed to be covered with firm, protective scales. Sharp teeth protruded from her upper and lower lips, and her eyes were large and round.

Despite expecting pressure to build up in my ears, it didn't. I cleared them anyway by pinching my nose and blowing, releasing small bubbles, just as I'd been taught in a scuba diving class. Daris studied me curiously. My main concern was not knowing when or how I would take my next breath of air. I needed to find a way to create an air pocket. Daris had mentioned having Teragos and Aquane magic, so I might have to find a way to utilize it.

Daris stopped swimming and held me still, facing him as we slowly began sinking feet first. I glanced down, but he grabbed my face, making me look into his eyes. With two fingers, he pointed at my eyes, then his own, before pointing at my teeth and touching them, followed by his own teeth. I shook my head, knowing we didn't have time for this. I motioned the diver's "out of air" signal, which he wouldn't understand. I was going to pass out.

Swimming away from him, I put my hands out, hoping to create an air pocket. Suddenly, a blast of air shot from my hands, pushing me right into Daris. We were thrown off course, and in the chaos, Orion's staff was ripped from my hand. I'd lost sight of it, but we had to find it! However, I was blacking out, drowning. I spied Daris nearby and flailed in the water, screaming. He just swam there, a few feet away, waiting.

I knew I was dying, drowning. I'd have to breathe in at any moment. Except—I didn't. My body refused. Elena passed by me, swimming on her back, while Daris continued to swim in front of me as my body sank further toward the bottom, feet first.

No ear pressure. No desire to breathe. Now I was getting angry. Why didn't Daris tell me? How much didn't he tell me? Of course, I realized he hadn't exactly had the time to tell me, but I was still angry having to find out this way.

And I didn't have my staff. I didn't know which way to go. My feet hit the bottom, its surface covered with beautiful iridescent pebbles. I scanned the area and took in the lovely underwater world.

Green plants swayed like wavy trees, some with broad leaves and others with thin grassy tendrils. Schools of silvery fish swam by, followed by a long black eel. Two large fish, almost as big as me but colored like a rainbow, wriggled close to my arm and then swam off.

I was so entranced that I almost forgot why I was there until Elena swam up in front of me and presented me with my staff in her mouth. I nodded a thank you and grasped it once more. Holding it and turning it in different directions, the light flared again more brightly in one direction, and so I headed that way.

Daris, swimming above me, cocked his head to ask if I were all right. Aside from being a bit miffed, I gave him the okay sign. He grabbed my arm, and pulled me to him, then hugged my body close. Using his Aquane magic, he was able to push us through the water to the center of the lake where we needed to be.

We dropped down to a rounded mound that rose up on the floor of the lake, standing out amidst the otherwise flat surroundings. The mound was brown and rocky, a stark contrast to the iridescent pebbles that covered the rest of the lake floor. Daris set me down, and Elena circled the area, keeping a watchful eye for anything approaching.

I had never witnessed Daris work Teragos magic before. In fact, most of the magic I'd seen him perform had been small, almost unnoticeable. But as he swam back up above the mound and positioned himself over it, I realized I was about to witness something on an entirely different level.

The tattoos on Daris's wrists began to glow a bright white, and light radiated from his hands. He aimed his hands at the earth mound and the ground shook. His first attempt yielded no results. Undeterred, he repositioned himself and used intricate finger motions along with his hand movements, spreading his hands apart. In addition to the white light, red light accompanied the glow on his tattoos and hands. Still, the earth remained unmoved.

Summoning what seemed to be his entire inner core, Daris's tattoos not only on his arms but also the swirls around his ankles and calves lit up, shining in vibrant white, red, and emerald-green. He raised his hands and moved them apart, causing the earth to rumble. Water bubbles obscured my view of him, and I lost my footing. Then, through the bubbles, I caught a glimpse of fire.

The earth mound began to crack and split apart, revealing a fiery core within. The water around the mound started to boil, and I could feel the heat emanating from the opening. Daris continued to focus his magic, his tattoos glowing even brighter as he poured more energy into his efforts.

With the earth now open, it was my turn to act. I prepared to go in, but suddenly, something huge knocked me sideways. Elena was there in an instant, countering the attack. I caught a glimpse of orange and green stripes and sharp fins. I was lucky those fins hadn't sliced across me, and I prayed that Elena's scales were strong enough to withstand them. I couldn't waste this opportunity; Daris had to be holding the earth open.

I tried as hard as I could to push myself through the water, remembering my need for air. Maybe I could use it to propel myself forward. "Cielo," I thought, but all I managed were bubbles. My swimming was painfully slow, and I felt frustration building within me.

Then, a memory flashed through my mind. At the Obsidian Mirror—the Reflection of Chaos—when I dripped my blood onto it and gazed into it with Master Coeus, I had been granted one gift to choose. Based on my fear of not being able to swim, I had selected it. Could it be true? Did I possess Aquane power? It wouldn't hurt to try.

Closing my eyes, I focused on the tiniest little shove, picturing myself moving forward like a fish, with water pushing me ahead. *Aquane*, I thought, concentrating all my energy on this single desire.

As I focused, I felt a subtle shift in the water around me. It began to swirl and churn, creating a gentle current that started to propel me forward. The sensation was strange at first, but I quickly adapted, letting the water guide me towards the fiery cocoon.

Elena passed by, locked in battle with the giant orange fish monster. She pushed it away with her front fins, snapping at it with her long, curved teeth. In a swift motion, she used one of her giant back flippers to catapult me toward the earth mound and the flames. My body tumbled through the water until I collided with the fiery barrier and bounced off, the heat searing my skin.

Or that works, too, I thought wryly, regaining my bearings.

Now closer to the fiery cocoon, I could feel the intense heat radiating from it, the water around me bubbling and swirling. I steadied myself, preparing to make another attempt to reach the Queen. The Aquane power within me grew stronger, and I focused on creating a more powerful current to push me through the flames.

With a deep breath, I summoned all my strength and launched myself forward, the water propelling me like a torpedo. As I hit the fiery barrier, flames licked my body, but my Ignitor power made my form resistant to their heat.

Still, as the flames wrapped around me, I felt a claw of darkness slash across my mind, and I heard the throaty taunt of Seraphina's voice. <<*Murderer! Your family is dead because of you. You failed them then, and you will fail them now. You are undisciplined, uncontrolled, weak, and insignificant. You will go to Lethenthril. They will rip your mind out and send you to oblivion—and it's what you deserve!*>>

I faltered. Was she here, somehow? Had they let her go? Was she right? I'd killed my parents. I was out of control.

Why was I here? What if I didn't know what I was doing? What if I was killing the Queen?

Immediately, I wanted to pull back—to run—to swim away somehow from the fire and the cocoon. Maybe I wasn't good enough for this. Who—what was I anyway? I didn't even know who I was or what I was. I just got here a few days ago. I'd only recently gone through the Blaze Ceremony and walked through The Eye of Chaos. I knew nothing. I was nothing. And I couldn't really swim.

The staff glowed bright, and a voice deeper within me drove the black claw away—pushed it back from my mind. <<*Fight, Nix. For your true self, for Elena, for Daris, Elias and Jessamine, and others counting on you. Fight. Don't give up! The Queen is in there. She will be lost if you don't get her!*>>

My tears merged with fire and lake water as I saw all their faces. I imagined the horror of the charred faces of my family alongside the memories of who they were when we'd laughed and had good times at county fairs and other events. Elena, Jessamine, Daris, Elias—Orion, and others who'd died who I did not know. Others who might die if we failed. We had to win.

I gritted my teeth, and pushed all darkness away from my mind, realizing that this might be part of a spell, something to cause people to second-guess themselves. I pushed the staff forward, pressing the crystal orb into the cocoon. I hoped it was the right thing to do. It just felt right.

As I pressed against the cocoon, the heat intensified, and the air inside grew thick with energy. I could sense the Queen's presence, her spirit trapped within this fiery prison. Reaching out with my mind, I tried to establish a connection, hoping to let her know that help had arrived, but I was met with silence. It was clear that I needed to break through the barrier.

Orion's vision had shown me the Queen existing in two dimensions: Arnexis, our current dimension, where her body was trapped in this cocoon, and the ninth dimension, known as Novdim. Although I didn't fully understand the complexities of these dimensions, I hoped that if I could penetrate the cocoon and find a way in, I might be able to reach her. The earth rumbled at the outer edges of the fire, reminding me that time was running out.

Grasping Orion's staff, its light pulsed in sync with my heartbeat. I reflected on how the staff had been lifeless until I'd held it. I had assumed it was because of the paintings and our use of it as Orion intended. But what if the issue was that the staff was meant to belong to me, and I hadn't fully accepted or embraced it? I still thought of it as Orion's staff, taken from him and never truly given to me.

Though I knew Orion was no longer in this world, I sent out my thoughts, reaching for his presence. *"Orion, I don't know what to do. This staff was yours, stolen from you after Variant killed you and then given to Seraphina. I don't feel right using it,"* I confessed, waiting for a response.

In the midst of the swirling flames that burned around me and within my mind, I felt Orion's blissful and mirthful presence. His voice echoed inside my head, filling me with a sense of peace and purpose. *"The staff is for you, my dear Nix, and for many days to come. Use it well. And know this. As you bring the Queen home, do not live with this one guilt. You did not kill your parents, and your brother escaped and lives in hiding. You will find their killer when your brother finds you. For now, complete your task and live well."*

Tears welled up in my eyes, a mixture of relief, gratitude, and newfound determination. Orion's words lifted a weight from my shoulders, absolving me of the guilt I had carried for so long. With renewed purpose, I gripped the staff tightly, feeling its power thrumming through my veins.

I focused my energy on the staff, pouring my intentions and desires into it. The crystal orb began to pulse with a brilliant

blue light, growing brighter and more intense with each passing second. I aimed the staff at the cocoon, channeling all my
strength and will into breaking through the barrier.

A beam of pure blue energy erupted from the staff, striking the cocoon with a force that sent ripples through the surrounding water. The surface of the airy cocoon, enveloped
by its fiery prison, shuddered and cracked. I maintained my
focus, pushing harder—determined to break through.

With a final surge of power, a section of the cocoon burst
open, and I was engulfed in a blinding light. I felt myself being pulled forward, my consciousness slipping from Arnexis
and into the Novdim. The sensation was disorienting, but I
clung to the staff, using it as an anchor to guide me toward
the Queen. A string of light seemed to act as a tether from
where I'd entered.

As the bright light around me faded, I glanced around to
find a string of white light tethering me from where I'd entered. I turned my eyes forward and realized I was in a Realm
unlike anything I had ever experienced. The air shimmered
with an ethereal quality, and the landscape was a kaleidoscope of iridescent colors that defied description—and yet
it was also disorienting with no real shape or form to it.

In the distance, I saw a willowy figure bathed in a soft, radiant glow. As she neared, I saw she wore robes of soft blue,
red, and gold.

I remembered how the Lord and Lady had chided me for
kneeling, but as this woman drew nearer, her spirit was luminous, and her eyes were filled with such wisdom and kindness that I found myself down on one knee without thinking.

"Queen Inferno," I tried to make my voice strong, but
it came out soft and lilting, almost like a song in this
place, "I am Apprentice Nix Emberwind of Skia Guild. Our
team has come to remove you from this prison, but I must
apologize. Guildmaster Devereux plans to hold you hostage

to get Grand Guildmaster Seraphina back, who has been arrested. She is a Demomancer."

The Queen smiled at me, a gesture of gratitude and understanding, her face lined with age that still probably did not accurately tell the number of years she'd lived. "I understand," she said, her voice resonating through the space. "Your bravery and dedication have brought us to this moment. Together, we shall restore balance to our Realm, have no fear."

I nodded; my throat tight with emotion. The Queen reached out, her spirit intertwining with mine. "We must hurry, Nix. The moment you opened this section of the Novdim, it began to collapse and seal itself. We need to leave before your thread is cut. It's why I haven't been able to leave. My body is buried separately beneath this mound."

Two parts of the Queen. Her body and her spirit. I hadn't known—hadn't realized. I gazed down at my own hands—translucent. Ephemeral. Was my body still outside this cocoon? I had no time to worry about it now. The Queen's spirit was strong. Together, we raced, following my thread.

As we sped through the Novdim, my mind raced with thoughts of the past and the future. I thought of my parents, of the guilt I had carried for so long, believing I was responsible for their deaths. Orion's words echoed in my mind, offering a glimmer of hope that my brother was alive and that the truth would be revealed in time.

But the weight of the present moment bore down on me. The Queen's spirit, though strong, was weary from her long imprisonment. I could feel her essence intertwined with mine, her strength waning as we navigated the collapsing Realm.

The landscape around us shifted and warped, the iridescent colors fading to a dull grey. The thread that tethered me to the physical world grew thinner, more fragile with each passing moment. I gripped the staff tighter, pouring every ounce of my will into maintaining the connection.

Tears streamed down my face as we raced against time, the enormity of our task and the consequences of failure threatening to overwhelm me. I thought of Daris and Elena, waiting outside the cocoon, their fates intertwined with ours. I thought of the Skia Guild, of the corruption that had taken hold of the GOC, and the difficult path that lay ahead for Arnexis and all the Realms.

But most of all, right now, I thought of the Queen. I had to protect her. Her spirit, though weakened, still radiated a quiet strength and resolve. I drew upon that strength and used it to fuel my own determination.

As we neared the end of the thread, the cocoon's opening came into view, a sliver of light in the growing darkness. With a final burst of energy, we surged forward, the Queen's spirit and mine merging into one as we crossed the threshold back into Arnexis—into the flames.

The moment we emerged, the cocoon shattered, its fiery prison dissipating into the water. I felt my consciousness snap back into my body, the sudden rush of sensation nearly overwhelming me. My lungs burned reminding me how much my Sangor body wanted breath.

My body Nix. Below the earth mound.

The Queens's voice inside my head. Part of me swore that the inside of my head had become a party place for voices ever since I'd come to Arnexis. In the Mortal Realm, they'd assess me, diagnose me, and treat me for a disorder like schizophrenia or something. My eyes darted to Daris, who'd already let the edges of the earth mound go and come to my side. I didn't know how to tell him the Queen's spirit was inside me. I could only motion "under" the mound and make a figure of a crowned Queen. I was so afraid we were running out of time. Daris face so pale. The venom laced blood he'd taken from Jessamine was affecting him—but to what extent, I wasn't sure. I didn't even know if it was lethal, though I suspected it was if he didn't get an antidote. How long did he have? My heart pounded.

Elena had managed to subdue the monstrous orange fish thing by pinning it down with some sort of immobilization spell. I didn't know how long that would last, but Elana's web-footed monster eyes betrayed the anxiety it felt because they were even wider and wilder than before.

Just under the mound. Your staff should show you where.

I motioned to Daris and showed him the staff and the mound. He understood that was how we would find her body, then he could tunnel and dig her up.

As old as the Queen is and as old as Orion was, I wondered if the Queen knew each Orion. I was betting she did.

I stretched out my staff. I did seem to act like a locator, though it was hard to see with the silt stirred up from the movement underwater. Daris noticed this and instantly cleared the debris away.

I held out the staff again. It pulsed faster the closer I got to the Queen's body until I was sure I had found the perfect location. From under the mound, we found the Queen's body in perfect stasis in a gilded box. Elena carried her to the surface in her mouth while Daris helped me to the shore.

When we arrived, the Queen's box was on the grass, Elena was still in monster form, and Variant had his knives aimed at her. Elena roared, opened her maw, and prepared to attack Variant as Devereux whipped his hands around Elias. We raced toward them.

"Elena, no!" Daris shouted.

DARIS

JUDGEMENT

It took all my faith that Nix would know what I was thinking—would know what to do. We were naked, vulnerable, and exposed. I was weakened from the venom I'd sucked from Jessamine's blood, but the sun was going to rise soon. With the rising sun, Devereux would once again have his shadows to use on the beach, and then Nix risked becoming a victim. Our one chance was now.

I still held Nix's hand, and for the briefest second, I squeezed it and nudged her toward Devereux. Then, I raced at Variant, my heart pounding in my chest, my muscles tensed and ready for battle.

Elena roared again, a sound that shook the very earth beneath our feet, and she charged at Variant as his knives flew toward her, glinting in the pale light of the fading night. His blades bounced off her armored skin, but one found its mark, sticking into her eye. She yelped in pain, her voice a mix of fury and agony.

Just as quickly, if not quicker, my grip was around Variant's neck, my fingers digging into his flesh, determined to end this once and for all. But he'd anticipated my attack and was already spinning and slashing, one of his knives cutting across my arm, leaving a trail of searing pain in its wake. Still, I didn't stop, my resolve unwavering.

Out of the corner of my eye, I spied Nix. She'd raced to Devereux and, curiously, placed her staff right at his neck. To my surprise, he'd stilled—frozen, as if under some spell.

Elias managed to peel Devereux's fingers away from his throat, coughing and gasping for air. Then, seeing Elena yowling with a dagger in her eye, his rage consumed him. He let loose a primal roar.

His body transformed, shifting and morphing into a hulking green Marsha with a long, thick, and powerful lizard tail, massive back claws, and long, razor-sharp front talons. His elongated lizard face was a mask of fury, his razor teeth gleaming as he lunged toward us, a primal roar tearing from his throat.

I dodged, my reflexes honed by years of training, as Elias caught Variant's throwing arm in his maw, his teeth sinking deep into the flesh. Variant screamed, a sound of pure agony that echoed across the beach.

Elena loomed over him, her massive form casting a shadow that seemed to swallow the world. As he grabbed a throwing knife with his other hand, she opened her froggish mouth, revealing those long, deadly upper and lower teeth, and snapped at him but missed. His blade found its mark again, striking her wounded eye and sending a fresh gush of blood cascading down her face.

In her anger and pain, Elena twisted her neck, her movements a blur. This time, her mouth found his arm, and she gripped it tight, her teeth sinking deep, her jaw locking in place. Variant's screams intensified his face, a mask of pure terror and agony.

I'd like to say I was a better man. A compassionate man. A man who trusted in a governing system to handle legal affairs have a proper trial and sentence a young man like Variant. A youth who might have some chance at rehabilitating himself in the future, a chance to see the error of his ways and seek redemption.

But deep down, I knew there would be no rehabilitation. What awaited Variant was a one-way trip to Lethenthril, a fate worse than death unless he managed to escape—and Variant was resourceful. I wasn't taking that chance. Maybe, in the end, I was being compassionate for everyone—except myself. By ending his life here and now, I was protecting countless others from the harm he would undoubtedly cause if given the opportunity.

I stared him in the eyes, those eyes that had once held a glimmer of humanity, now replaced by a cold, unyielding hatred. There was no remorse in his screams; they echoed across the beach, a chilling reminder of the monster he had become.

Then, abruptly, he stopped. His chest heaved, rising and falling with each labored breath. He stared at me with the hatred of a thousand hells, his eyes boring into mine, and he spat—a final act of defiance.

"You have no idea what is coming," he gasped, his voice ragged and strained. Even the seers can't see it; it's so dark." Elias and Elena pulled on his arms again, and he screamed, a sound that pierced the night. But he also laughed maniacally, a twisted, unhinged cackle that sent shivers down my spine. "You have NO idea!"

I didn't even *want* the taste of his blood, tainted as it was by the darkness that consumed him. But then again, after a thousand years, a certain darkness consumed me too.

My gaze flicked to Nix. I had a choice. I could drain him and learn everything—all that he knew. But then, I'd have the memories of everyone he'd killed, how he did it. I'd see how

Hemere died. I'd see his corpse. Or I could keep his laughter alive in my mind. My last memories of him were good ones. Of how we bantered and drank at the Oneg Run together. I could be selfish just this once. Save something bright, something beautiful for myself.

I hoped she understood and could see past the monster I was because she would learn that the monster was in her, too. *This is who I am.*

My fingernails elongated, transforming into razor-sharp claws, a physical manifestation of the beast within. With a steady voice filled with conviction, I let him hear his last words, a final judgment for his crimes.

"For Hemere, for Orion, and for all the others whose lives you stole . . ." I said, my voice barely above a whisper yet carrying the weight of a thousand souls.

With a swift, decisive motion, I plunged my hand into his torso and gripped his spine. Then, I hissed into his ear as my fangs slipped into his throat, and I began to drain him slowly, my mind merging with his, "You will pay for their souls by telling me all you know until your last breath!"

Variant's life played before my eyes like a symphony of sorrow and horror—the deaths he was part of—his role in Hemere's death. He'd killed far fewer than I supposed, but he had been an accomplice for many of Devereux's terrifying murders.

As I searched his mind, I found the Demomancers, Seraphina, the Sevvirs—more Sevvirs than I imagined, and the plans Variant had overheard. Then, unexpectedly, a black wall shut down on my mind, as if something had locked me out. Dissatisfied, I pulled away, realizing I'd get no more from him. I yanked my hand from his torso and slit his throat with my nails, watching what was left of his lifeblood trickle from the wound, staining the carpet of grass beneath him a deep, crimson-red.

I held his gaze as the final light faded from his eyes, and I didn't know how to feel. Part of me was satisfied. Another part of me still raged. And still, another part of me felt empty—hollow—as if a section of my soul were missing. Was it the Sevvir venom? Or something else?

As I stood there, watching the blood congeal around Variant's lifeless feet, I couldn't help but reflect on the choices that had led us to this moment. The paths we had walked, the sacrifices we had made, the friends we had lost along the way.

I thought of Hemere, of his unwavering loyalty and bravery as he stood by my side through the darkest of times. I thought of Orion. In the short time I'd known him, he'd shown wisdom and compassion and guided me with a gentle hand and a kind heart. My mind flew to Nemar, and I asked him to come and bring Leander. Hopefully, Leander understood.

I thought of all the others, the victims of Devereux's and Variant's cruelty, the lives cut short by their insatiable hunger for power. They were the reason I had done what I did, the reason I had taken on the burden of judge, jury, and executioner.

Now, we had to figure out what to do with Devereux. One thing I knew we needed. We needed his blood because we had to have an antidote, and fast. For Jessamine and for me. And there would be others.

"Drop him," I nodded to Elena and Elias. "It's done."

Variant's corpse fell to the ground with a thud, his lifeless eyes staring up at the slowly brightening sky. Elena and Elias returned to their Arnexin forms, their bodies shifting and morphing in a way that never ceased to amaze me. Elena still had two of Variant's daggers lodged in her left eye, the blades glinting in the early morning light.

Elias rushed to her side, his strong arms wrapping around her as blood continued to pour from the wound, staining her fur a deep crimson. I hadn't realized before how much he seemed to care for her. Maybe I hadn't wanted to.

I glanced over to see Nix maintaining her hold on Devereux with her staff in place. Her eyes were locked on his frozen form, her muscles tense, ready for any sudden movement. "I can't move it, Daris," she called out. "If I do, he'll be free. We need magic restraining cuffs and maybe something else to keep him from his other power—he's a Sevvir? And we need his blood for you, too."

"Yes," I answered both of her questions with the word, my mind racing with the possibilities and the implications of what we had just done. We all were still naked, our bodies exposed to the cool morning air. I was acutely aware that the sun was rising, its warm rays beginning to peek over the horizon.

Just then, I heard the flapping of wings, a sound that filled my heart with a sudden, overwhelming sense of relief.

Nemar! Cobalt!

"We should probably get . . . " I started to say, but before I could finish my sentence, Leander appeared through his Guildmaster Portal, his eyes wide with surprise as he took in the scene before him.

His gaze swept over us, taking in our state of undress, and for a moment, I thought I saw a flicker of amusement in his eyes. That was probably not too surprising. We were at the Celestial Waters, after all, where clothing was not allowed if one went swimming.

But then his eyes fell on Elena, with two daggers still lodged in her eye, on Variant's lifeless corpse, on Nix naked, holding her staff to Devereux's frozen body, and on me, blood-stained and standing next to a gilded box that held the Queen.

He sucked in a breath, his eyes widening even further, and uttered, "Oh, my."

I do believe it was the first time I'd ever heard Leander utter a surprised expression. Under any other circumstances, I might have found his reaction amusing, a brief moment of levity in an otherwise dire situation. But before I could say anything, before I could even begin to explain, I felt a sudden, overwhelming weakness wash over me.

My body collapsed to the ground.

NIX

OMNISCOR

L eander! My mind called out.

I probably should have been embarrassed, standing there in all my naked glory with my crystal staff at Devereux's throat, but I wasn't. My mind was consumed with thoughts of Daris as he collapsed on the grass, his body crumpling to the ground like a marionette whose strings had been cut. Every fiber of my being screamed at me to rush to his side, to hold him, to do something, anything, to help him. But Devereux—I could not let loose of Devereux, not even for a moment.

"Leander!" This time, my words finally came out loud, my voice cracking with the intensity of my emotions. "Daris—Daris drank Jessamine's blood to put her into paralysis, or stasis until you could create more antidote. He's been poisoned with Sevvir venom, too!"

Leander's eyes widened with understanding, and he rushed to Daris's side, his movements a blur of speed and purpose. Two more Immaru arrived on the beach, their white robes billowing in the early morning breeze. Leander pointed to Elena and Elias, his expression grave.

Elena cried out, her voice raw with pain and desperation, "No! I need to ..."

The sweetheart needed to know when it was time to go, to heal, and let others take over.

"Elena, you've done enough!" I blurted in a commanding tone, my voice rising above the din of the crashing waves. "Take Elias and make sure you both are okay. I'll see to Daris. Jessamine will need you at Immaru Guild soon."

They looked at me with surprise, their eyes wide and uncomprehending. But then, to my amazement, Elena took the hand of a white-robed female, and Elias joined her. They were gone, disappearing in a flash of light that left spots dancing in my vision.

Two Immaru gently curved in beside me, their faces set with determination. They both drew needles and some vials, their movements precise and practiced.

"Normally, we ask patients for permission," one said, his voice calm and measured, "but given the circumstances, we are foregoing that procedure at this time. Life and death emergency."

I watched as they siphoned several vials of blood from Devereux, more than were probably necessary to save Daris and Jessamine, but they'd hear no arguments from me. I just hoped someone would find a way to properly restrain Devereux so I could remove my staff and finally clothe myself since no one seemed the least concerned with my modesty.

Unfortunately, others started arriving as well: two junior Arcane Alliance members deemed not to be Demomancers and security staff. I wondered where the senior ones were. Those who got there early got an eyeful. At least the two junior members had the decency to conjure a blue drape to wrap around me until someone could decide what was best to be done with Devereux.

More Immaru arrived. I watched as they transported Daris and Jessamine to the Immaru Guild. Leander explained he'd stabilized Daris but had to treat him at the Guild, and he wasn't sure if they'd be able to save Jessamine. He drifted close to me before he left, his palm stretching out to rest on the crown of my head.

"Rest easy in your mind, Nix." And there it was, that fresh air—that breath of freedom. Yes, I was outside, but Leander, he just... did that. He never really smiled, but his face was serene, like a bright sunrise after the darkest night. "The Alliance will stay with you, then you'll see the others soon."

I wanted to nod, but I stood perfectly still as he faded into his Guildmaster Portal—a gentle mist this time. Tears welled in my eyes and threatened to spill over, but I blinked them back.

Not long after, my hands trembled, and I thought I could no longer endure holding the staff in that one position for much longer. A bright light flashed, and the new Magus Guildmaster I'd met with Lord and Lady Inferno, Lux Amber, emerged, the scent of citrus and vanilla following in his wake.

"Apprentice Nix." His voice was calm and reassuring, though I dared not to do more than glance briefly at him, afraid of letting my attention waver. "The senior members of the Arcane Alliance had just completed their emergency meeting. Our problem was that we knew nothing of the Sevvir as a people. Even our historians only know of them as an extinct reptile. We never imagined this would happen. We never knew their species existed. The Alliance has decided the only answer to neutralizing Devereux while you stand here is to take his memories right here and then we will sentence him to Lethenthril, or execute him. On the last part, we are undecided."

Upon finishing his words, a team of sixteen members arrived, and then another four. Two from each Guild to witness the procedure, and four to operate the equipment that would remove Devereux's memory. I only caught peripherally what they did to him, but I saw the bio-electronic machine they brought toward him. It was crafted like a lotus flower on one end and the root of a lotus on the other. The cyber petals of the flower wrapped around Devereux's head, one of them planted on each of Deveraux's temples.

As this happened, I heard the Queen's voice inside me. *"Nix. What they are about to do will be very dangerous for you, for me—for all of Arnexis. You must pull yourself away the second before they turn on the machine. Tell them!"*

I shouted, "Magus Amber—the Queen's spirit is with me. She said you must let me know one second before you turn the machine on so I can pull away. We cannot be connected to Devereux when you do. Our lives and all of Arnexis depend on it."

There was a pause as if uncertainty filled the air. *"Tell Magus Amber I have more Agon stories to tell if he's willing to listen on Celeste night."*

This time, I made sure my voice carried, "The Queen says to tell you, Magus Amber, that she has more Agon stories to tell you if you're willing to listen on Celeste night!"

"Yes, your Majesty!" Magus Amber now sounded even more resolute but reverent. Everyone dropped to their knee, and I wished they would get up.

I was so tired. *"You are doing well, Nix. Just a little more, my girl,"* the Queen's gentle voice encouraged.

"Quick," Magus Amber instructed, "secure the root in the container now."

What I'd seen of the container appeared to be a clear but brownish liquid in a jar, with a mud on the bottom. Then, the Magus was beside me. "We are ready. The machine is timed. I will tell you to go just before as timer is on the final second—then you must move."

What seemed like a lifetime went by. I felt a fresh breeze. Then Magus Amber's voice. "Nix, get ready. One, two, three—go!"

I fell away, dashing as quickly as I could, but my muscles were so stiff that my reaction was delayed. I heard the gentle spark. I felt a flutter. Surely, what I felt was the blue drape over my body. I'd moved fast enough—exactly as Magus Amber told me. I searched my mind. Then, "Your Majesty?" I sent my thoughts through my mind. Are you . . ."

"I'm here, Nix. You did well."

Relief flooded through me as I stared at Devereux's body, slumped, standing on a support they'd brought to transfer it with. The snakes on his suit no longer slithered and writhed. His shadows, his venom, couldn't hurt us anymore.

My next thought? *Damn, I'm hungry . . .*

The ceremony to merge the Queen's spirit with her body was a private affair. Magus Amber escorted me to the palace and, after being showered and clothed, led me to Queen Essembra's Presence Chamber. It was a magnificent room unlike any I'd ever seen.

The ceiling had the illusion of an open sky, and small friendly sprites and fairies flitted through the air, performing comical antics among the clouds and overhanging branches of virtual trees. Flowers bloomed along the sides of the ceiling and the walls rotated through a number of paintings and pictures. Sometimes of royal family, sometimes of interesting art. I spied what I suspected were her favorite written passages of poetry or meaningful lines from books. It was a true menagerie dedicated to some of the things Queen Essembra Inferno treasured most.

At the front of the room, on a raised gilded platform accented with wildflowers of various kinds—some I'd never seen before—was the gold gilded box that Daris, Elena, and I had dug up from the Celestial Waters—the one that contained the Queen's living body.

I also had pleasant surprises awaiting me there. On comfortable seats of blue, gold, and red sat Lady and Lord Inferno, their regal bearing and commanding presence filling the room with an air of anticipation. They were talking with Daris, Elena, Elias, and Jessamine, their voices low and urgent, their expressions grave.

And then I caught that scent of fresh air that eased me, a familiar, comforting scent that I had come to associate with only one person. I turned to see Leander's luminous blue eyes behind me, his gaze steady and unwavering.

I couldn't take it anymore, the constant pull of his presence, the way my thoughts always seemed to drift to him when I was stressed or worried. I had to know the truth. "Okay, Leander. What gives?" I asked, my voice barely above a whisper. "I love that peaceful air you give off, but it's creepy how I'm always thinking of you when I get stressed. I get worried, and suddenly, I'm smelling fresh air and feeling relaxed. Is it an Immaru thing?"

Leander's gaze widened ever so slightly, a flicker of emotion passing behind his eyes. He seemed as if he wanted to say something, his lips parting as if to speak, but then the Queen interrupted inside my head, her voice a gentle whisper that filled my mind. *My dear Nix, I believe it's time. Are you ready to meet me?*

My question had to go unanswered for now, pushed aside by the urgency of the moment. My body warmed, and little sparks sputtered from my hands, though I tried to control them, tried to keep them contained. I nodded my head, though no one else could hear the Queen but me, and said, "Yes."

"Whoa, Sparks—you okay?" Elias piped up, raising an eyebrow, his expression one of concern.

Daris sauntered to my side, his presence a solid, comforting warmth beside me. I nodded again and addressed Lord and Lady Inferno, telling them the Queen was ready to start.

I'd carried my staff with me, its weight a constant reminder of the power that flowed through me. I couldn't imagine going anywhere without it ever again. Respectfully proceeding up to the gilded box, which reminded me of a coffin, though it wasn't shaped like one—it was rectangular and decorated with magical designs—I stood before it and closed my eyes to listen to what the Queen had to say.

"Seraphina didn't worry much about protection on my physical form since she'd locked away my spirit," the Queen said, her voice a gentle murmur in my mind. *"The staff should be able to unlock the box if you can find the correct magical frequency. Then simply touch my body, and we should merge."*

I had no idea what that was. Correct magical frequency? That sounded like music.

"Yes."

But I'm not musical, and that's not an Elemental Power. This sounded like an impossible task. Something an Apprentice was supposed to do in class for a higher level.

"Nix, I need you. Arnexis needs you. Just think. Focus. Think about what you've learned your entire life."

I took a deep breath and blotted out everything around me. Forgot about Daris, Elena, Leander, the Lord and Lady—all of it. Music. Frequencies. Magical Frequencies. It made me think of best frequencies for the brain. Something I'd read once by

Nikola Tesla about finding secrets of the universe and thinking in terms of frequency, vibration, and the universe, or something like that. Where was the Internet and Google when I needed it?

Okay. But what frequency? What music? I remembered how I felt at The Eye of Chaos—like I was in the Wizard of Oz movie. And now? Now, instead of ruby slippers, I had a crystal staff. Instead of being Dorothy, I was the Wizard. Except I wasn't fake. This wasn't a dream.

I held the blue crystal staff in my hand and moved forward, placing my other hand on the box. I had no clue what I was doing, but no one else knew what to do. They were trusting in the Queen, trusting in me. And if I failed, did I doom Arnexis?

"Keep going, Nix."

I pressed the crystal of my staff to my forehead. The blue crystal was cool at first, then warm, then searing hot, but my body burned with it. I searched for the Queen in my head and found her voice.

"Stay with me—right here—as I find that sound." I urged her.

I felt her presence with me, and in my mind's eye, I heard the ethereal music of the universe pulsing throughout space and time. Stars were born and died, galaxies swirled and collided, and at the center of it all, there was a single, pulsing heartbeat, a drumming rhythm that echoed through the very fabric of reality.

And then, in that vast expanse of sound and light, I saw it—a single point of brilliance, a shining beacon that called to me like a siren's song. I focused on that point, letting it fill my mind, my body, and my very soul.

As I did, I heard the music change, shifting and morphing into something new, something ancient and powerful. It was the sound of life itself, the primal melody that had echoed through the universe since the dawn of time.

I saw a seed sprouting, its roots digging deep into the rich, dark soil of time. I saw those roots spreading out, reaching for the stars, and then I saw the branches, the leaves, the fruit of the future. It was the Tree of Life, the source of all creation, the wellspring from which all magic flowed.

I felt, saw, and heard the frequency of that tree, the vibration of its essence. It was a sound, a vision, a feeling unlike any other, resonating through every fiber of my being and to unlock the secrets of the universe itself.

I focused on the vibrations, colors and harmony as it filled me and guided me. A word sang out with a perfect chime, the tone so sweet it flooded my heart, my mind, my very soul with tears of joy.

Vikara!

Then, with a blinding flash of purest light, I felt the box beneath my hand click open. The lid slid back to reveal the Queen's living body, her skin pale and perfect, her hair a shimmering cascade of white.

I reached out, my hand trembling, and I touched her skin. In that instant, a rush of power unlike anything I had ever experienced before overcame my senses. It was like a vast bolt of lightning coursing through my veins, like a supernova exploding in my chest.

I felt the Queen's essence detach from me, our minds separating, and yet—somehow, I thought, still linked. I peered through her eyes, experienced the heart of her emotions in that moment, and I understood what I had failed to grasp since I'd come to Arnexis. The true nature of magic.

The Eye of Chaos had shown me, but I wasn't ready. It was too much then. It was too much now, but I understood more.

The Queen rose out of her box, her spirit now one with her body. I saw she had Cielo magic as she used air power to bring herself to her feet in front of me. She appeared weary, and the Lord and Lady Inferno were ready to take her away to her chamber to rest and probably be seen by an Immaru as soon as possible. Still, she paused.

"Thank you, Nix. And thank you, Daris, Elena, Elias, Jessamine, and my dear Leander," she said, calling everyone by name. "Jessamine, please stay at the palace. Your quest is fulfilled." Everyone heard Jessamine's bracelet drop off her wrist. "Our Senior Guard will find you a place among our ranks if you would like to serve among my Guard. You have proven yourself worthy."

Jessamine took a knee before the Queen, and her face was immediately overcome with emotion. It was clear she had not expected this. "Your Majesty is too kind. I accept." Jessamine gave us hugs farewell and immediately exited following her Senior Guard new employer.

The Queen continued, "Nix, before I go, it is extremely important that you know that your parents left Arnexis and changed their names. Your father, by birth, was an Inferno. He was in line to inherit the throne should his sister die, and sadly she did. He left long before that, not desiring to compete for any inheritance. Apparently, he was killed despite his efforts—and I'm so sorry about your parent's deaths. That said, you are now the next in line after me to inherit the throne. You will return to the Guilds of Chaos, and you will learn all you can. You must prepare yourself, Nix. I will work on healing now, and I will see you soon. But war is coming, and you need to be ready."

Of all I thought I was going to hear today, this was not it. I figured it was going to be a "*Hey, Nix, get the Queen out of the box. Yay!* (pat on the back) *Let's return to the GOC, find some blood—get some sleep!*" Then, I'd finally have alone time with Daris for the rest of the day. I didn't think I'd hear, "Oh, by the way, you are the next heir of Arnexis, and we're going to war soon, so be ready . . ."

And I didn't particularly like the way the Lord Inferno and Lady Inferno were eyeing me right now. They smiled, but their eyes glittered, and I wasn't seeing the warmth there I had seen before.

I started to take a knee when the Queen swept me into her gossamer arms. "I think we're beyond that now, my dear Nix, don't you?"

She caught me off guard, her embrace warm, firm, and caring. I hadn't had a hug like that since my mom died. I almost started sobbing in front of everyone in the room but gulped the tears back.

Before she pulled away, the Queen whispered into my ear. "By the way, Leander is an Empath, and he's an Inferno by blood, too. He's one of your cousins." She pulled away and smiled before a group of Immaru led her away.

I gazed over at Leander. He tilted his head, his blue eyes a shade deeper, his face a bit brighter, though he still didn't smile. I wasn't sure where to go from here, but I wasn't leaving without telling Leander thank you, so I strode up to him before he could disappear.

"I understand now. And I've been meaning to say thank you, *cousin*. You've helped me so many times." I could have been wrong, but those thin, pink lips on his narrow face might have moved up a little on one corner.

Daris, Elena, and Elias huddled together, and I noted that Elena and Elias were holding hands. That was so cool. Young monster and monster hunter love.

"Meet me back at Skia Guild?" I whispered into Daris's ear. "We'll break the Guildmaster and Apprentice fraternization rules before we start classes again? Just this once?"

Everyone's Celcom started buzzing. I pulled mine out. My first real announcement.

We all turned to look at Daris. He was still staring at his phone. Without even participating in the vote, he'd just been voted by the Arcane Alliance to serve as Grand Guildmaster.

"Congrat . . ." started Elena.

But Daris had already portaled me to his room and thrown me to his bed. His black satin sheets were cool and slippery against my skin. His passionate kiss was hot and demanding.

"I've waited for you for so long. I'm not your Guildmaster now, and I might be your Patron in time. Or, depending on you, your Bond-Mate." He kissed me again, his lips trailing over my neck where I felt his teeth, and oh, how I wanted him again like we had done before.

"Nix." Daris's voice was thick with desire. "You've gone through so much and learned so much; I know your mind is reeling. But I have more to tell you—more that changes how we can be together and what you know about who you are."

I wasn't sure I wanted to hear this. I mean, I'd walked through The Eye of Chaos. I'd become a Sangor. I—

"You *aren't* a pure Sangor, Nix," Daris held me, his eyes locked with mine, his gaze intense and unwavering. "When you hold your staff and use it, your eyes turn blue, like Orion's did. You hold multiple powers—more than most Sangors. You have two Elementals but then three Ariparz. No one's told you, but that is extremely rare. When you looked into the Obsidian Mirror—The Reflection of Chaos—with Master Coeus, what did you ask for?"

I was sure now that he already knew, even though at the Celestial Waters, I hadn't shown any indication of it. I didn't swim worth squat and barely showed any skills. I rolled over on him, straddling his hips, my body pressed against his. "Aquane."

Daris reached up, his fingers tangling in my fire-red hair. I'd forgotten how long it had grown, the silky strands cascading down my back. I usually had it trimmed by now, but it was much longer now, a wild, untamed mane. "That makes you extremely powerful. You'll be feared. You'll also be a target. As Grand Guildmaster and as someone who is Protection Bonded to you, I will make sure you learn how to protect yourself. Not coddle you, but train you. Understand?"

I thought I did and nodded, a shiver of fear running down my spine at the thought of the challenges that lay ahead.

"What you are—is what Sangors have not seen in an age. I've only heard stories of them. It's called an Omniscor. They are essentially of the "old" Sangor heritage, part from the Celestials and Zeleel itself, part old Grasha and original Elsh. It's what allows for your many magic powers at once. And, because of this, because you are not true Sangor, you can still be my Prime."

When he said the last part, my temper flared, hot and bright. "Really, Daris? Is this about a meal?"

"No," he laughed, his hands clasping mine, his touch sending sparks of electricity dancing across my skin. "Seriously, *dazi*. Remember what we had together. Our time on Zeleel. Think of how it might be if it were more . . ." He paused, and here I think he almost blushed, a hint of color rising to his cheeks, which would be saying something for a man over a thousand years old: " . . . intimate."

I was quiet—probably too   quiet.   I   conceded,   my voice barely above a whisper, "I know I bound myself to you as your Prime. But then I walked through The Eye. I became a Sangor. I thought I couldn't be a Prime anymore."

Daris held up one calloused hand, his expression serious. "I'm not done."

I raised an eyebrow, my heart hammering in my chest. He grasped my hands again, his touch firm and reassuring. I hadn't noticed before how large his hands were compared to mine.

"You'll like this part, maybe, or you'll find it weird. But as an Omniscor, I can be your Prime, too." With that, he let me go, his eyes searching my face, waiting to see what I would do. "It's why we still smell so good to each other—attract each other—in that way."

I thought about that, my mind reeling with the implications. Daris could be my Prime, too, so I could experience that sensation, like what he did to me on Zeleel. I became acutely aware that my heart rate and my breathing had both accelerated, my body responding to the mere thought of it. I glanced down, and the sheets were on fire, the flames licking at the fabric.

"Shit, Daris! I'm sorry!" I jumped off, trying to summon water to put the fire out and failing, my powers still too new, too untamed.

Daris flicked his fingers once, and the fire was gone, the sheets pristine and untouched. Another flick of his fingers, and the bed was as good as new.

"Don't worry about it." He chuckled, pulling me back down on top of him, his arms wrapping around me. "I'd say it happens all the time, but if I did, I'd turn scarlet."

We laughed, the tension broken, and then we locked eyes, the air between us charged with something electric, something primal.

"What do you say," he asked, his voice low and rough. "Want to give it a try? You're a *nacen*, but you've come a long way. I trust you. It's probably one of the most intimate things we'll do, especially when we combine it with lovemaking, should we get there in the future."

Should we get there? Oh, dear God, I wanted to be there already, my body aching for his touch, for the feel of his skin against mine.

I ran my hands across his chest, my fingers tracing the hard planes of his muscles. I lifted his shirt over his head, throwing it to the floor, my eyes drinking in the sight of him. I admired his sculpted abs, his muscular arms, and the scars that crisscrossed his body, each one a testament to the battles he had fought and the challenges he had overcome.

My gaze was drawn to the pulse of his neck. I inhaled the heady scent of cinnamon and cedar that rose up from his skin, a scent I had missed having time to enjoy for so long.

I leaned in toward him, my body lengthening against his, my mouth nuzzling the curve of his jaw, his stubble rough against my lips.

"Are you sure?" I whispered into his ear, my breath hot against his skin. And I wondered if he'd ever had anyone feed on him this way, if he had ever surrendered himself so completely, so utterly. I'd know in just a few seconds.

I'd also know everything I wanted to know if I decided to. I'd have access to what he saw in Variant's mind on the grassy beach when he ended Variant's life. Did I want to see that now?

I realized it shouldn't matter. I was here *now*, with a stake in Arnexis, a stake in the Realms. I shouldn't run away. The Demomancers, the Sevvir, were a threat. Whatever happened, happened.

"Yes," Daris growled, his voice rough with need, with desire. And he gripped my body, his hands rough and demanding, his touch setting my skin on a different kind of fire. "Do it."

I wrapped my arms around him and grasped his head tight, my fingers tangling in his hair. As my fangs slid into his neck and his hot, rich blood entered my mouth, our thoughts and emotions merged. Here, I reached that sweet peak moment of no return—the thrilling apex pause before the careening plunge—and my hungry mind caressed his and offered him a choice. With a gentle mental whisper filled with desire, I sent one question to his mind.

Do you want to feel everything?

REVIEW THIS BOOK

Gratitude and joy. That's what I feel every time I know someone has picked up a book or a story of mine and read it, particularly if they've enjoyed it.

Creating worlds and writing my tales is a true love and passion of mine. I'd love to hear your thoughts about the Guilds of Chaos and the magical creatures living in it!

You can find more information about the Guilds of Chaos at https://www.malferasinclair.com

~Malfera Sinclair

ABOUT THE AUTHOR

Malfera Sinclair is an author, Navy Veteran, martial artist, and an avid reader. She lives in the wilds of Virginia with her dog, Trapper, and her cats Echo and Kiwi. You might catch her hiking in the Blue Ridge Mountains or visiting a winery or brewery in the local area. If you see her, stop and say hi!

www.ingramcontent.com/pod-product-compliance
Lightning Source LLC
Chambersburg PA
CBHW071445170626
46811CB00007B/2484